TRUTH LIES BENEATH

JACK STAINTON

ALSO BY JACK STAINTON

A Guest To Die For
You're Family Now
Mother
Last One To Lie
He Is Here
The Boss's Wife
Dead Ever After

This novel is entirely a work of fiction and any resemblance to actual persons, living or dead, is purely coincidental.

An imprint of Windmill Streams *Publishers* Limited

Truth Lies Beneath

Copyright © Jack Stainton 2025
All rights reserved.
ISBN: 978-1-7385768-2-1

All rights reserved. No part of this publication may be reproduced, stored in a retrieval system, or transmitted, in any form or by any means, electronic, mechanical, photocopying, recording or otherwise, without the prior permission of both the copyright owner and the publisher of this book.

This book is sold subject to the condition that it shall not, by way of trade or otherwise, be lent, re-sold, hired out or otherwise circulated without the publisher's prior consent in any form of binding or cover other than that in which it is published and without a similar condition including this condition being imposed on the subsequent purchaser.

PROLOGUE

ADAM

THE NIGHT OF THE ACCIDENT

The sound of the engine revving grew louder, the BMW racing back towards me like a predator closing in for the kill. I couldn't move, couldn't cry out. Pain wracked my body; every nerve on fire. My vision blurred, and the street around me dimmed. I closed my eyes tight, waiting for the inevitable. A deserved finality to the misery I'd caused.

Then, a voice. Sharp. Desperate. "Stop!"

The BMW's tyres screeched, the car coming to a halt by what felt like only inches away, before shifting gear once more. It sped off along the narrow street, its sound soon lost as the howling wind returned, echoing around the tall buildings.

Peering through the tiniest of gaps my eyes could manage, I saw Kevin and Vicky, who had been silently witnessing my demise, turn and bolt back into the flat, the door slamming shut behind them. You bastards, I thought, and even in the midst of my hideous predicament, I considered how sweet revenge would be. They'd lured me there, knowing that Bob's children were waiting in the shadows as soon as I departed their flat. They let me go, allowed me my freedom, but they knew…

I tried to speak, to scream, but my lungs wouldn't cooperate. My breath came in short, ragged gasps. The cold bit at my skin as my limbs refused to move. I was sinking deeper into the blackness.

And then I heard her. Footsteps. Quick and purposeful. The figure that emerged from the gloom was a blur of motion and shadow. She knelt beside me, her breathing uneven as she looked me over, trying to assess the damage. I could barely see her through the haze of pain, but her presence was a strange comfort in the growing dark.

Her hands hovered over me, uncertain where to touch. My head spun as I tried to piece together how she had found me, why she had come. However, having her near offered me a moment's peace, a reformation.

"Stay with me, Adam," she whispered, her voice trembling, the desperation in it cutting through the fog in my brain. Her hand gripped mine, pulling me back from the brink, anchoring me to the world. I tried to respond, but the pain swallowed me whole.

She leant closer. "Who did this to you?" she asked, her tone soft but insistent, searching for answers.

Through the haze, I endeavoured to form words, my mind barely functioning. The names tumbled out, a jumble of thoughts and half-conscious mutterings. "Vicky… Kevin…" I croaked, each word burning in my throat. The taste of blood was thick on my tongue. "Nathan… Belinda… Bob's children…"

I sensed her tense beside me, her grip on my hand tightening. "What are you saying? What about them?"

My mind swam, fighting to stay afloat as more names flooded in. "Luke… Sandra… the business… Every single person has betrayed me…" It all felt so distant now, slipping further from my grasp with each passing moment. "You need to stop them. Retribution…"

The woman's voice broke through again, but I couldn't focus. Everything was blurring. The street. Her face. The sharp edges of the world around me began to fade, softening into a void that pulled me under. I was losing the battle, slipping deeper into the abyss.

Then her voice again. It grew louder, more urgent, but her words were garbled now, distorted by the pounding in my head. She asked me something, but I couldn't make it out. All I felt was her hand on mine, and her breath close to my ear. She spoke softly, almost a whisper. A promise.

Something inside me knew it was important, that those would be the last words I ever heard, but I was unable to process them, couldn't hold on to the meaning. All I could do was sink.

The world darkened further, the street vanishing as if swallowed by a black hole. The pain dulled, replaced by a strange, numbing sensation that spread through me. The sirens in the distance grew closer, their high-pitched wail a backdrop to the chaos in my mind.

I wanted to stay awake, to cling to whatever thread of life remained, but my body was betraying me. I tried to move, to speak, but my limbs were heavy, my mouth refusing to cooperate.

I felt her grip tighten, her hand warm and firm around mine. She was still there. Still holding on. But I was slipping away, the darkness beckoning me, pulling me deeper.

Her fingers slowly slid from mine. Then footsteps, running.

Then, everything went quiet. Silent. Peaceful.

But her voice stayed in my head. Her words, barely audible through the fog. One last whisper as everything faded to black. I smiled. I knew she would honour me

And then, nothing.

1

THREE WEEKS LATER

ADAM CHAPMAN'S FUNERAL

THE BITTER COLD seemed to penetrate Kat's skin as she stepped out of the hearse. It was the first Tuesday of the new year and consecutive nights of frost had left the ground frozen solid. She pulled her coat tighter around her, shivering; a combination of the enormity of the situation and the biting wind that whistled through the graveyard.

Thankfully, her son, Tom, was staying with his friend Max, but even amid burying her husband, Kat couldn't shake the unsettling unease over Tom's recent behaviour. Ever since she'd sat him down and gently told him that Daddy had fallen asleep and wouldn't be waking up, Tom had become distant, almost eerie in his actions. Although she couldn't possibly understand how a six-year-old would take such devastating news, Kat certainly hadn't expected the transformation that had overtaken her child.

It started with the silence—Tom, always chatty and full of questions, had withdrawn into a shell, speaking only when absolutely necessary. His once-bright eyes now held a darkness, an unsettling emptiness that made Kat's skin crawl. But it wasn't just his quietness that disturbed her; it was the way he would stare, unblinking, at nothing in particular, his small face devoid of emotion, as though something else was looking out from behind his eyes.

She'd caught him on more than one occasion staring out of the living room window at Imogen's house opposite, his slight frame completely motionless as he gazed at the now dilapidated property. The overgrown garden, once pristine, only added to the sense of unease that had settled over their home ever since the night Adam died.

Kat forced herself to focus on the present. She scanned the gathered mourners as they huddled together, seeking comfort from the cold and each other. Luke and Sandra stood a few feet away, the distance between them palpable. Kat noticed Luke glancing at her, a brief smile tugging at the corners of his mouth. Her heart skipped a beat and she was unsure how to respond. She quickly averted her gaze, hoping Sandra hadn't noticed. But the next time it happened, Sandra did see, her expression unreadable, leaving Kat to wonder what the hell she must be thinking.

Did she know?

As the vicar spoke his solemn words, Kat's gaze drifted to the back of the small crowd. There stood Kevin and Vicky, their presence irritating her. She'd already confronted Kevin at work, demanding to know what had really taken place that night. But he and Vicky denied any wrongdoing. They hadn't known a car had hit Adam, insisting they only invited him over to meet Vicky and not knowing anything had happened until the sound of sirens filled the street below. Kevin claimed Adam was angry. Luke had already met Vicky, and Adam still hadn't had the pleasure. He declared he thought it churlish to complain of such a thing, but was concerned about his boss's wellbeing and only wished to maintain the peace. Kevin insisted he and Vicky were sickened when they heard the news that Adam had died. Kat wasn't sure who or what to believe. It certainly sounded like Adam. Jealous of Luke, and if he'd been introduced to the infamous Vicky before him, she could just imagine Adam's fury; as if the world were against him once again.

Kat's parents, William and Edwina, stood stoically beside her. They had never liked Adam, and they'd already advised her to move on, their words striking her as heartless given how little time had passed. Yet, in her heart, she understood their point. Adam had been a ticking time bomb, teetering on the edge of revealing everything to the authorities. He was vulnerable, close to breaking under the pressure of his secrets: their secrets. The missing terracotta pot in their garden, the way he reacted when William had found Tom's football, days after Adam had searched in the same vicinity. Various other occasions when Kat was convinced he was on the brink of a breakdown. Oh, and the evening of Luke's supposed sleepwalking in their house. Although Kat knew it wasn't the occasion to indulge in her naughtier side, she still had to stifle a grin as she glanced at Luke out of the corner of her eye.

As they slowly lowered the coffin into the freezing ground, Kat felt a strange sense of release. She wasn't sure if it was the finality of Adam's death or the cold realisation that it might be the best outcome for all. The dark cloud that had hung over their lives for so long was gone, buried with her husband. But as she looked at the people who remained—Luke, Sandra, Kevin, Vicky, her parents—Kat couldn't help but wonder if it really was the end. There was nobody left who really knew what happened, nobody but her, of course. But she also had renewed reasons to doubt all those around her.

The wind whipped through the churchyard, scattering dry leaves across the graves. Kat tightened her grip on the bouquet she held, stepping forward to toss the flowers onto the casket. The petals fluttered in the air before landing softly on the polished wood, a splash of colour against the starkness of the day.

And then, it was over. Adam was gone, and with him, the deceit, the guilt, and the fear that had threatened to unravel her life.

But as she made to leave, Kat caught a glimpse of somebody standing motionless amongst the trees, far in the distance. She shivered as the figure turned and slowly walked away. Although convincing herself that they weren't even looking at her, she also knew that the past had a way of resurfacing, no matter how deep she tried to bury it.

2

KAT DECIDED to walk home from the church, the mile-long journey offering her a rare moment of solitude. She told her parents she would collect Tom on the way, and they had taken a taxi, promising a hot meal upon their arrival. The cold air stung her cheeks, but it wasn't the biting wind that made her numb—it was the memory of the funeral, how no one cried, not even her.

As she walked, the events of the past weeks played heavily in her mind. She thought about Adam and the man he had once been—loving, attentive and protective. How they had fought back from adversity and the hours he worked to rid themselves of their once crippling debt. Those qualities had remained with him throughout, right until the day he slept with Imogen. That was when everything changed. Kat knew. It was what she had to believe. The story she had to stick to. Otherwise, she had to believe he was right…

Looking back, Kat realised something must have happened and how she'd been so stupid not to recognise it straight away. Ever since that night, Adam had become more distant, withdrawn, as if a part of him had died that day. Or maybe, she thought grimly, it was the good part of him that had died, leaving only his bad side to remain.

The crisp crunch of her footsteps on the frost-covered pavement echoed in tandem with the rhythm of her thoughts. Memories swirling in her mind—their wedding day, the birth of Tom, and those quiet moments when they had just been happy together. Kat realised she had been living in denial for far too long, refusing to confront the reality of their life after Imogen. She had never really forgiven Adam, and she wondered if that resentment had poisoned everything, driving him to his breaking point. She had always suspected that something might have happened between them, but she had no proof, just a gut feeling that gnawed at her. Not that she could talk—she smiled bitterly, recalling her own indiscretions.

Kat sighed heavily as she turned onto Lauren's street, the house looming ahead. She hadn't wanted to leave Tom for too long, but he needed the distraction, and she had needed the space to breathe, even if just for a moment. As she reached Lauren's front door, her heart sank. What if Tom played up? Asked awkward questions about where she had been. Kat hadn't told him of his dad's funeral, desperately trying to keep everything to a routine. But Tom had been acting strange, and his behaviour over the last couple of weeks had been unsettling, to say the least.

She knocked on the door, and it swung open so quickly it caught Kat off-guard. Lauren stood there, her face pale, eyes wide with concern. "Kat," she began, her voice trembling slightly, "Come in." Lauren scooted towards the kitchen, leaving Kat with little choice but to follow.

"Whatever's wrong?" she asked when she caught up.

Lauren leant her back against the work surface, picking at her fingernails. "I know you're going through a lot right now, and you must be having the most awful of days…" Lauren paused, as if expecting a reaction from Kat. The silence forced her to continue. "But Tom… he's really scared me."

Kat's heart jittered. "What do you mean?"

Lauren hesitated, glancing over Kat's shoulder, checking to see if Tom was within earshot. "It was earlier, soon after you dropped him off. Max had gone to his room, and I wondered why it was so quiet. Then I found Tom in the living room, sittting cross-legged on the floor, staring at the TV."

Kat allowed a slight sigh of relief to escape. "Oh, he often does that. We're…"—she caught herself—"I'm forever telling him he's too close to the—"

"No. You don't understand," Lauren interrupted. "He hadn't even turned on the TV. Instead, it was as though he could see someone in there. And he kept saying, 'She's coming home,' over and over again. But it was the way he said it, Kat… with this huge grin on his face, like he wasn't even there. It was as though he was in a trance, lost in some other world. I didn't know what to do."

Kat felt an icy chill crawl down her spine. Tom's behaviour had been odd since Adam's death, but this was something else, something far more disturbing. "I'm so sorry," Kat stammered, her voice thick with guilt. "I'll talk to him."

Tom appeared from behind the door, his expression blank and distant, as if he hadn't heard a word of their conversation.

"Tom, get your shoes and coat on, now," Kat instructed, her tone sharp with urgency.

He moved slowly, almost mechanically, as he gathered his things. Kat apologised profusely to Lauren. "I don't know what's got into him," she muttered. "He's just... I don't know."

Lauren nodded sympathetically, though the fear in her eyes hadn't subsided. "It's okay. I just... I thought you should know."

Kat forced a smile. "Thank you. I'll make sure it doesn't happen again." She pulled Tom close, more to reassure herself than him, and stepped out into the freezing air. The cold seemed to bite deeper than before, extending farther down and seeping into her bones.

As they walked away from the house, Kat intended to speak to Tom, to demand an explanation, but before she could say a word, her phone rang. She fished it out of her coat pocket, glancing at the screen. It was her mum.

"Kat." Edwina's voice crackled over the line. "We just got home, and... the house opposite... it's been sold. There's a sign up in the garden."

Kat froze, her grip tightening on Tom's hand. "Sold? How?" she asked, her thoughts whirling. The house opposite. Imogen's house. Empty and decaying since…

As far as Kat was concerned, it wasn't even on the market.

"We couldn't believe it either," her mum replied. "The sign must have gone up while we were at the funeral."

Kat's thoughts churned with uncertainty as she ended the call. She looked down at Tom, who was staring straight ahead, unblinking, his small hand cold in hers. "Come on, darling," she whispered, more to herself than to him, as they continued walking.

But the unease wouldn't leave her. Who had bought Imogen's house? And why did they erect the sign that day of all days? Kat's mind whirled with questions, none of which she had an answer to. And then she recalled what Lauren had told her. The thing Tom had allegedly repeated over and over again.

"She's coming home…"

3

Kat hurried home, her breath emerging in puffs of white as soon as it hit the cold air. The sight of the 'Sold' sign in Imogen's front garden sent a fresh wave of unease through her. She forced herself to stay calm, telling Tom to go and find his grandparents. He offered her a strange smile, almost as if he knew something she didn't. She watched him skip into the living room, his carefree attitude clashing with his otherworldly side, making her doubt herself once more.

In the kitchen, Kat joined her parents, who were waiting patiently, sitting at the table. The smell of home-cooked food at least offered her some form of day-to-day comfort. However, the prospect of new neighbours, in that house of all places, still whirled around her head like a tornado. "Who could have bought it? How could it have been sold?" she asked, noticing the slight tremble in her voice. "Liam and Imogen didn't have any living relatives."

William cleared his throat and turned his iPad to face her. "I've just Googled it, love," he said, his tone reassuring yet cocky. Kat thought what Adam's reaction would be, and she caught herself glancing at the empty chair at the table. She smiled inwardly towards her husband.

"There's a concept called 'bona vacantia'," her dad continued, his chest puffing out at discovering something useful on his latest toy. "Well, I think that's how you say it." He pushed the iPad across the table and Kat leant forward to read the screen. "When someone dies without a will or any known relatives," William proceeded, "their estate passes to the Crown, I suppose anybody can apply to buy the property after that."

Kat frowned, the explanation made sense but did little to ease her discomfort. The house had been a constant in their lives, a silent reminder of the tragedy that she and Adam had played such a fundamental part in. "So, just anyone could have bought it?"

William nodded. "Yes. It was only a matter of time before someone snapped it up. A property like that, in this area. It was never going to stay empty for long."

Edwina, again in a reassuring tone, added, "It might be a good thing, darling. A new family could bring some life back to the place, help everyone move on. You never know, they may have children too, someone for Tom to play with. It's an extremely desirable family house."

Kat tried to absorb what they were saying, but the timing still felt off. Adam had only just been buried, and now this? The logical side of her knew her parents were right, that it was inevitable the house would eventually sell. Yet the speed of it all, so soon after the accident, left her feeling as if the ground beneath her feet was shifting.

"I guess you're right," she said, her voice wavering. "I'm just being paranoid."

But as much as she tried to push it aside, the unease lingered. Her thoughts drifted back to Tom, to the unsettling conversation she'd had with Lauren earlier. She passed the iPad to William and began busying herself by making fresh coffee. "Lauren mentioned something about Tom that's been bothering me," she said, turning, her gaze flicking between her parents. "She said he scared her today."

Edwina's expression softened with concern, but her response was quick. "He's been through a lot, darling. Losing his dad so suddenly—it's bound to affect him in ways we can't fully understand. The best thing you can do is keep things as normal as possible. Routine is what he needs now."

Kat desperately wanted to believe her mother's words, to put it all down to trauma and grief, but the way Tom had been acting—staring out of the window, talking about someone coming home—felt like more than just a child's way of coping. It was as if something darker was creeping into their lives, a thought she quickly chastised herself for.

"I hope you're right," she said. "It's just… he's not acting like himself."

Edwina stood and joined Kat, taking her hand in her own. "Give it time, love. He's a strong boy, just like his mother. He'll get through this, and so will you."

Kat squeezed her mum's hand, nodding even as her mind raced with a thousand worries. She wanted to believe that time would heal the wounds, that routine and normalcy would bring them back to the life they once had. But something deep inside her whispered things would never be the same.

Just as she was about to check on Tom, who had since dismissed himself to the sanctuary of the living room, her phone buzzed on the table. She picked it up, her heart skipping a beat when she saw Luke's name on the screen.

"Kat, when are your parents leaving?" Luke's voice was casual, but there was an undercurrent of something that made her pulse quicken.

"Friday," she replied, trying to keep her tone light. "Why do you ask?"

"Great," he said, the lightness in his voice fading. "Can I come round after work, then?"

Kat agreed and hung up, her mind racing. It didn't feel like a routine call; she could sense it in his voice. If Luke had something important to say, she didn't know if she was ready to hear it.

4

THE HOURS CRAWLED BY, shrouded in numbness. Kat knew her parents were right, and she had to focus on getting Tom back into his routine. The very next day, she took him to school, the first day of a new term, and watched as he trudged reluctantly through the gates. She knew it was important for him to regain some semblance of normalcy, but she couldn't ignore the nagging feeling that sending him back so soon might not be the best decision. She was also worried about how he might behave.

She spent the rest of that day at home, perched on the edge of the sofa with her laptop open, attempting to work but making little progress. The idea of going into the office felt overwhelming, yet it was inevitable. Adam's absence left a void that she would have to fill, and the thought of it made her chest tighten with anxiety. She hated the office environment, but she was no longer the boss's wife: she was the boss. But for now, she simply wasn't ready to face her colleagues, the whispers, the sympathetic glances. Instead, she stared blankly at the screen, her mind wandering to the events of the last few weeks.

The constant presence of her parents in the house did not help her mood that week, hovering over her with well-meaning attention yet somehow infuriating her more as the hours and days passed by. They fussed over Tom's meals, his bedtime routine, and even how she should manage the household in Adam's absence. At first, she appreciated their support, but as the days wore on, their existence grated on her. Their insistence that she was better off without him became a recurring theme in their conversations, and while Kat knew she had to move on, hearing it from them felt like an insult to the man she once loved. It was down to her how she moved on from Adam, not them.

"Adam was losing his grip, darling," her mother said after dinner on the Thursday evening. "By the end, he was… well, he was bordering on schizophrenia."

Kat nodded absently, though her stomach churned at the words. She didn't want to admit it, not even to herself, but her mother wasn't entirely wrong. Adam's behaviour had become increasingly erratic before his death, but it wasn't something she wanted to discuss with her parents, especially then. She caught herself glancing out of the window, her gaze once again drawn to Imogen's house across the street, its once-pristine garden presently wild and untamed. The memory of that day—the cold metal of the spade in her hands, the sickening thud as it connected with Imogen's skull—flashed in her mind. The dreams had been relentless, waking her in the middle of the night drenched in sweat, her heart pounding with guilt. But only since Adam's death. How had she coped so easily before? And what was different now?

By Friday morning, the tension between Kat and her

parents had reached boiling point. It started with another of their unsolicited opinions about Adam and ended with Kat snapping.

"Maybe Adam was right about you two!" she yelled, her voice shaking. "You don't know when to stop. I'm not a child anymore, and I don't need you hovering over me, telling me how to live my life. I'll call you if and when I feel like it."

William and Edwina exchanged glances, obviously hurt and amazed by the sudden outburst, yet neither of them said a word. They silently packed their suitcase and gathered their belongings, as if hoping she might take back what she'd said. But Kat stood her ground, arms crossed, watching as they trudged out of the door. She closed it behind them but immediately felt the weight of guilt settle on her shoulders. They were only trying to help. But it was too much. Everything was too much. She watched from the window as they climbed into a taxi to take them to the station, and for a fleeting moment, she considered running after them to apologise. Instead, she sank onto the sofa, burying her face in her hands.

That evening, with Tom in his bedroom playing, the doorbell rang, jolting her out of her thoughts. Opening the door, she found Luke standing there, a bottle of wine in one hand and a bouquet in the other. He gave her a small, reassuring smile, but she could see the tension in his eyes.

"Thought you might need these," he said, stepping past as she moved aside to let him in.

"Thank you, Luke," she replied, taking the flowers from him and leading them into the kitchen. The bouquet's scent was sweet and calming, a welcome contrast to the emotions swirling inside her. "You didn't have to."

"I wanted to," he said, setting the wine on the worktop. He glanced around, his gaze lingering on the cluttered kitchen table. "How are you holding up?"

Kat shrugged, trying to keep her voice steady. "I'm managing. But it's been difficult."

Luke nodded, his expression softening. "I know it's been hard, Kat. But you're strong. You'll get through this."

She looked at him, attempting to gauge the seriousness behind his words. "What did you want to talk about?"

He hesitated again, and for a moment, Kat thought he might change his mind. But then he sighed, running a hand through his hair. "I was waiting for your parents to leave because I didn't want to say this in front of them. It's about Adam, and… well, about everything that's happened."

Her heart skipped a beat, fear and curiosity mixing. "What do you mean?"

"Let's sit down," he suggested, gesturing to the table.

Kat couldn't shake the feeling that whatever Luke was about to say might change everything. He uncorked the wine, his back turned to her as she collected a vase from the cupboard, ignoring his request to sit. As he poured two glasses, she raised the bouquet to her face, inhaling the soothing fragrance of the blooms.

A faint smile broke out across her face. It was a slight comfort, a fleeting moment of regularity in a world that felt increasingly unstable. But as she lowered the flowers into the vase, she looked back at Luke and knew he had something important on his mind.

5

KAT FINALLY SAT at the table as Luke requested, the cold weight of the argument with her parents still making her feel uncomfortable. She would need to call them, make sure they got home okay.

She watched as Luke moved around the room, before setting one of the glasses of wine in front of her. He was calm, almost too calm, as if the past few weeks hadn't happened. His attitude was unsettling, but Kat reached for the glass anyway, the need for alcohol heightened by the tension of the day.

"Kat," Luke began, his voice steady. "I've been thinking about the business a lot now that Adam's gone."

She nodded, not quite meeting his eyes. Losing Adam had left a gaping hole in her life, not just emotionally, but practically. The thought of running the business without him was overwhelming. Luke continued. "You can't do it all by yourself, especially if you want to maintain some distance and keep working from home. It's just not viable."

Kat took another sip of wine, allowing his words to

sink in. She knew he was right, and it was a subject she'd visited a few times since Adam's accident. The business was too much for her to handle alone, especially now. She'd rarely been into the office—mostly after hours to avoid the tongue wagging—and the thought of going there regularly made her stomach churn. "I know," she admitted softly. "I'm not an office person, anyway, but I realise somebody has to be there, keeping their eye on things."

Luke leant forward, his smile returning. "I could help. But I think we need to make some changes."

"What kind of changes?" she asked, her curiosity piqued. She couldn't help her heart skipping a beat. Being so close to Luke with no interruptions had a calming effect on her. She desperately tried to push the image of Adam standing in the corner of the kitchen from her thoughts.

"I've been thinking," Luke continued slowly, as if choosing his words carefully, "that it might make sense if I had a stake in the company. Become a fellow director."

Kat wavered slightly, surprised by the suggestion. The idea of giving up part of the business hadn't even crossed her mind. She had inherited it alongside Adam, and despite everything, it felt like one of the last things she had left of him. Yet Luke's proposal made sense. It would relieve some of the pressure and allow her to keep her distance, to continue just as she had before. Look for new business, visit clients. If she could drum up the enthusiasm, of course.

"I don't know…" she began hesitantly, but he cut her off.

"Just think about it. It would be a fresh start for both of us. You could focus on what you need to, and I could take care of the day-to-day. We'd make a great team."

Kat nodded slowly, allowing the logic of his suggestion to seep in. After everything that had happened, perhaps it was the best way forward. They talked more about the business, discussing clients and finances, and as they began their second glass of wine, she felt herself relax a little more. She found the conversation easy, natural, and the topics of death and loss slowly slipped away.

Luke also mentioned Kevin, citing that his interest in his work had definitely waned since the accident. According to Luke, Kevin had confided that he thought someone had been wandering around outside Vicky's flat. But when they checked, no one was there, but Kevin couldn't dismiss the unease. Luke's mention was meant to be casual, an obvious ploy that he was the right man to keep his eye on things, but it set Kat on edge. Had they really seen somebody lingering outside their flat, or was it all in their imagination? Kat knew exactly how that felt.

As the conversation flowed and the wine took effect, Luke reached out and held her hand across the table. Kat didn't pull away, though a part of her screamed it wasn't right. Adam was barely cold in the ground, yet here she was, sitting with Luke, holding his hand like they were something more. She glanced at the empty place next to her once more, as if seeking some kind of approval.

Luke grinned, a mischievous twinkle in his eyes. "Remember that night Adam caught me sleepwalking?" he asked with a chuckle, as if reading her mind.

Kat couldn't help but giggle, despite the pang of guilt that twisted in her stomach. "How could I forget? You nearly gave him a heart attack."

"He was so serious about it," Luke continued, laughing. "I had to act my way out of it, make up some nonsense about stress at work. I thought he'd never let it go."

Kat smiled, but the memory was bittersweet. Adam had been suspicious, she knew that, but at the time, she'd told him it was all in his head. The more she thought about it, the more she realised just how close they'd come to getting caught.

"Do you think he ever suspected anything between us?" Luke asked, his tone dropping to something more serious.

Kat shook her head. "I don't think so. Adam… he had many issues towards the end. I don't think he could focus on anything properly."

The conversation lapsed, and Kat found herself lost in thought, still holding Luke's hand. It was comforting in a way, familiar, but it didn't feel quite right. She looked at their interlocked fingers as she spoke.

"How are things with Sandra? You know she caught you smiling at me at the funeral, don't you?"

At the mention of his wife, Luke's expression changed. He stood abruptly and began pacing the room. "It happened before the funeral," he confessed. "She suspected something between us weeks ago." He turned to face Kat. "She's left me. I've pulled out of buying the flat just along the road. I'm staying at my place near Russell Square for a bit. Until I find my feet."

Kat stared at him, shocked at the way Luke spoke, but not with the content. There was a sense of relief in his voice, as if Sandra's departure was exactly what he wanted. She felt a shiver of unease, but before she could respond, Luke was beside her again, his hand resting on her shoulder.

"It's just us now," he said softly, his tone a little possessive. "We can finally be together, without anything or anyone in the way. I adore Tom too. It could be just perfect, Kat. A new beginning for all of us."

Kat's heart pounded in her chest, a mix of fear and confusion swirling inside. She watched as Luke strolled around the kitchen, retrieving the bottle to refill their glasses, as if he was already part of the scene. She caught the scent of the fresh flowers, and a slight smile crept across her face, but deep down, she couldn't dispel the sense that the entire scenario had been planned months in advance.

6

They sat together in the living room, talking about nothing in particular. After a while, Luke reached out to touch her hand, and again, she didn't pull away.

When Luke made a move to kiss her, Kat allowed it, but the guilt troubled her. They hugged for a long moment, and spurred on by the alcohol, they kissed again. It wasn't as innocent as before; it was tinged with something deeper, something that frightened her as much as it excited her.

But just as things were heating up, the doorbell rang. Kat jumped, pulling away from Luke as if caught doing something illegal. It was the pizza delivery. Grateful for the interruption, she excused herself to get the food, using the time to regain her composure. She called Tom down from his bedroom, flattening her hair that didn't need flattening.

Luke smiled at her as she set the pizzas on the table, and she could see the desire in his eyes. He wanted more, but she wasn't ready to give it. Not yet. Not ever?

Luke stayed the night, but in the spare room. The

next morning, he kissed her playfully on the cheek before leaving, his hand lingering on her back a moment too long. Tom was oblivious, but Kat knew she needed to be careful. Luke's presence was comforting, but there was a kind of possessiveness in him she didn't like.

A few days after her parents had left, Kat finally decided to FaceTime them. She'd let them stew for a while, partly out of stubbornness and partly because she wanted space to think. The conversation started off strained, but when she mentioned Luke was interested in helping with the business, she could see the delight on their faces. The tension dissipated almost immediately, on their side at least.

"That's a wonderful idea," Edwina exclaimed. "It'll take a huge burden off your shoulders, something Adam never helped with."

Kat instantly felt the familiar irritation rise within her. Even now, they couldn't resist criticising Adam. Her mum smiled knowingly. "Not only is Luke good at business decisions, but I always thought he was very dishy too."

Kat forced a laugh, but the conversation left her feeling unsettled. Her parents' approval should have been a comfort, but instead, it felt like pressure. They didn't know everything, and Kat wasn't sure she wanted them to.

As the next two weeks passed, Kat found herself meeting Luke at the café more often than necessary, discussing the business and the future. But it annoyed her as he continued to cross her boundaries, reaching out to hold her hand or brushing his leg against hers under the table.

She reminded him, again, that they needed to take things slow. He agreed, but there was a definite flicker of disappointment in his eyes.

However, despite her reservations, the idea of bringing Luke into the company made more sense with each passing day. He had great ideas and good contacts in the city. Almost two weeks after their initial conversation, Kat contacted her accountant to get the ball rolling. Luke would be made Managing Director.

But even as she reached the decision, her mind was often elsewhere. She couldn't help but think of Tom. Fortunately, as far as Kat was aware, he had settled into school as if nothing had changed, but at home, his behaviour remained worryingly unsettling. He refused to speak about his feelings, barely acknowledging her once inside the confines of the house.

One evening, Kat heard him moving around upstairs long after he should have been asleep. She climbed the stairs quietly, pausing outside his door. She could hear him talking to someone, his tone a constant murmur. Her heart raced. Was he talking to himself? Or did he believe there was something, or someone, else in the room with him?

She knocked gently and opened the door, her eyes flicking everywhere. Tom was sitting on the floor, his back to her, drawing on a piece of paper. When he turned to look at her, his expression was untroubled, almost otherworldly in its calmness.

"I've made this for you, Mummy," he said, holding out a picture.

Kat's heart melted as she took it, but when she flipped it over, her blood ran cold. It was a drawing of the house opposite. The windows, doors, planters in the upstairs windows; all were meticulously detailed as much as a six-year-old could muster. And standing in front of the house, smiling, was the woman she recognised all too well.

"Who's this?" she asked, pointing, her hand shaking.

"Aunty Imogen, of course," Tom said matter-of-factly.

"Why have you drawn her, darling?" Kat begged, her voice trembling.

"Because she's coming home," Tom replied, his eyes wide and unblinking.

The drawing remained on the kitchen counter well after Tom had gone back to bed. Kat couldn't bring herself to throw it away, but neither could she look at it for too long. The likeness was haunting in its simplicity, even with the imperfections of a child's hand.

That night, she barely slept. She tossed and turned, her thoughts churning over Tom's behaviour, Luke's advances, and the creepy drawing that seemed to hold some kind of sinister significance.

By morning, she was exhausted, both physically and mentally. She went through the motions of getting Tom ready for school, her mind elsewhere. As she watched him walk through the school gates, a sense of dread settled in her stomach.

Driving home, she couldn't shake the feeling that she was being watched. Every pedestrian seemed to look in her direction, every car followed too closely. As soon as she stepped into her house, she shut the door behind her and locked the Chubb. Her breathing was erratic. Once in the kitchen, she placed a coffee pod in the machine, quickly realising that caffeine was the last thing she needed for an already pounding heart. So, instead, she poured herself a glass of wine, despite it only being nine thirty on a Friday morning. "What the hell is becoming of me?" she said to the empty chair on the far side of the table.

Sitting down, Kat found herself staring at Tom's drawing once again. The house opposite, the smiling woman, and Tom's words echoing in her mind. *"She's coming home."*

But Imogen wasn't coming home, Kat kept repeating. She couldn't be. For Imogen Daley was dead.

7

THE START of a new working week found Kat dragging herself through the motions of daily life. The weekend had been a blur of sleepless nights, punctuated by the persistent image of Tom's drawing. It haunted her, its details ingrained into her mind.

Monday morning came with January clinging onto the short days and forever dull skies. Kat decided she had to confront the issues at work. Luke's comments about Kevin slacking had cemented themselves in her brain. Not only was she worried about the figure Kevin and Vicky had reportedly seen near their flat, but Luke's observation about Kevin's waning commitment needed addressing. She couldn't afford to have someone on the team who wasn't fully invested. Or had she been looking for the ideal excuse ever since that night?

After dropping Tom off at school, she drove to the office and took a deep breath, steeling herself for the inevitable confrontation ahead. She found Kevin hunched over his desk, his back turned to her. For a moment, she hesitated, wondering if she was overacting.

"Kevin," she called, her voice sharper than intended.

He turned slowly, his expression a mix of surprise and annoyance. "Kat. I wasn't expecting you here."

"Can I see you in my office, please?"

Kat intentionally averted her gaze from Luke, although she could feel his eyes boring into her.

After Kevin sat down, Kat closed the door and didn't waste any time on pleasantries. "I've been hearing some concerning things, Kevin."

Kevin's eyes narrowed. "What kind of things? And who's been telling you?" He turned his head to look through the glass wall towards Luke.

"Don't play dumb," Kat snapped, regaining his attention. "I've heard your work has been slipping. Is it true?"

Kevin's face flushed with anger. "You're accusing me of slacking? I've been working my ass off! Is this to do with Adam being at our flat on the night he was killed? You can't take that out on—"

Kat's temper flared. "Don't be so facetious," she snapped. "I expect answers, not excuses. If your heart's not in this job anymore, just say so."

The tension in the room was tangible. She hadn't expected the meeting to go downhill so rapidly, but Kat knew she only had herself to blame for that. Kevin stood up, surprising her, before pushing his chair back with such force it nearly toppled over. "Fine. You want me to leave? I'll go. I don't need this shit."

Kat felt Luke's observations of Kevin had been vindicated and, with a stiff smile, said, "Good. I accept your resignation."

Just as the words left her mouth, Luke appeared in the doorway. "What's going on?" he asked, though it was clear he had heard everything.

"Kevin was about to leave," Kat said, her voice calm

yet her anger not subsiding. It wasn't helped by Luke just inviting himself in.

Luke nodded, stepping aside as Kevin stormed past him, muttering curses under his breath. Once Kevin was gone, Luke closed the door and turned to Kat, a strange look in his eyes.

"You did the right thing," he said, but there was an element in his tone that Kat didn't like.

For a moment, they stood in silence, each waiting for the other. Kat couldn't help but notice the way Luke was looking at her, a mixture of admiration and something darker, something she couldn't quite place.

At home later that day, Kat replayed the events in her mind. She was unable to shake the image of Luke's face after Kevin left; the way his eyes had lingered on her, almost as if he was enjoying the moment, as if it was all down to him. She felt a shiver run through her, though the house was warm.

She wandered to the window, her gaze drifting to Imogen's old place across the street. The 'Sold' sign still stood starkly against the dreary backdrop. Kat pressed her hand against the glass, staring at the house as if it could offer her some answer, some explanation for the growing unease inside her.

Tom was quiet at dinner, his pupils distant as he pushed his food around his plate. Kat tried to engage him, but he barely responded, retreating to his room as soon as he finished eating.

Kat picked up her phone and hesitated before dialling her parents' number. They answered on the second ring, and the familiar sound of her mother's voice brought a small measure of comfort.

"Kat, darling, how are you holding up?" Edwina asked, concern evident in her tone.

Kat sighed, trying to keep her voice steady. "I'm okay, I guess. It's just… there's so much going on, and I feel like everything's spiralling out of control."

"Of course, it's going to be overwhelming," her mum replied sympathetically. "But you will get through this."

"It's not just that," Kat said, her voice trembling slightly. "Tom's still acting strange. He barely speaks at home, and when he does, it's like he's in his own world. I'm scared, Mum. What if it's more than just grief?"

There was a pause on the other end of the line before Edwina spoke again. "Tom's going through a lot, sweetheart. Losing his father… it's bound to affect him. But I really think it's just part of the grieving process. You're doing everything you can for him."

Kat wasn't convinced, but she didn't argue. "And then there's Luke," she continued. "He's been coming on really strong. About the business and… personally."

"That's wonderful, darling," Edwina said, her voice brightening. "You need someone to lean on right now. Luke cares about you, and he's willing to help. That's a good thing."

"But I'm not sure I'm ready for anything like that," Kat admitted. "It's too soon…"

"Give it time," her mother reassured her. "But don't push him away. You deserve to have someone who cherishes you. And as for the business, it sounds like Luke is stepping up just when you need him the most."

Kat hesitated before bringing up Kevin. "I had a confrontation with Kevin today. He handed in his notice after I asked him about his performance."

"Well, good riddance," Edwina said, taking Kat by surprise. "If he wasn't doing his share of the work, you're better off without him. And it's a good job Luke was there to back you up. You need someone strong in your corner, especially now."

"How do you know Luke backed me up?" Kat asked, standing and pacing to the window.

Edwina replied after a brief pause.

"You told me," she said. "Just now."

Although Kat couldn't recall saying that, she still placated her mum. "I suppose you're right."

"Hang in there, darling," Edwina said softly. "It'll all come good in the end. Just take it one day at a time."

They ended the call, but Kat's unease hadn't lessened. She stared at her phone for a long moment before her gaze drifted across the street to Imogen's house. The curtains remained drawn, as they had been for days, and the place looked as empty and silent as ever. But just as she was about to turn away, something caught her eye; a fleeting shadow in the upstairs window.

Kat froze. She strained her eyes, trying to focus on the spot where she thought she'd seen movement, but when she looked back up, the window was empty.

8

THE WEEK WAS a mixture of unsettling changes and creeping dread for Kat. Kevin's abrupt departure from the company left her feeling uneasy. Kat insisted on his immediate exit, encouraged by Luke's warning about Kevin's potential to manipulate the company's software. The thought of Kevin having access to sensitive data prompted her to pay him in full, if only to confirm he could cause no further harm. However, attempting to put Kevin behind her wasn't as simple as Kat hoped.

Twenty-four hours after he stormed out of the office, Vicky phoned her. Kat was supposed to be working from home but, as usual, her was mind was elsewhere.

"Hello?"

"Kat." Vicky's voice was tight, barely controlled. "You've made a mistake."

"Oh?" Kat's utterance was as neutral as she could make it, masking the flicker of curiosity rising within her.

"Yes," Vicky continued, her tone hardening. "You shouldn't have let Kevin walk away like that."

Kat's brow furrowed. "What exactly are you getting at, Vicky?"

There was a brief silence on the other end of the line before Vicky spoke again, her words laced with bitterness. "Let's just say my aunt Pauline was onto something. She'd been watching, observing... and she knew more than anyone realises." The last part came out like a dare, as though Vicky wanted Kat to react.

Kat's heart skipped a beat, but she forced herself to remain calm. "Your aunt Pauline?" she echoed, careful to keep her tone measured. "And what did she know, exactly?"

"Enough to raise some eyebrows," Vicky replied, a sly inflection creeping into her voice. "Secrets that made Adam uncomfortable. Ones I'm sure you wouldn't want to be dragged out, either."

Kat's fingers tightened around her phone, but she laughed, keeping her tone light. "I have nothing to hide, Vicky. I'm just surprised you're suddenly so concerned about secrets."

"Oh, come off it, Kat," Vicky snapped. "Everyone has skeletons, and don't pretend you're any different."

A chill swept through Kat, but she held her ground. "What are you getting at?"

There was a pause, and then Vicky's voice softened, almost sweetly. "Did you ever meet Bob's children? Nathan and Belinda Lane?" She let the words hang, as though inviting Kat to make the connection.

Kat's mind raced. Why would Bob's children—Nathan and Belinda—have anything to do with all this?

"I don't see what they'd know," Kat said, forcing nonchalance, though her pulse accelerated.

"Believe what you want," Vicky replied, her voice

Truth Lies Beneath

thick with disdain. With that, she hung up, leaving Kat in stunned silence.

As the call ended, Kat sat motionless, Vicky's words reverberating in her head. Kat knew about her aunt Pauline. But Nathan and Belinda were somehow tangled up in all this too? Her heart pounded as she wondered what it all meant. Had Adam kept further secrets from her?

Her mind spiralled with questions. One thing was becoming clear: Vicky, Kevin, and now Nathan and Belinda were all connected somehow, tied together by something dark involving Adam.

Kat didn't sleep that night, forever wondering how much Vicky might actually know and how much she was bluffing. Although she had caused nowhere near as much carnage as Adam had, Kat still feared somebody being able to prove her part in Imogen's death. Tom's drawings and mutterings of her coming home only added to her increased risk of developing a psychosis. Had the same thing happened to Adam?

On Friday evening, at the end of an endless week, Kat watched the sun dip below the horizon, finding a rare moment of respite. Lauren had agreed to take Tom for a sleepover alongside Max. She seemed reluctant at first, given Tom's strange antics the last time he was there, but Kat persuaded her it was just his way of coping with the loss of his dad. Lauren took pity and gladly agreed to have him. The peace and quiet allowed Kat the opportunity to reclaim some semblance of routine and perhaps spend some time in the company of the person she found herself relying on more and more. She invited Luke over.

When he arrived, armed with a bottle of wine, it felt

like a breath of fresh air. His presence had an instant soothing effect. They settled in the living room, choosing one of Kat's favourite movies and as they watched, she could feel the tension physically ease from her shoulders.

The wine flowed freely, too freely, and with each glass, the barriers between her and Luke receded. His charm soon won her over, and as they snuggled up on the sofa, Kat felt a flicker of excitement run through her.

As they kissed, Kat sensed both a pang of guilt and a desperate longing for the comfort Luke offered. The transition from the sofa to the bedroom took her by surprise, driven by her need for closeness and intimacy. The night was a blur of sensations, a whirlwind of lost inhibitions and desires. As they came together, it was as though her world of problems ceased to exist, leaving only the two of them safe in each other's arms.

By the time the first light of day filtered through the curtains, Kat and Luke lay entwined, their bodies a tangle of exhaustion and contentment. Sleep was rare, their passions keeping them awake but Kat reluctantly untangled herself from Luke's embrace. She had promised to pick up Tom from Lauren's and, as she kissed Luke one last time, the reality of her responsibilities made her curse. Oh, to spend the day in Luke's arms.

After Luke left, Kat dressed quickly, her mind hazy from the wine and the night of passion. She pushed aside the lingering thoughts of Vicky's call and the uncertainty of everything else that messed with her head. As she stepped out of her house, the crisp morning air greeted her, invigorating and welcoming. She took a deep breath, and for the first time in months, believed that all might be okay after all.

But then, her eyes fell upon a figure standing at the end of her footpath. For a fleeting moment, her heart skipped a beat. It was Sandra, her expression unreadable, a mask of calm that did nothing to quell the storm brewing inside Kat.

Sandra stood still, her posture rigid, her gaze fixed intently on Kat. Did she know Luke had slept over? Had she waited until he left?

Kat's mind raced, the memories from her night with Luke quickly overshadowed by Sandra's unexpected appearance.

"Morning, Sandra," Kat managed to say, her voice wavering slightly despite her best efforts to sound composed.

Sandra's eyes remained locked onto Kat's, a cold, calculating gaze that seemed to pierce right through her. "Kat," Sandra said, her voice smooth but laced with an undercurrent of tension. "I was hoping to have a word."

Kat's heart pounded in her chest, a sense of dread filling her as she wondered what the hell Sandra wanted.

Sandra took a step closer, her expression softening slightly. "I'd like to discuss a few things, if you don't mind. It's important."

Kat nodded, her thoughts racing. She knew she had little choice but to deal with Sandra, but the weight of the night with Luke and the ongoing turmoil in her life made her feel unprepared.

Sandra followed Kat inside, the warmth of the house hitting Kat hard in contrast to the chill outside. She offered Sandra a seat, her hands trembling as she filled the coffee machine.

Finally, after accepting her drink, Sandra spoke, her voice low and measured. "I know things have been difficult lately. Luke told me a bit about the situation, and I'm here to offer my support."

Kat's heart skipped a beat. Support? She forced a

smile, trying to read Sandra's intentions as she responded. "I appreciate that. It has been a difficult time, and any help is welcome."

Sandra nodded. "I'm sure you've got a lot on your mind, especially with everything that's happened. But I want you to know that Luke is committed to helping you through this. He's been a rock, hasn't he?"

Kat swallowed hard, the edge in Sandra's tone doing little to ease the restlessness that had settled in her stomach. "Yes, he has. He's been very supportive."

Sandra's smile appeared genuine. "That's good to hear. We all need someone we can rely on during difficult times."

With that, Sandra stood to leave, her coffee untouched. The conversation had been ambiguous, leaving Kat with more questions than answers. She watched as Sandra left, her thoughts tangled with uncertainties, yet she was genuinely pleased to see the back of her.

9

The drive to Lauren's house was a blur, Kat's mind preoccupied with Sandra's visit. Sandra's calm demeanour had only deepened Kat's feeling of unease. And if she knew Luke had stayed over, why hadn't she confronted her? And why had she spoken so cryptically about Luke being a good friend? None of it made sense.

But she needed answers, and she couldn't wait any longer. Pulling over to the side of the road, Kat took a deep breath and dialled Luke's number. It rang a few times before he picked up, only adding to her torment.

"Hey, Kat," Luke said cheerily. "Missing me already?"

"Luke, did you tell Sandra you were staying overnight at my house?" Kat's voice was harsher than she intended.

There was a brief pause. "No, why would I?"

Kat felt her frustration boiling over. "Because she just showed up at my house about twenty minutes after you left! She talked about you being a good friend, someone I could rely on. It felt... weird, like some kind of cryptic message. Then, she just upped and left. It had to be you."

"Kat, I swear, I didn't talk to Sandra," Luke replied,

his tone defensive. "I've only seen her once since we separated a month ago, and that was at Adam's funeral. I don't even know where she's staying. I presumed she was with her friend on the south coast."

But Kat remained unconvinced. "Sandra said something else strange. She told me we all need someone we can rely on during difficult times. She was talking about you, Luke. What did she mean by that?"

"I don't know," Luke admitted. "It doesn't sound like her. But, as I said, I haven't been in touch with her. You have to believe me."

Kat ended the call, feeling no closer to the truth. Luke's reassurances seemed genuine, but she couldn't rid herself of the sense that something still wasn't quite right. She already regretted spending the night with him.

When she arrived at Lauren's house, she found Tom playing happily with Max, his carefree demeanour a welcome relief. At least it was something positive, and Kat thanked Lauren for allowing Tom to stay.

"Anytime," Lauren replied genuinely. Her warm smile, at least, made Kat feel a bit better about someone. "Are you okay?" she added, obviously noticing Kat's jumpy behaviour, her eyes darting everywhere.

After reassuring Lauren that she was just stressed because of the business, she thanked her once more before driving home in near silence.

But as she turned into her street, her heartbeat increased. Standing in front of Imogen's house was a large removal lorry, its back open as removal men carried furniture and boxes into the house. Kat had no inclination her new neighbours would move in so soon.

She parked her car and hurried towards the lorry, Tom following close behind. One guy, a burly man with a clipboard, looked up as she approached.

"Excuse me," Kat said, trying to keep her voice steady. "Who's moving in?"

The man shrugged. "We're just shifting her furniture."

Her?

"She arrives on Monday."

Kat's stomach dropped. "Who is she? Do you know?"

"Can't say, ma'am. We simply follow the orders."

Kat stepped back, her mind whirling. "Come on, Tom," she said, taking his hand and leading him home. But as they walked away, she noticed Tom glancing back at Imogen's house, a subtle smirk playing on his lips.

When they got inside, Kat set her keys down and looked across the street, the removal lorry obstructing the view of the house. Tom stood beside her, staring too.

"Why are they putting Aunty Imogen's things back?" Tom asked quietly.

Kat forced a smile. "They're not, darling," she said. "Somebody else is moving in."

But as she looked down at Tom, her heart sank. He was still smiling, his eyes fixed on the removal lorry across the street. His expression sent a chill down Kat's spine.

"Why are you smiling?" she asked softly.

Tom turned to her, his grin unwavering. "I'm just happy, Mummy. Aren't you?"

10

Kat spent much of the weekend wrestling with what to do about Tom. Should she contact her local GP and try to book an appointment, or go direct to a more specialised consultant? Or was she simply overreacting? Besides, Kat didn't even know if there were such things as child psychiatrists; she'd never thought she would need such a service.

Monday morning arrived, and Kat was wide awake before the sun rose. The feeling of unease that had taken root in her chest refused to leave. She got Tom ready for school, grateful for the routine that temporarily diverted her thoughts. Tom seemed in better spirits, as if his comments about Imogen hadn't taken place at all. He chattered excitedly about the possibility of building a snowman as flurries of snow drifted through the air. His sudden shift back to being a playful, loving boy only heightened Kat's sense of anxiety, as if the questions regarding Imogen's furniture had been from an entirely different person. Maybe her mum was right, and he was just grieving?

Truth Lies Beneath

After dropping Tom off at school, Kat returned home, her nerves still on edge. The house across the street was quiet, with no sign of life, no car in the driveway. The anticipation tormented her, and she soon found herself back upstairs, staring out of her bedroom window once more.

Then, at eleven o'clock, a sleek four-by-four pulled into the driveway. Kat's heart skipped a beat, and she inched closer to the window, careful to stay hidden behind the curtain. She watched as the driver's door opened, her pulse quickening with each passing second. The first thing she saw was a pair of knee-length boots stepping out, followed by tight jeans hugging the figure as the occupant stood up while keeping her back to Kat.

Kat's breath caught in her throat as she observed the woman reach up and pull a mass of long, shiny black hair free from her jumper, cascading down to the centre of her back, strikingly similar to Imogen's. Kat could barely breathe, the fear in her chest morphing into something closer to terror. It can't be, she thought, desperately trying to rationalise what she was seeing.

The woman moved with a familiar grace as she approached the front door of the house, her height, her build, everything about her was reminiscent of Imogen. Kat's mouth went dry, and her hands trembled as she clutched the curtain. It had to be a coincidence, she told herself, but Tom's words echoed in her mind.

"She's coming home…"

As the stranger reached the door, she paused, hesitating, as though she felt someone's eyes on her. Slowly, she turned her head, glancing to her right, offering Kat a partial view of her face. Olive skin, sharp features; Kat's heart was pounding so hard she was sure the woman would hear it from across the street. And then, as if sensing her, the woman's gaze landed directly on Kat's house.

Panicking, Kat jumped back from the window, her breath coming in shallow gasps. Had the newcomer seen her? She waited, frozen in place, for what felt like an eternity before finally daring to peek out from behind the curtain again.

The figure was gone. The front door of the house was closed. But Kat knew, with a sickening certainty, that she had indeed been seen watching. The way she had looked in Kat's direction was no accident.

Kat spent the rest of the day in a daze, unable to focus on anything. Every sound, every creak of the house made her jump. She couldn't shake the feeling that something was terribly wrong, that this new neighbour was more than just a stranger moving in across the street. She retrieved Tom's drawing once more, staring in disbelief at the figures depicted in the garden. Kat ripped it in half and in half again until all that remained were tiny bits of confetti.

As the afternoon stretched on, Kat kept glancing out the window, half expecting to see the woman again. She tried to tell herself that it was all in her head, that she was letting her fears get the better of her.

By the time the school day ended, and she picked up Tom, Kat's nerves were frayed. She made small talk with him on the drive home, but her mind was elsewhere, back on the stranger across the street.

When they arrived home, Tom immediately ran upstairs to his room, leaving Kat standing alone in the hallway. At least he appeared to have forgotten about their new neighbour moving in, which Kat found disturbing in its own right. Why would he be so preoccupied and certain that Imogen was coming back one minute, and then apparently oblivious to anybody being in the house at all?

She glanced out of the window one last time, and her heart skipped a beat when she saw the front door slightly ajar. There was no sign of the woman, but the sight of the open door filled Kat with deep foreboding.

What was happening? Where had she gone?

Kat pulled out her phone and called her parents. She needed to talk to someone, to get some reassurance that she wasn't losing her mind. But as the phone rang, she couldn't shake the feeling that the woman might be in her rear garden, or worse still, somewhere in the house.

11

Kat's parents had been typically dismissive when she called them, but at least her unwanted suspicions about the woman being in the house diminished as soon as she heard her mum's soothing voice. "Stop being so paranoid, darling," Edwina chided. "Why don't you take a cake over tomorrow and introduce yourself? That way, you'll see it's not Imogen, and you can put your mind at ease. You never know, she could be just the neighbour you need. A friend to call upon."

It made sense, Kat supposed, but the idea of confronting the woman across the street filled her with dread. She couldn't ignore what happened the last time she set foot in that house.

Sleep eluded her yet again that night, her thoughts an endless loop of fear. The next morning, as she bundled Tom in the car for school, she noticed that the snow was settling, the icy February wind biting.

The drive to school was a blur. Tom chattered away in the rear seat, something about building a snowman, but it barely registered as she responded with nods and smiles. By the time she returned home, the street was quiet, the snow a thin blanket over the road and footpaths. But the sight of the four-by-four still parked in the driveway opposite caused Kat's anxiety to flare again.

She spent the morning trying to drum up the courage to take her mother's advice. She'd stopped at the supermarket on the way home and bought a cake—chocolate, always a safe option—but still she hesitated by the window, her eyes locked on the house opposite. Each time she decided to go, she pulled back; her fear winning over her logic.

Finally, her phone rang, breaking the cycle of indecision. It was Luke.

"Kat, we need to talk." Luke's voice was steady, but there was an edge to it that made Kat's stomach drop. She felt a wave of guilt. She had been neglecting the business, and it was becoming clear that Luke was holding things together in her absence.

"What's wrong?" she asked, trying to keep her tone neutral.

"I got a call from Kevin," Luke said. "He told me not to get involved in the business. Said something's off." Luke paused again, as if waiting for Kat to reply. "Is there anything you're not telling me?"

Kat's heart raced. "What? No, of course not!" she replied, a bit too quickly. "Kevin's just trying to stir things up because he's pissed off that I let him go so easily. You know how he is."

Luke sighed on the other end. "I pressed him for more, but he clammed up. Said I should work things out for myself. I need to know if there's something going on."

"No, Luke, I swear. Kevin's just being spiteful," Kat insisted, though her thoughts immediately turned to

Vicky. The memory of her threatening call sent a shiver through her.

Luke was silent for a moment, then his voice softened. "Alright. I trust you, Kat. But if there's anything… please…"

"There isn't," Kat lied. "Just ignore him."

After they hung up, Kat remained standing by the window, the phone still clutched in her hand. She had convinced Luke for the moment, but both Vicky's, and now Kevin's threats, were something she didn't need. But how much did he really know? And why call Luke and then clam up? And then there was Vicky—what had her aunt Pauline really dug up about Adam?

As the thoughts swirled in her head, a darker one surfaced. How much simpler her life would be if Kevin and Vicky were no longer around. The idea was both terrifying and strangely soothing, like a solution she hadn't allowed herself to consider until then.

By mid-morning, Kat was still pacing the living room, her thoughts circling around the events of the past few days. Luke's calming presence had been a comfort, but there was something unsettling about how easily he appeared to be stepping into Adam's shoes. He was supportive, almost too supportive, and he'd handled things well since Kevin's departure. He was efficient, maybe too efficient.

Kat shook her head, trying to dispel the unjustified suspicion that was creeping in. She needed to get a grip. She couldn't afford to lose herself, not having come so far. But it was so much easier from the outside looking in, like her parents, than it was when you'd played such a fundamental role in everything. Not only that, but Kat had once taken great delight in Adam's exploits. The way he had *disposed* of all those who stood in their path. It's what she'd always wanted, her own business. What they had both desired all their lives. An inseparable duo. Kat chuckled to herself as she glanced at Adam's reading chair in the corner of the room.

The snow outside was falling thicker, covering the ground. Kat wrapped her arms around herself, feeling a chill that had nothing to do with the weather. And yet, she still couldn't shake the sensation that Kevin and Vicky were on the brink of taking things further.

She found herself thinking about the flat they shared. The last place Adam had been. The impromptu invitation continued to play heavily on her mind. Maybe it was time she paid them a call. If they were plotting something, she needed to know what it was. And if they were just trying to scare her, she needed to put an end to it.

But as she turned away from the window, a fresh fear gripped her. What if Luke was involved? What if *he* was hiding something? The thought sent a jolt of terror through her, but she pushed it aside. She couldn't afford to distrust Luke, not now. She needed him. He was the only one holding everything together.

Kat took a deep breath, trying to steady herself. She must stay focused. As she looked back out at the snow-covered street, she made up her mind. She would confront Kevin and Vicky, get to the bottom of it all. And if she found out that Luke was involved… well, she would deal with that too. Everybody was disposable.

But for now, it was necessary for her to introduce herself to her new neighbour, and that in itself made her skin prickle.

12

Kat stood in her hallway, gripping the packaging around the cake tightly in her hands. She had spent the entire morning working up the courage to walk across the street, feeling the weight of all her burdens from that house pressing down on her. The memories of the times she and Adam were there with Imogen and Liam were bittersweet, filled with laughter and friendship, until everything began to fall apart.

Taking a deep breath, Kat crossed the road, each step becoming heavier than the last. The thin layer of snow crunched beneath her boots; flurries still filled the air. The house loomed ahead, familiar yet somehow different.

When she reached the door, she hesitated, her heart racing in her chest. The thought of being inside that place again, of facing the ghosts of her past, made her stomach churn. But she needed to do this, to confront whatever was left of those memories and finally move on.

Kat rang the doorbell, the sound evoking memories of Tom pressing it, a huge smile across his face with the promise of another gift from his aunt Imogen. She remembered his drawing. The windows, doors, planters. And standing in front of the house, smiling, was his favourite aunt.

She tensed as she heard footsteps approaching from the other side, the heavy sound of boots on the wooden floor sending a jolt of anxiety through her. When the door opened, Kat held her breath, bracing herself for the worst.

And for a dizzying second, she believed Imogen had returned. The resemblance was almost supernatural—glossy black hair cascading over olive skin, and a delicate bone structure that mirrored Imogen's perfectly. But, blinking hard, Kat realised she had to be mistaken.

On closer inspection, the woman was close in appearance, but as Kat took in the subtle differences—her shorter height and warm brown eyes instead of Imogen's sparkling blue—Kat exhaled. She felt foolish for even thinking it, but for that brief moment, she'd been so certain.

The woman was attractive, undeniably, and Kat couldn't help but think what Adam would make of her. She found herself looking over her shoulder, waiting for the curtains to twitch as Adam tried to catch a glimpse of their new neighbour. Kat managed to swallow the rising tide of emotions that had briefly surged within her. She offered a smile, the kind that concealed more than it revealed, still unconvinced by the amazing similarity.

The woman smiled warmly, her expression friendly. "Hello. Can I help you?"

After a few moments, Kat came to her senses, realising she was just standing there, staring. Quickly, she found her voice. "Hi, I'm Kat. I live across the street with my six-year-old son, Tom. I wanted to welcome you to the neighbourhood." She knew she was babbling, her tongue tripping over the words. Awkwardly, she held out the cake, still in its supermarket wrapper with the price sticker clearly visible. Kat felt herself redden.

The woman took the cake with a smile. "Thank you, that's really kind of you. I'm Clara. Clara Denton. Nice to meet you. Would you like to come in for a coffee?"

Kat hesitated before nodding unconvincingly. She took another glance over her shoulder at her living room window. She knew Adam would approve.

Clara stepped to one side, but the thought of going inside that house made Kat waver. Should she really accept the invitation or just leave Clara with the cake? The memories of laughter and shared meals, along with the painful reminder of how it had ended, all echoed around her mind. Clara must have noticed her hesitation and asked, "Are you alright?"

Kat forced a smile and nodded again, following Clara into the house. The interior was much the same as she remembered, though the furniture was different. The space was familiar, yet strange, filled with remnants of laughter that seemed to linger in the air.

Clara led her into the kitchen, and Kat felt a pang of nostalgia as she stepped inside. She could almost see the four of them sitting around the table, the sound of Imogen's giggling ringing in her ears. Her head spun, and she reached out to steady herself against the counter.

"Please, sit down," Clara urged, her concern genuine. "I'll get you a glass of water."

Kat sat at the table, her eyes scanning the room. It was surreal to be back in that place where so much had happened. When Clara returned with the water, Kat took a sip, trying to calm her racing heart.

The conversation started off slowly, with Kat still reeling from the flood of memories and the undeniable similarities between Imogen and her new neighbour. But Clara's warmth and friendliness gradually put her at ease. They chatted about the neighbourhood and the house, and Kat found herself asking the question that had been on her mind since she first saw the 'Sold' sign.

"How did you get to buy this place? I didn't think it was even on the market."

Clara's expression shifted slightly, a flicker of something unreadable. "No, it wasn't," she began. "But I'd been interested in the area for a while. I used to drive by here, and when I saw the house was empty, I made some calls. It took a bit of digging, but I found out who the solicitor was handling the estate. They eventually agreed it could be sold, and I bought it as soon as they did."

Kat nodded, though something about the story didn't sit right with her. It seemed too convenient, too simple. But she didn't know enough about how such things worked to question it further. And what had her dad said that day?

"When someone dies without a will or any known relatives, their estate passes to the Crown. I suppose anyone can apply to buy the property after that."

After fifteen minutes of friendly yet stilted chat, Kat left Clara's house, experiencing a mix of relief and trepidation. Clara seemed genuine, but there was something about her that Kat couldn't quite put her finger on. Perhaps it was the way she had spoken about buying the house, or maybe it was just the uncanny resemblance to Imogen that left Kat feeling unsettled.

Back home, she tried to shake off the lingering doubts. She had done what she needed to do—introduced herself and stepped back inside the house she always doubted she would ever visit again. But as she stood at her window, looking across the street, she couldn't help but feel that something was still amiss.

The memories of Imogen, Liam, and Adam wouldn't leave her alone, and the house, once a symbol of friendship and happiness, now felt like a dark reminder of everything that had gone wrong.

Kat clenched her fists, trying to push the thoughts away. She wanted to believe that she could finally move on, but deep down, she wondered if the past would ever be over.

13

Kat bundled herself in a thick coat, wrapping a scarf around her neck as she prepared to leave the house to pick up Tom from school. As she stepped outside, her gaze fell on Clara's driveway, and she noticed that the car was gone. Fresh tyre tracks were visible in the otherwise pristine snow leading down the street. Kat frowned, trying to recall if she had heard the car depart, but her mind drew a blank.

She shook her head, dismissing the creeping unease. Of course, Clara had every right to come and go as she pleased. Still, something about the quiet departure somehow bothered her, even though she realised she wasn't being at all rational. She drove to collect Tom, trying to shake off the odd sensation that had settled over her.

The cold air bit at her cheeks as she waited by the school gates, glancing around at the other parents, believing their eyes were on her. Were they all feeling sorry for the woman who lost her husband in a hideous hit-and-run accident? Raising a child by herself, so soon after being caught up in the deaths of her close neighbours too? How *is* she coping?

As she tried to make herself as small as possible, a tap on her shoulder sent a jolt through her, making her gasp in surprise.

"Whoa, sorry! Didn't mean to scare you," Lauren said, stepping back with a concerned look on her face.

Kat forced a smile, willing her heart to slow down. "It's okay. I'm just a bit on edge, that's all."

Lauren studied her, only adding to Kat's restive state. "Are you sure everything's alright, Kat? You seem a bit… well, out of it. I noticed it the last time I saw you too. Is everything okay at home?"

Kat hesitated, unable to articulate what was really on her mind. She didn't want to sound crazy, didn't want to reveal her concerns about Kevin or Luke or Sandra, or indeed an innocent woman who had happened to move in across the street.

The one who looks just like the woman I killed.

"I'm fine, really. Just… you know, life."

Lauren nodded, though she didn't seem entirely convinced. "Well, I was thinking, if you're up for it, maybe we could go for a drink this Friday? I'll see if my mum can babysit the boys."

Kat felt a pang of anxiety at the prospect of socialising once more. It had been so long, apart from within the confines of her own house with Luke. "Sure, that sounds nice."

Lauren smiled, relieved. "Great! I can pick the boys up from school and take them direct to Mum's house. She lives less than a mile from me, so it's not far."

Kat nodded, though a part of her balked at the idea of Tom being somewhere that Kat wasn't familiar with.

She forced herself to push the worry away. "Where should we meet?"

"How about the Sunset Wine Bar? It's about halfway for both of us and easy on the tube line. It's near your office too, isn't it?"

Kat's heart lurched at the mention of the bar. Why suggest there, of all places? The Sunset Wine Bar held so many memories, some good, some not so good. She vividly recalled the time she and Imogen had walked in on Adam and Liam drinking with two women—Sharon and Beth. The memory of Imogen's furious outburst. And Sharon… something had happened to her, hadn't it? Pushed down the steps of the local tube station? Kat hadn't thought about that incident in a long while. However, she smirked without realising, causing Lauren to tilt her head curiously. "What's so funny?"

Kat quickly masked her expression. "Oh, nothing really. Just… fond memories of the Sunset."

Lauren obviously didn't want to rake up the past. "Hey, if you'd rather go somewhere else—"

"No, no, it's fine," Kat interrupted, suddenly feeling a strange sense of déjà vu. "The Sunset is perfect. Let's meet there."

Lauren nodded, smiling. "Great, I'll make the arrangements and let you know."

As Tom ran up to her, his face flushed with cold and excitement, Kat parted ways with Lauren and sensed a sudden unexpected wave of happiness. The prospect of returning to the Sunset Wine Bar, once a place of mixed emotions, now felt like an opportunity to move on. Just as she had overcome stepping inside Imogen's old house. She also knew how much Adam loved going there.

The drive home was peaceful, Tom chattering away in

the backseat about his day, his words filled with a familiar lightness that made Kat's heart swell with pride. She often glanced in the rear-view mirror, watching her son as he chatted continuously, looking out of the side window, oblivious to his mum's looks. There was no mention of Imogen, nothing to darken the mood. Kat cursed herself for considering taking him to the doctors. He was just grieving, just as her mum had said. But as they turned onto their street, that feeling of ease began to dissipate once more.

Clara's car was back in the driveway, and as Kat climbed out of the driver's seat, she noticed something that made her skin crawl. Standing in the window, framed by the blinds, was Clara, staring directly at her.

Kat's breath caught in her throat. There was something unsettling about the way Clara watched her, her expression blank, almost too still. The hairs on the back of Kat's neck stood on end and an icy feeling crept down her spine.

Although Clara raised her hand, Kat quickly ushered Tom indoors, glancing back at the window one last time. Clara was gone, but the sense of being watched lingered, pressing down on her with an almost tangible weight.

Inside, Kat tried to shake off the unease, but it clung to her like a shadow. The brief moment of happiness she had felt earlier was already fading.

As Tom settled in to watch television, Kat stood at the window, staring across the street at Clara's house. She had met the woman, spoken to her, and yet…

14

Despite the unease of Clara standing at the window, the remainder of Kat's week passed in a surprisingly positive manner. She felt lighter, almost as though she had finally started to shed the weight of the past few months. Work was picking up, thanks to Luke, and her mood was the best it had been in ages. She managed to dismiss her feelings towards her new neighbour as being the connection to the house and realised that Clara was not to blame for who lived there before; or indeed what had happened.

Kat had a couple of productive meetings with Luke. Despite his growing obsession with the business, she appreciated his dedication. Sure, he might be intense, but it seemed to be a genuine concern for the company. She had even heard from their accountant and it wouldn't take long to rubber stamp Luke's place as a bona fide director. Kat tried not to let it bother her that Luke's focus on work also edged into her personal space. After all, wasn't she the one who'd been distant recently after inviting him to stay the night? Maybe this was his way of making sure everything was still okay between them.

On Friday evening, as she prepared for her date with Lauren, Kat felt a sense of anticipation she hadn't experienced in a long time. It was almost strange to be excited about something as simple as going to a bar, but it felt like an enormous step towards normalcy. She spent extra time getting ready, wanting to look her best. Kat wanted to feel good about herself and secretly hoped for an admiring glance or two in the Sunset. Not that she would take it any further, but she'd missed the confidence boosts, despite Luke's over-the-top compliments.

In the middle of deciding which shoes to wear, the doorbell rang, distracting her from her thoughts. Surprised, Kat hurried downstairs, wondering who it could be. She selfishly prayed all was okay with Tom as she was now so looking forward to her night out. When she opened the door, she was met by Clara standing on the porch, a small dog on a leash by her side.

"Hi, Kat," Clara said warmly, a smile spreading across her face. She looked Kat up and down, obviously surprised by her attire. "I hope I'm not interrupting anything."

Kat tried to hide her discontent at the timing. "No, not at all. I was just getting ready to go out."

"Oh, I see," Clara replied, her gaze sweeping over Kat's outfit once more. "You look lovely."

Was that a hint of sarcasm in Clara's tone? Kat silently kicked herself.

"Thank you," she forced her reply. "And who's this little beauty?"

Kat didn't like dogs, but thought it polite to give the small brown and white pooch some attention.

"Oh, this is Charlie. I only collected him two days ago. He's been in kennels while I moved." Clara glanced over Kat's shoulder. "I thought I'd bring Charlie over to meet Tom. You mentioned your son when you popped over and I've seen him in the car when you take him to school. I thought he might like to meet the latest member of my family. He's only nine months old. Isn't he adorable?"

Kat allowed herself an inner smile. She'd been wrong earlier in the week when she caught Clara watching from the window. She'd spotted Tom getting in and out of the car. It was pure coincidence, and Kat needed to quell her overactive mind.

"That's kind of you, Clara, but Tom isn't here right now. He's staying over at a friend's house."

Clara's smile didn't waver, but there was a fleeting look in her eyes that Kat couldn't quite decipher. "Oh, I didn't realise. Well, maybe another time then?"

Just as Clara spoke, Charlie suddenly lunged forward, jumping up at Kat. The dog's muddy paws smeared slush across the front of her dress. Kat gasped in surprise, stepping back.

"Oh no, I'm so sorry!" Clara exclaimed, though Kat could have sworn she saw a tiny smirk at the corner of her mouth before she quickly masked it with a look of concern. And had Clara's foot twitched slightly beforehand, as if she had nudged the dog intentionally?

Kat bit back a sharp retort, instead brushing at the mud on her dress. "It's okay, really. I'll just change."

Clara apologised again, but Kat couldn't shake the feeling that it hadn't been entirely accidental. Still, she didn't want to make a scene.

"Don't worry about it," she said. "I'll be fine."

Clara nodded, seeming genuinely remorseful. "Well, I'll let you get on with your evening. I didn't mean to disturb you. And again, I'm so sorry. He can just be a little over friendly, and—"

"Seriously," Kat interrupted. "It's not a problem. These things happen."

Clara's expression softened. "Of course. I hope you have a good night."

As Clara walked away, Charlie trotting beside her, Kat closed the door and leant against it, her thoughts racing. Was she overthinking things again? Surely Clara had meant no harm? Who would make a dog jump up at someone when it was obvious they were ready to go out for the evening?

With a sigh, Kat headed back upstairs to change. The mud on her dress was a minor annoyance, but it had left her feeling off balance. She quickly changed into another outfit, trying to shake off the strange encounter. This was supposed to be a good night, a step towards a fresh routine.

By the time she reached the Sunset, Kat had pushed the incident from her mind. The underground ride and short stroll to the bar were uneventful, and on reaching her destination, Kat was determined to put the incident behind her and focus on enjoying the evening. She hadn't been out in ages, and she was eager to catch up with Lauren in a more relaxed setting. It was exactly what she needed to clear her head and move forward.

Inside, the bar was warm and inviting, the familiar sounds of clinking glasses and soft chatter wrapping around her like a comforting blanket. Kat scanned the room, half expecting to see Adam, a bottle of wine and two glasses before him. Dismissing the sensation, she soon spotted Lauren at a table near the back. As she made her way over, she couldn't help but feel a sense of déjà vu. The last time she'd been there, things had been so different.

"Kat! Hi!" Lauren called, waving her over, her eyes crinkling at the corners.

Kat returned the smile, her earlier unease fading as she slid into the seat opposite Lauren. "Hey, sorry I'm a bit late. I had an unexpected visitor."

"Everything okay?" Lauren asked, her eyes narrowing in concern.

"Yeah, just the new neighbour," Kat said casually, not wanting to dwell on it. "She stopped by with her dog to meet Tom, but, as you know, he isn't home."

Lauren nodded, offering Kat a glass from the bottle of red wine which sat between them. "That's nice of her. How's everything else been?"

Kat shrugged, trying to keep the mood light. "Not bad, actually. I've been getting back into work and endeavouring to move on, you know?"

"That's great," Lauren said, smiling warmly. "It's about time you had some fun."

As they settled into their conversation, Kat felt herself beginning to relax. The worries seemed to melt away in the cosy atmosphere of the bar.

Yet, as the night wore on, she couldn't help but wonder if Clara's visit had been as innocent as it seemed. And when she returned home later that night, she found herself checking the windows of the house across the street, half expecting to see Clara watching her again. But the windows were dark and empty, and Kat forced herself to breathe a sigh of relief.

But as she got ready for bed, she couldn't shake the feeling that Clara knew Tom wasn't home when she'd stopped by. The thought sent a shiver of unease through her, but she pushed it aside, telling herself it was just her imagination. After all, she'd had a good evening, and that was all that mattered.

15

KAT WOKE the following morning with a sense of peace she hadn't felt in ages. The best night's sleep she'd had in months left her feeling refreshed, and she wondered if it was her mind finally settling or if the wine and the previous evening's company had been the key contributory factor. The shower's warm water soothed her as she reflected on her night out. She couldn't help but smile as she thought of Lauren and how much they had in common. Both had lost their husbands—albeit in different ways—they had sons of the same age, and they had laughed and joked like Kat hadn't experienced in a long, long time. From their love of obscure indie films to a mutual fondness for walking, something Kat had neglected for a while, but now felt eager to take up once more, the more they talked, the more Kat felt she had found a new best friend in Lauren Croft.

As the wine flowed, Kat had grown more comfortable and opened up more than she'd intended. She recounted the tragic events that had shaped the last year of her life —the deaths of her neighbours, Imogen and Liam, and the terrible accident that took Adam's life. She probably said too much about Adam's downfall towards the end, the day he went crazy about the missing football and the terracotta pot moving by itself in the garden. However, she didn't disclose too many of the details, conscious of not discussing events which Lauren could interpret as the wrong side of the law. After all, Lauren had met Adam previously at Tom's birthday party, and Kat didn't know how much they had talked or indeed what they'd even spoke about. By the end of the night, she wondered if she'd said more than she should have.

Lauren, however, was a good listener. She soon placated Kat when she mentioned the new neighbour, Clara, especially when Kat expressed her doubts over how quickly Clara had bought Imogen and Liam's house. Lauren dismissed her concerns, offering a reasonable explanation that if there was no next of kin, the property would naturally go back on the market. Again, Kat recalled her dad saying the same thing to her.

However, when Kat mentioned Kevin and Vicky, Lauren's demeanour had shifted slightly. As Kat explained about Kevin telling Luke not to get involved in the business and then how Adam's accident had happened just outside Vicky's flat near Liverpool Street, Lauren asked Kat if she thought the accident was indeed that—an accident. The question lingered for a while, again Kat not wishing to divulge too much of the past, but the very mention of wondering if it were an accident rekindled the question Kat had deliberated many times before.

In return, Lauren shared bits of her own life. She told Kat about her separation from her husband, Sean, who was now living abroad in southwest France, working on a grand renovation project of a château. She didn't go into too much detail about the reasons for their breakup, but she did talk about how their son, Max, had taken it hard. Sean had promised Max a holiday in France the following year, but Lauren was doubtful it would ever happen. As she spoke, Kat could sense the pain in Lauren's voice, and knew the separation had hit her hard.

By the time they parted at the tube station, both a little tipsy from the wine, Kat felt lighter, her spirits lifted by the new friend she'd made. It had been so long since she'd allowed herself to truly relax and enjoy someone's company, and for the first time in what felt like forever, she felt like she might be able to move forward.

As she stepped out of the shower, she focused on the prospect of her new friendship. Lauren seemed like someone she could trust, someone who understood what it was like to carry the weight of loss and still try to move on. And that was something Kat desperately needed—someone who wouldn't judge her for her past, but who would instead help her look towards the future.

As she finished getting dressed, Kat caught a glimpse of herself in the mirror. Her reflection seemed different somehow—softer, less burdened by the weight of the past. She smiled, deciding that maybe this was the start of something good, something that could help her rebuild her life.

Later, when she was on her way to collect Tom, the memory of the evening before still warmed her. Kat hoped it would be the first of many nights like that, where she could simply enjoy being herself again. For now, though, she focused on the day ahead, determined to keep hold of her newfound sense of peace for as long as she could.

But as she stepped outside into her street, her feeling of contentment wavered slightly. Clara's car was in its usual spot, but something about its presence made the hair on Kat's arms stand up. She quickly dismissed the feeling, cursing herself and determined not to let anything ruin her good mood. After all, it was just a car, and Clara was just a neighbour. There was no reason to be suspicious, no reason to worry.

Still, as she started her car and pulled out of her driveway, Kat glanced up at Clara's house. She couldn't help but feel the familiar knot of anxiety tighten in her chest. Of course, Clara wasn't at the window, but the mere thought of her was enough to bring back a shadow of doubt. And then the dog jumping up at her, muddy paws and that slight movement in Clara's leg as if she'd pushed the damn thing forward.

Kat shook her head, refusing to let her mind spiral. She had a son to pick up, a day to enjoy. Whatever lingering fears she had about Clara would have to wait. For now, she was determined to focus on the good things.

16

On the Wednesday of the following week, Kat met Luke at the café for another impromptu meeting, the hum of mid-morning chatter filling the air. She hadn't yet mentioned Clara's dog to Tom, though she was aware she should have. After all, isn't that exactly why Clara brought the bloody thing round in the first place? She knew she wasn't helping herself by not sharing the news with Tom, and if Clara told him how long ago it was when she initially suggested meeting Charlie, Tom would definitely fly off the handle at Kat. And who could blame him?

So what was it? Didn't Kat want Tom getting too close to their new neighbour? But why? He hadn't mentioned his aunt Imogen for a while now and the drawings had ceased too. In fact, Kat couldn't give herself one reason she was keeping Tom from meeting Charlie.

Apart from who Clara looks like, of course.

She desperately tried to push the image aside as Luke sat down across from her.

"So, I've put out a few feelers for Kevin's replacement," Luke said after taking a sip of his coffee. "We can't wait forever. What do you think?"

Kat nodded absently. "Yeah, makes sense. We need to move forward."

She remembered promising herself to visit Kevin and Vicky's flat. Why was she putting that off? Maybe Lauren would go with her, now that she'd told her where Adam was killed and the interest she had shown as a result?

The conversation continued to flow between Kat and Luke. Work had become a safe topic between them, something concrete to cling to, while the undercurrents of their personal relationship remained murky. But that day, with the formalities out of the way, Luke seemed less interested in business. After a few minutes of discussing potential candidates, his tone shifted.

"Kat, I've been thinking," he began, leaning forward slightly. "What do you say we go away? Maybe over Easter or in the summer. Just you, me, and Tom. We could use the time together. Somewhere warm."

Kat balked, caught off-guard. She could feel the weight of his suggestion settling over her like a blanket—one that was suddenly too heavy. Luke reached across the table for her hand, but she pulled back instinctively, glancing around the café as if someone might be watching.

Someone like Adam, you mean?

He frowned, clearly hurt. "What's wrong? I thought… I mean, isn't there something between us? Don't you think going away would be good for us?"

"I don't know, Luke," she said carefully. "I'm not sure I'm ready for that. Besides, Tom… it's all a bit complicated."

She could tell his frustration was simmering just below the surface. A vein protruded from his temple. "I'm not asking for lifelong commitment," he replied. "It would just be a chance for me to get to know Tom better, for us to figure things out."

Kat hesitated, the silence between them growing thicker. She didn't know what to say. There had been a time when she thought maybe Luke could be the answer to all her problems, when Adam had been at his most vulnerable, although she kicked herself for laughing about the sleepwalking incident with Luke. She glanced around the café once more. Who was she expecting?

"I'll think about it," she said finally, knowing it wasn't the response he wanted.

Luke leant back in his chair, disappointment clear in his eyes. "I don't want to feel like I'm being used, Kat."

Her breath caught in her throat. "Used? What are you talking about?" She looked at the couple at the adjacent table, convinced they would judge her.

"You keep pushing me away," he said quietly. "I need to know where I stand."

Kat sighed, rubbing her temples. "Am I why you and Sandra split up?" she asked, the question hanging in the air between them.

Luke didn't respond immediately, but his hesitation told her all she needed to know. Kat's stomach twisted. She had her answer. He had left Sandra, at least in part, because of her. But Kat had never asked him to, never given the impression that they had a future together. Had she?

After another awkward pause and a convoluted conversation about a client, they parted amicably, but the tension was impossible to ignore. As Kat got into her car and headed home, her mind buzzed with conflicting thoughts. She couldn't keep leading Luke on, but the idea of him walking away from the business terrified her. He had been her anchor for so long, and she knew the company would be in dire straits without him at the helm. She'd lost Adam, and Kevin had walked out. Even if Luke took on a new programmer, she was aware of how long it would take to get them up to speed.

When she pulled into her driveway, something caught her eye across the street—Clara's wheelie bin, set out for collection the next day. She glanced at the house, noticing Clara's car wasn't in its parking spot. The bin lid wasn't closed completely, and a bag of rubbish sat on top.

On impulse, Kat got out of her car and stepped across the road, her head twisting both ways. As she neared the bin, her heart skipped a beat. There, on top of the rubbish, still in its supermarket wrapping, was the cake she had taken over the day she'd introduced herself.

It hadn't even been opened.

Kat stared at it, her mind spinning. Why would Clara throw it away? Why not just eat it, or at least open it and discard a slice or two in the bin? The gesture suddenly felt meaningless, like an unspoken rejection of her attempt to be neighbourly. Or maybe there was something else going on that Kat couldn't yet see.

17

Kat's parents arrived on Friday evening. Their presence should have filled the house with a sense of comfort, especially with February's lingering chill outside. But instead, it felt oppressive. Their familiar remarks regarding Adam and how he was never good enough for her, reared its ugly head within an hour of their arrival. And then, their attempts to steer her towards Luke, as if her life were a puzzle they could easily fix, made her stomach turn. They didn't understand, yet they couldn't resist continuing to interfere. Her resentment bubbled beneath the surface, making their visit feel like an intrusion rather than a reprieve. So, on Saturday morning, after a hurried breakfast, Kat excused herself, explaining she needed to go into the office for a few hours to catch up on some work. She preferred it when it was quiet, and with her mum and dad around to watch Tom, she made her excuses, much to their disdain.

As she took the underground into the city, she reflected on the recent changes in her life. Her mood had lifted during the past few days, until her parents rubbed her up the wrong way. Her night out with Lauren had helped, providing a much-needed distraction. Still, something nagged at the back of her mind. She'd tried to dismiss Kevin's contact with Luke, warning him about the business, and Vicky's follow-up call. She also convinced herself Luke would see sense soon enough and might back away a little until she found her feet. After all, she hadn't ruled him out altogether. So what was bugging her so much?

After a productive few hours at work, Kat decided to make the most of the crisp winter sunshine and took a stroll through Regent's Park. It would also allow her to put some distance between herself and her parents. Another lecture was the last thing she needed.

The air was fresh, the kind of cold that invigorates rather than chills. She inhaled deeply, feeling a sense of calm settle over her. The park was unusually quiet, the customary crowds absent. She felt herself relax, her shoulders dropping as the tension eased.

She reluctantly returned home mid-afternoon, energised by her day. But as she walked along the garden path, she heard a noise that made her pause. A dog barking. Her heart sank. Kat glanced across the street and saw Clara's car in its usual spot, parked perfectly in the driveway, as if measured out with a ruler. She didn't need to guess who was inside her house. The bark grew louder as she approached the door, and as soon as she inserted her key into the lock and pushed it open, Charlie came bounding down the hallway, barking excitedly.

"Good grief!" Kat exclaimed, stepping back as the dog leapt up at her, its paws scraping at her jeans. She already wasn't fond of dogs, but this one seemed to be particularly oblivious to her personal space. She wanted to kick the fucking thing so hard she could watch it as it skidded on the wooden floor, yelping in pain.

"Charlie, no!" Clara's voice echoed from inside the house as she rushed into the hallway, laughing. "I'm so sorry! He's just excited to see you."

Kat forced a smile, though irritation simmered beneath the surface. She tried to gently push the dog down, but Charlie was insistent, his paws scrabbling at her legs. Tom appeared behind Clara, giggling at the sight of his mum being ambushed by the little dog.

"Isn't he cute, Mummy?" Tom said, his voice filled with joy.

Kat bit back her annoyance. "Yes, he's quite adorable," she replied through gritted teeth, trying to hide her sarcasm.

Clara finally pulled Charlie away, still smiling. "He really loves people, doesn't he, Tom?"

Kat was surprised by her familiarity with her son, despite having just met him.

Tom nodded enthusiastically. "Can we take him for a walk, Mummy? Please?"

Before Kat could respond, her parents chimed in from the kitchen. Kat, Clara, and Tom joined them, and found them sitting at the table with freshly made cups of tea. "Clara came over to introduce Charlie to Tom," Edwina explained, her face lighting up with approval. "And did you know Clara's a financial advisor? She works for herself and has some huge clients. Isn't that fascinating?"

Kat gave a tight-lipped smile, her patience wearing thin. She knew her parents meant well, but their newfound enthusiasm for Clara was already beginning to grate on her nerves. They'd only just met Clara and she couldn't recall them heaping such praise upon herself in recent months, despite the hell she'd been going through.

"Oh, it's just a job," Clara said modestly, brushing off the compliment.

"Nonsense! It's amazing!" William added, his eyes beaming. "Imagine having such a successful woman living right across the street."

Kat forced herself to stay quiet, but inside, she was seething. It wasn't just the bloody dog or the way her parents were fawning over Clara—it was everything. The staring out of the window, the cake discarded on top of the rubbish, and now this uninvited visit. She glanced at Clara, trying to read her expression.

After some polite conversation, Clara finally gathered Charlie and prepared to leave. "Tom, you're welcome to walk Charlie with me anytime," she said, giving him a warm smile.

Tom's face lit up, but Kat quickly interjected. "We'll see," she said, her tone firmer than she intended.

"Mummy, why not? I want to!" Tom protested, his voice rising in frustration.

"Katrina, darling. Really," Edwina said, her tone chastising as if Kat were the child in the room. "There's no harm in it. You're being far too protective."

Kat bit her tongue, unwilling to get into an argument in front of Clara. "We'll talk about it later," she said, signalling the end of the conversation.

Once Clara had left and the house had settled down, Kat found herself alone with her thoughts. That evening, her parents had retired to bed earlier than normal, and Tom was playing quietly in his room. He still hadn't properly forgiven her, and Kat thought it wise to get into his good books by allowing him to stay up a little longer than usual.

Pouring herself a glass of wine, she stepped out onto the patio, hoping the chilly night air might help clear her head. She fished a cigarette out of an old pack she'd found in Adam's drawer, something she hadn't touched in years. She'd noticed his old mobile phone there too. The first drag felt amazing, almost comforting, as if Adam's smell was part of the cigarette itself.

She stood there, gazing up at the night sky, trying to make sense of the tangled mess of emotions inside her. Clara had charmed everyone, even her parents, but something about the woman just didn't sit right with Kat.

Lost in her thoughts, she extinguished one cigarette and quickly lit up another. The nicotine made her head spin, and she caught herself smiling as she looked at the packet in her hand.

Minutes later, her phone pinged, and she pulled it from her pocket. She smiled, as if expecting it.

The message was brief—just one sentence.

> I didn't know you liked dogs

Kat just stared at the screen, her heart thudding in her chest.

18

THREE DAYS after her parents left, Kat paced the kitchen, reliving the frustration of the weekend. She'd re-read the text message several times, but she didn't want to share it with anyone, least of all her mum and dad. She had smoothed things over with Tom about walking Charlie, promising they'd go on Saturday, but her parents' insistence had escalated into yet another argument. By the time they left, Kat was questioning why she kept them in her life. Adam's dislike for them now made perfect sense; they were driving her mad with their constant interference.

To give herself a break, Kat decided to satisfy her curiosity and call on Clara, on the pretence of organising a dog walk for Tom. She also had another question on her mind. However, once outside her neighbour's front door, Kat wondered if she'd made the right decision as a pang of disquiet swept through her.

Clara greeted her with open arms, clearly delighted to see her, and quickly invited her in. But as soon as she stepped inside, that familiar feeling washed over Kat again—a strange mix of nostalgia and discomfort, the memories of Imogen prickling at her senses, not helped by the similarity of Clara's looks. She noticed Clara had begun to put her own stamp on the house, with the hall and living room walls already painted in darker shades.

Clara caught her glancing around. "I'm planning to make some more changes," she said casually. "I'm thinking of carpeting the floors—hardwood feels too cold in the winter. And I found a local gardener to redo the back once the weather improves."

Kat nodded, but her mind was elsewhere, especially as she followed Clara into the kitchen and her eyes were drawn to the garden. She barely heard Clara as she spoke. "Oh, that thing," Clara added, catching Kat staring. "I'm thinking of having that summerhouse taken down."

The words hit Kat like a punch to the gut. She fought to keep her expression neutral, but her mind reeled. The summerhouse. The place where she and Adam had ended Imogen's and Liam's lives, burying their secret deep within the garden. Cold sweat prickled the back of her neck. She couldn't believe Clara would even consider removing it. And more importantly, why?

"That sounds like a big project," Kat said, her voice faltering. "Won't it leave a vast space?"

Clara shrugged. "Exactly. I think it would open up the entire area, give the garden a larger feel. Besides, I'm not much of a fan of such structures—they make an outside space look cluttered." She smiled, oblivious to the turmoil brewing in Kat's mind.

Kat forced a smile and accepted the offer of coffee. Despite the familiar surroundings, everything somehow felt foreign. Clara's warm hospitality at least helped put Kat's mind at ease. But as they sat at the table, Kat struggled to focus on the small talk, unsure how to steer the conversation towards what she had really called round for.

Fortunately, Clara was in a chatty mood, and soon broached the subject herself. "Tom's such a sweet boy," she said, beaming. "You've done a wonderful job raising him. He's so polite and bright. I'd love to take him and Charlie for a walk…" she paused. "Only if it's okay with you, of course."

Kat nodded, offering a distracted smile, but Clara continued. "That's great. Oh, and your parents… such lovely people. I can see where you get it from. You're lucky to have such a supportive family."

Kat felt a twinge of guilt. Had she been too quick to judge Clara, to dislike her without cause? And was she being too hard on her mum and dad? Clara had been nothing but kind, offering compliments and being so nice to Tom. Kat's discomfort slowly shifted into sympathy as Clara spoke more about herself.

"I've never had a family like yours," Clara said, her voice softer now. "I have an estranged sister, but she moved abroad years ago, and we've spoken little since. It's been hard, but life goes on."

Kat felt a pang of empathy. Clara's life had clearly not been easy, and here she was, trying to make a fresh start. Kat scolded herself for having allowed her suspicions to cloud her judgement. How could she have let herself dislike someone when she'd never given her a chance?

"Have you ever been married?" Kat asked, hoping to steer the discussion away from more painful subjects.

Clara shook her head. "No, never married. I had two long-term boyfriends, but neither ended well. I guess fate didn't intend it to be."

Kat offered a sympathetic smile. The conversation

had taken a surprising turn, and she felt less suspicious of Clara by the minute. Perhaps she had been wrong all along, letting her imagination get the better of her.

As they finished their coffee and Kat prepared to leave, she finally worked up the courage to ask, "Did you enjoy the cake I brought over the other week?"

Clara looked slightly uncomfortable. "Oh, I meant to mention that. I'm so sorry, I had to throw it away."

Kat tried to sound surprised. "Throw it away?" At least she didn't deny it.

Clara nodded, apologetic. "I was saving it to share with Tom, but the night I put the bins out, I noticed the cake on the side, and the use-by date had passed. By several days, actually. I didn't like to say, but the use-by date was *before* you brought it round. I hope you're not offended, Kat, but I didn't want to risk it."

Kat felt her face flush with embarrassment. "Oh, I didn't realise… I'm so sorry."

"Please don't worry about it," Clara said kindly. "It was such a thoughtful gesture."

But as Kat walked back across the street, the encounter nagged at her. How could she have missed the cake's expiration date by so much? She had bought it fresh. Could the supermarket really be that careless, leaving out expired stock?

19

THE FOLLOWING DAY, Kat couldn't put off visiting Vicky's flat any longer. She knew she couldn't face it alone and asked Lauren at the school gates if she would accompany her. On their night out, she'd explained how Adam had been knocked down just outside the flat near Liverpool Street, and Lauren had asked if she thought the accident was indeed only that—an accident. The question had plagued Kat ever since.

As they left the boys at the school gates and boarded the tube, Kat felt her pulse quicken. She told Lauren how nervous she was, recalling Luke's stories of Kevin suspecting someone lurking outside the flat. She questioned whether he actually saw someone or if it was simply his imagination. But now, with the prospect of standing in the place where Adam met his fate, her confidence faltered.

Lauren, ever the supportive friend, agreed it seemed odd and leant her hand on Kat's arm. Kat smiled in return. As they sat side by side, the train clattered and echoed through the tunnels, and Kat took a deep breath before confiding in Lauren about the night Adam died.

"I got a phone call... around midnight," she began, staring at the window opposite, her reflection pale and still. "Apparently, Adam had left Vicky's flat only minutes before. The car... it hit him, but he wasn't dead straight away. I remember praying he'd pull through, that somehow his injuries wouldn't be that bad."

Lauren appeared to falter slightly, but squeezed Kat's hand, her face softening with empathy. "So, when did he actually pass?" she asked quietly.

Kat forced a smile and squeezed her friend's hand in return. "He died a few hours later. Sometime in the early hours, I believe. Internal bleeding. Too much damage. By the time I got to the hospital, he was gone."

Silence enveloped them. Kat's chest felt heavy, weighed down by the memories she had tried so hard to bury. But they were resurfacing, and it was nearly more than she could handle. As they arrived at Liverpool Street, Kat couldn't shake the unnerving feeling that someone was watching her. Her eyes darted around the crowded station, searching for something—anything—out of place.

"You okay?" Lauren asked, noticing Kat's tension.

Kat nodded quickly, forcing a smile. "Yeah, just... I don't know. It's probably just nerves about being here."

They exited the station, stepping into the cold air. The streets were busy with the usual crowd, people going about their routines, oblivious to the turmoil churning inside Kat. They walked along Old Broad Street, Lauren matching Kat's slower pace.

Kat pulled out her phone, checking the directions again, even though she knew the way. Her stomach twisted when she saw the familiar name of the office building across the street: Wheelwright Solutions. It was the company Adam had briefly worked for before his betrayal of Kevin. Lauren noticed Kat slow further and the colour drain from her face.

"Are you sure you're okay?" she asked gently.

Kat nodded, but she wasn't sure. She swallowed hard, forcing herself to keep walking. "It's just…" she faltered. The air felt thick, almost suffocating as they finally approached a myriad of small, confined streets.

They entered a narrow turning marked by a no-entry sign, and Kat's breath hitched. "This is it," she whispered. Her voice was hoarse, as if the mere act of speaking was too much effort.

Lauren's expression shifted, her brows furrowing as she read the street sign above. "This is where he…"

Kat looked at her sharply. "Lauren, are you alright?"

Lauren let out a nervous laugh, shaking her head. "I'm fine. Just… it's just a bit eerie, that's all."

Kat frowned but let it go, too consumed by her own emotions. They stood at the door to Vicky's flat, the buzzer panel gleaming in the faint winter sunlight. Vicky's name was listed among the others.

As Kat turned, her gaze swept over the narrow street, and a strange sensation pricked at her skin—a subtle, cool touch on her arm, almost like a whisper. She froze, the feeling unmistakable. It was as though Adam himself was there, standing just behind her, close enough to brush against her. Her heart beat faster, and she felt an overwhelming mixture of grief and warmth flood through her.

This was the place. The spot where Adam had fallen, where he had taken his last breath. She looked at the road, her vision blurring as she imagined him lying there, broken and alone in his ultimate moments. Her knees weakened, nearly giving way beneath the weight of the grief she'd been carrying, the grief she'd tried so hard to keep at bay. For a moment, it felt as though Adam was beside her, binding her to the tragic place where their lives had been irreversibly changed.

Without warning, the tears came. They spilled down her cheeks and she collapsed to her knees, sobbing, her entire body trembling. Lauren rushed to her side, wrapping her arms around Kat and clenching her tightly.

"Let it out," Lauren whispered, her voice thick with emotion.

Kat clung to her, burying her face in Lauren's shoulder, as months of pent-up pain eventually surfaced. It was too much. All of it—Adam's death, Imogen, Liam, everything she had been trying so hard to forget.

When her sobs finally subsided, Kat looked up at Lauren, her vision blurry from the tears. That's when she noticed. Lauren's eyes were red and watery too. She had been crying alongside her.

"You okay?" Kat asked, her voice cracking.

Lauren smiled weakly, wiping her eyes. "Yeah, I'm fine. Just seeing you like that. It really got to me."

Kat took a deep breath, her chest still tight but the worst of the emotion seemingly over. She stood, shakily, with Lauren's help. "I'm sorry," she mumbled, embarrassed by her outburst. "I didn't mean to—"

"Don't apologise," Lauren interrupted. "You needed that. We all need to let it out sometimes."

Kat nodded, and they stood in silence for a few moments before Kat glanced at the door to Vicky's flat again.

Lauren quickly brushed her tears away, turning towards the flat door, her face hardening. "So, this is where that bitch lives, is it?"

Truth Lies Beneath

Kat, a little taken aback, nodded slowly. "Should we… should we press the buzzer?"

Lauren hesitated for a moment, then shook her head. "No. I think you've been through quite enough."

Kat didn't argue. She wasn't ready. And she doubted if she would ever be.

20

Saturday arrived, and following her more enjoyable chat with Clara earlier in the week, Kat finally agreed to let Tom walk Charlie to the park with Clara, who had stopped by the day before, casually asking if Saturday morning would be okay. Kat had hesitated initially, but found herself feeling more at ease after her visit to her neighbour's house. Also, being at Vicky's flat had somehow made her more upbeat. The sensation of Adam's presence felt as if he were guiding her.

Since then, her mood had lightened considerably. She even arranged to go out again with Lauren the following weekend, just the two of them. The connection she felt with her new friend was something she hadn't expected, and in a strange way, Kat didn't want to share her with anyone else. She thought it might be because there was no history between them, allowing them to bond so well. Lauren had even cried when Kat did, and that shared moment made Kat feel understood in a way she hadn't in a long time. It was a comfort she hadn't appreciated she needed.

Tom had barely been gone an hour when Kat heard voices outside along her front path. She assumed it was Clara and Tom returning from their walk with Charlie, but as she stepped towards the door, she realised there was a third voice—Luke's.

Broad grins and the sight of Charlie barking excitedly, his tail wagging frantically, greeted her as she opened the door. Kat backed off a little, not wanting the dog to jump up at her again.

"Look who I found!" Clara beamed, her eyes briefly meeting Luke's with a look that Kat couldn't quite place. Was it admiration? She wasn't sure, but something about the interaction didn't sit comfortably with her.

"I was walking back from the tube station when I thought I saw Tom with a dog, so I followed to see what the fun was about," Luke explained with a smile.

"Oh," Kat said, forcing a grin. "That was a bit of luck." She couldn't help but notice how at ease Luke and Clara seemed with each other. It felt as though it wasn't the first time they had met, such was the unspoken familiarity between them.

Everybody stepped inside after Kat asked if they would like a coffee. Tom, looking exhausted, took Charlie into the living room, where the little dog promptly settled down on a cushion. Kat watched as Tom whispered to the dog, his admiration for his four-legged friend tangible. She wondered if she should get one of their own, as it was obviously having a positive effect on him, but the thought of a canine forever running around her feet almost made her squirm in anguish. She recalled the anonymous text message and smiled to herself.

> I didn't know you liked dogs

Meanwhile, in the kitchen, Clara and Luke sat around the table, chatting. They were laughing about something they'd seen in the park, something Kat had missed. Their connection was evident, and Kat began to feel like an outsider in her own home.

She watched Luke closely. Was he doing it to get at her? To punish her for not giving him an immediate answer about the holiday? She hadn't yet made a decision, and she knew it must have frustrated him. But seeing him there, laughing easily with Clara, Kat couldn't help but wonder if Luke was trying to make her jealous. Or maybe it was worse, maybe he actually found Clara attractive. Just as Adam had fallen for Imogen.

The thought ate away at her as they continued talking. Kat forced herself to smile, but found it increasingly difficult to join in the conversation. Instead, she let them carry on while she continued to make them drinks.

Thirty minutes passed, and eventually Clara made her excuses to leave. She called Charlie, who bounded out of the living room, tail wagging furiously as he trotted towards the door. "Thanks for letting Tom come with us," Clara said, smiling warmly at Kat. "He's a delight to have around."

"No problem," Kat replied, her voice polite but distant. She couldn't shake the discomfort she felt as she watched Clara leave, Charlie trotting happily beside her.

After Clara left, Luke lingered a little longer, but even he seemed to have one foot out the door. They continued to make small talk, though Luke appeared distant. He didn't mention the holiday at all. The trip he'd been so insistent on only a week before felt like some kind of distant memory. In fact, he didn't even bring up the business, which was odd, considering they usually discussed it whenever they met.

It was as if his mind was elsewhere, distracted.

Eventually, Luke made his excuses and left as well. Kat stood in the living room window, watching him until he disappeared along the street, feeling more alone than she had in a while. The whole interaction left her with a strange sense of isolation, as though something had shifted, and she wasn't sure why.

As she cleared the kitchen table, Kat's thoughts drifted back to how effortlessly Luke and Clara had got on. The way they laughed together felt like a personal affront, and it stung more than she cared to admit. She wanted to believe it was nothing, that Luke was just being amicable, that Clara was merely a friendly neighbour. But something about it didn't sit right.

And then there was the nagging feeling that Luke had purposely avoided talking about their holiday plans. Why hadn't he mentioned it? Was he no longer interested? Or had his interest simply shifted to someone else, as if she had had her chance and he'd already moved on?

21

A FEW DAYS LATER, around noon, while Tom was at school, Clara stopped by again. Although surprised by Clara's increasingly frequent calls to socialise, Kat silently remonstrated with herself for being so unreasonable. She also felt a tremendous sense of relief when she realised Clara had left Charlie at home. After inviting her in, they settled down in the kitchen for coffee, and within minutes, the conversation was flowing easily.

Kat took a sip of her drink and leant back in her chair, deciding to ask the question that had been on her mind for a while. "You seem to have a lot of spare time for someone who's so successful. Do you have a set schedule or something?"

Clara chuckled softly, shaking her head while placing her drink back down on the counter. "Not really. I work for myself, so I kind of set my own hours. It's much better than being tied down to a nine-to-five job. It gives me a lot more freedom."

Kat nodded, though a part of her still wondered if that was how things operated in the financial world.

Shouldn't she be visiting clients at their business premises? Kat smirked to herself. She didn't have the first idea about how it all worked. "I guess that makes sense," she replied, glancing towards the window, trying to hide her embarrassment. Changing the subject, Kat asked, "So… you mentioned you've had two long-term relationships before. What happened to them?"

Clara's expression shifted, but she still answered without hesitation. Kat's probing questions didn't appear to affect her at all. "Well, the first one was with a guy called James. We met at uni and were together for a few years, but he ended up moving to the US for a research position. We tried long-distance, but it just didn't pan out." She shrugged, as if it were an old wound long healed. "The second one was Dan, someone I met at work. But again, we drifted. We both worked long hours and I guess we were putting our careers ahead of our relationship." She looked at Kat before settling her eyes on her coffee mug between her hands once more. "It wasn't a nasty breakup. It just wasn't meant to be."

Kat listened, slightly relieved at how forthcoming Clara was. There didn't seem to be anything particularly unusual about her existence, at least not on the surface. But there was still something; her nagging feeling about how well Clara interacted with Luke the other day. How she was seamlessly stepping into Kat's life. And those looks, uncomfortably close to Kat's old neighbour and one-time friend, Imogen. Was Clara too perfect, too nice? Or was Kat overthinking things?

As if sensing Kat's uncertainty, Clara shifted the conversation again. "By the way," she said, "I wanted to ask. When are your parents visiting again? They're such lovely people."

Kat looked up from her coffee, surprised by the question. "Um… I'm not sure. Maybe next month?" She furrowed her brow, feeling it was an odd thing for Clara to query. "Why do you ask?"

Clara smiled, her tone casual. "Oh, no reason. I just think they're wonderful, that's all. It must be nice to have family around."

Kat nodded slowly. Clara was just being genuinely kind.

Clara glanced at her watch, then smiled brightly. "Speaking of having visitors, I'm having a few people over on Friday night—just drinks and nibbles. I'd love for you to come."

Kat stiffened. The idea of socialising in Imogen's old house made her squirm. She quickly tried to think of an excuse.

"I don't know. Friday might be tricky. Tom's at home, and I obviously can't leave a six-year-old alone," she said, hoping the mention of her son would quell the proposal.

But Clara was quick with a solution. Almost too quick. "Oh, that's no problem! Tom can come too. He can hang out in the TV room with Charlie. I'm sure they'll keep each other entertained and I can put on a movie or something for him."

Kat hesitated, feeling trapped. She didn't want to go, but Clara's offer was hard to decline without seeming rude. And Tom had been pestering her to see Charlie again since their walk in the park.

"I… guess that could work," Kat said reluctantly.

"Great!" Clara exclaimed, beaming. "It'll be fun. And it'll be nice to see you all again."

Kat frowned, her mind catching on the word. "All?"

Clara smiled. "Yes, you, Tom, and Luke."

Kat's heart skipped a beat. "Luke's coming?"

Clara nodded enthusiastically. "Yes. I invited him

when I bumped into him at the park the other day. He seemed more than happy to accept."

Kat felt a knot form in her stomach. The idea of being in that house unnerved her, but Luke was going to be there too. It especially grated when Clara had invited him *before* her. And why hadn't Luke mentioned it to her? They'd spoken on the phone since the weekend.

After Clara left, Kat grabbed her mobile and immediately dialled Luke's number. Her fingers trembled slightly as she waited for him to pick up.

"Hey, Kat," Luke's voice was cheerful, oblivious to any rising frustration.

"Did Clara invite you to hers on Friday?" Kat asked, cutting straight to the point.

There was a brief pause. "Yeah, she did. I was going to tell you—"

"So why didn't you?"

Luke hesitated. "I didn't think it was a big deal. I figured you'd be okay with it, especially since Tom's coming too."

He knows Tom is going?

"How do you know about Tom? I've only just arranged it."

"Oh, sorry." Luke sounded genuinely surprised, as if Kat was totally overreacting. "It's just that Clara mentioned it in the park. I assumed he'd told you."

Kat clenched her jaw, struggling to keep her voice steady. "It just feels weird, Luke. You could have told me sooner."

"Kat, it's just drinks and some food. Why are you making it into something it's not?"

She exhaled sharply. "I'm not... It's just... never mind."

Luke's tone softened. "Look, it'll be fine. Maybe it'll

be good for us all. To be able to relax in a different environment."

Kat didn't respond, muttering a quick goodbye before ending the call. She stared at the phone in her hand, her thoughts swirling in confusion. Clara's invitation, Luke's nonchalance. Did she have it all wrong?

22

As Kat walked into the office the following morning, the hum of the building's daily operations immediately greeted her. It felt strange being back in the familiar environment, one she had been absent from more than she probably should have. She missed Adam and his day-to-day running of the office, but Luke had stepped up and taken on much of the responsibility himself. And although it had been her choice to let him, it still left her feeling slightly out of place.

She greeted a few of her employees as she made her way to her desk, exchanging pleasantries. "How's everything going?" she asked Kathy in accounts, who smiled back at her.

"It's going great, Kat. Luke's been really supportive," she said. "We've been making good progress on the quarterly reports."

"Good to hear," Kat replied, forcing a smile. It was nice that things were running smoothly, but hearing Luke being praised again gave her a small pang of discomfort. Another team member, Sarah, echoed similar sentiments when Kat stopped by. Luke, as Adam often told her, had truly ingratiated himself with the staff.

The thought nagged at her as she moved towards her desk. She had let Luke handle things almost single-handedly, giving herself space to focus on other parts of her life, but perhaps it was a mistake. Still, the last thing she wanted was to be tied down to the office. The decision had been made, and she wasn't about to second-guess it just because of a few passing remarks.

When she finally reached her cubicle, she took a deep breath and pushed the thoughts aside. The day wasn't about her internal struggles; it was about replacing Kevin. Luke had arranged two interviewees for the analyst position, and she was determined to be part of the process, even if only to observe.

Luke greeted her with his usual warm smile as he finally joined her. "I'm pleased you've come in," he said, instantly putting her mind at ease.

"Yes, well," Kat replied, "I still need to know who we're paying the wages to."

They laughed and exchanged pleasantries before the first of the interviewees arrived thirty minutes later. Kat immediately felt more involved, but as the interviews progressed, she found herself saying very little. Luke, on the other hand, was professional, totally in command. His questions were good, his attitude confident. Kat couldn't help but admire how smoothly he conducted both evaluations.

When they finished, Luke fetched coffees, and they sat together at his desk, reviewing the candidates. As they chatted about the pros and cons of each, Kat's eyes flicked to the monitor behind him. Her breath caught in her throat when she thought she saw an email with Clara's name in his inbox.

She blinked and looked away, trying to focus on their conversation. No, it can't be, she told herself, but she was convinced of what she'd seen. She couldn't believe that Luke might have correspondence from Clara. What could they possibly be emailing about? Had they exchanged more than just pleasantries?

As Luke explained his choice of candidate, Kat couldn't help but glance at the screen over this shoulder once more, but Luke noticed and casually flicked the monitor to a different window. Her suspicions deepened. What was he hiding?

As lunchtime approached, Kat made a suggestion. "How about a walk in the park? We could grab a drink. It's nice out today."

Luke smiled, seemingly pleased by the idea. "Sounds good to me."

They strolled towards Regent's Park, the late February sun providing a hint of warmth in the chilly air. For a brief moment, Kat felt content. They bought drinks from a kiosk and found a bench to sit on, chatting about work and life in general.

Kat thanked Luke for everything he was doing with the business. "I honestly don't know what I'd do without you," she admitted. "You've been incredible."

Luke looked mildly taken aback by her praise, but smiled modestly. "I'm just doing what needs to be done."

Encouraged by the atmosphere, Kat leant in slightly. "Really, I mean it," she said, her voice softer now. "I'm so grateful."

Before she realised what she was doing, she leant in further, intending to kiss him, a small gesture of intimacy and gratitude that felt right in the moment. But Luke stood up abruptly, startling her. He looked around the park, his expression tense.

"What's wrong?" Kat asked, confused and embarrassed by his sudden reaction.

Luke continued to glance around, his eyes scanning the area as if searching for someone. "I just don't think it's appropriate to kiss in public like this."

Kat frowned, unable to believe what she was hearing. Only a couple of weeks ago, he had been the one chasing her, asking her to go on holiday, acting as if he couldn't bear to be away from her. Now, he was pulling back, as if the idea of being seen together was something to be ashamed of.

They stood in awkward silence for a moment before Luke gestured towards the office. "We should get back."

Kat followed him, her mind spinning. What had changed? Had Clara's presence somehow altered things between them?

As they neared the exit of the park, Kat caught a glimpse of a figure out of the corner of her eye. They were quite a distance away, standing on the footpath at the far end of the street. Her heart raced, and she quickly tapped Luke on the shoulder, gesturing towards where she had seen the figure.

"Can you see someone watching us?" she whispered.

Luke turned, following her eye line, but there was no one there. Whoever it was had vanished, leaving Kat to question why somebody who looked remarkably like her dead ex-husband would be watching out for her.

23

KAT SIGHED, staring at her reflection in the mirror. She did not know what to wear to Clara's party. Clara had described it as just drinks and nibbles, making it sound informal, so Kat opted for jeans and a jumper. Casual, comfortable, and simple. But still she couldn't relax. It wasn't just the party—it was everything. Luke was becoming increasingly distant, and although they had both agreed on the best candidate from the interviews, a guy named Prakash, Kat still couldn't help but feel that Luke was sending her mixed messages. He'd mentioned feeling "relieved" that the position was filled, and Kat wondered if it was a dig at how little she had been involved in the business lately.

As she prepared to leave for the party, Tom tugged at her sleeve. "Mummy," he said softly. "Is Daddy going to be there?"

Kat's heart sank. Her son hadn't asked about his father in so long, not since she had gently explained that he had "fallen asleep" and wouldn't wake up again. And although he'd referred to Imogen a few times, he hadn't mentioned her either in weeks. She'd thought her mum had been right, and it was just his way of grieving. So why ask about his 'Daddy' again now?

"No, sweetheart," she replied carefully. "Why would Daddy be there?"

Tom shrugged, looking down at his shoes. "I just thought he would. That's all."

Kat's throat tightened, and she forced a smile, stroking his hair. She put it down to distress, a coping mechanism. Kids often misunderstood things or created their own narratives to cope. Nevertheless, the comment left her feeling uneasy. She couldn't help but think of the person she thought she'd seen after leaving the park with Luke or the figure in the window across the street.

Finally, after a deep breath, Kat gathered Tom, and they crossed the road to Clara's. The house appeared to grow in size the closer she got, its upstairs windows surveying her as if contemplating whether or not she was welcome.

Clara greeted them at the door with a beaming smile. She looked stunning, wearing a free-flowing, off-the-shoulder, emerald-green dress that accentuated her figure without being overly formal. Her dark hair cascaded in loose waves, her makeup subtle yet classy. It reminded Kat of Imogen greeting her and Adam for any one of their infamous boozy nights. She could imagine Adam's eyes taking in all of Imogen's form. And not only that, but it was also a look that left Kat's outfit feeling woefully inadequate.

Kat's gaze drifted behind Clara, catching a glimpse of another woman gliding across the kitchen, dressed in a deep burgundy dress that looked equally striking. The sight made Kat's stomach turn. She suddenly felt so foolish, like somebody who had shown up to a black-tie event in fancy dress.

"I should... I should go home and change," Kat stammered, embarrassment burning her cheeks. "I didn't realise..."

"Nonsense," Clara interrupted with a laugh, stepping aside to usher them in. "You look perfect. It's just a little get-together. You don't need to change a thing."

Kat hesitated, feeling self-conscious, but knowing her excuses were thin. She stepped inside, the atmosphere immediately enveloping her in warmth and soft music. Clara took Tom into the TV room, and Kat heard Charlie bark in excitement. As Kat stood awkwardly in the hallway, she glanced around into the dining room, and her eyes fell on Luke.

He was standing near the fireplace, dressed in a sleek dinner jacket and bow tie. Kat couldn't believe it. Why hadn't he mentioned the formality of the evening? The sight of him looking so sophisticated and handsome made her feel even more out of place. She was in jeans and a jumper for heaven's sake, surrounded by guests in stunning outfits, and Luke, of all people, hadn't thought to give her a heads-up.

"Luke," she mumbled as she approached him, but he was deep in conversation with a man she didn't recognise. She stood awkwardly before stepping back, trying to avoid the growing discomfort yet not knowing where to go.

Clara reappeared at her side, holding a tray of champagne flutes. "Here, have a drink. Relax," she said with a smile, handing one to Kat.

Kat took the glass with a grateful nod, feeling the bubbles tickle her throat as she sipped the drink. Resisting necking the champagne in one, she stepped towards the corner of the room, trying to blend into the background. Her mind buzzed with confusion. What had Clara said?

"Speaking of having visitors, I'm having a few people over on Friday night—just drinks and nibbles. I'd love for you to come…"

But it was far from an informal gathering. It was… a party. A full-blown event, with guests dressed to the nines and conversations flowing as easily as the champagne. Kat couldn't help but wonder if Clara had done it deliberately, knowing that Kat would show up underdressed and looking like a fish out of water.

Clara floated around the room like a perfect hostess, mingling with the guests and making sure everyone had a drink in their hand. Meanwhile, Kat remained in the corner, sipping her champagne while wishing the ground would open up. Luke caught her eye from across the room and offered her a small smile. It came across as distant, like a reminder of his growing disinterest in her.

Kat felt more and more like a stranger in Clara's home, surrounded by people she didn't know and was unable to hold a conversation with. She glanced at Clara, who was laughing with a group of people by the fireplace, looking completely at ease.

Kat took another sip of her champagne, her mind swirling with thoughts she couldn't quite grasp. Something was off, but she was unable to put her finger on what exactly. All she knew was that this night, this party, was not at all what she had expected—and Clara, once again, was at the centre of it all.

24

Kat stood awkwardly, clutching her champagne flute tightly as Clara introduced her to more guests. They were all elegant, educated, and incredibly posh. It felt as though she'd invited the cream of London just to make Kat feel more inadequate. She became more and more convinced that their eyes were focused on her as though she was out of place, a mere owner of a tiny IT firm. Her jeans, which seemed fine when she left the house, now felt grimy, and she could swear her jumper had holes she hadn't noticed before. The sensation of being completely out of her depth began to overwhelm her.

The ambient music, initially a soft hum in the background, appeared to grow louder and louder. The surrounding chatter, the laughter, the clinking of glasses —it all merged into an oppressive roar. Kat's heart raced, and for a moment, she thought she might even pass out. The room seemed to shrink, the walls closing in around her, her breaths coming in shallow gasps. Her eyes darted to Luke across the room, who was in deep conversation with Clara. Her heart sank at the sight of them, comfortable in each other's presence, as if she didn't exist.

She wanted to get out.

Once Clara left Luke to mingle, Kat made her way past a few fellow guests, edging by the sleek dresses and the expensive perfumes, until she found Luke alone by the window. She could still feel the judgemental eyes of the other attendees burning into her.

"Why didn't you tell me this was a formal thing?" Kat asked in a low voice, trying to keep her frustration at bay.

Luke glanced at her, his expression impossible to read. "I thought you knew," he replied with a casual shrug, as if it was the most obvious thing in the world.

Her hands clenched around her glass. "You thought I knew?" she hissed through gritted teeth. "How the fuck would I know? And why the hell didn't you think to mention it?"

He looked at her, a flicker of something—maybe indifference—passing over his face. "Kat, it's not a big deal."

She felt her blood boil. "Not a big deal? Look at me!" She took a small step backwards, bowing slightly while waving her arm in a circular motion to bring attention to her attire. "Why are you being like this?" she continued. "Is it because I didn't commit to the holiday? Or is it about the business? Or..." She hesitated, but couldn't stop herself. "Is it because you like Clara? Have you gone off me as quickly as you went off your wife?"

Her voice cut through the air, and in that instant, the music stopped. Silence fell over the room as if the universe had conspired to ensure everyone heard her. Her cheeks burned, and she could feel the weight of every single pair of eyes upon her. The space filled with murmurs, and she caught Clara glancing their way from the far side of the room.

When the music recommenced, Luke's expression was hard, his jaw tight as he leant in closer. His voice was low but cutting. "Your behaviour lately, Kat… It's beginning to remind me of Adam."

Kat's breath caught in her throat.

"You're losing interest in the company," he continued. "Seeing or hearing things that aren't there, like that person in the park yesterday who didn't even exist."

Kat stared at him, momentarily stunned. He was twisting the knife, and he knew it.

"Adam couldn't stand you, you know that?" she spat, her voice trembling with a mix of rage and despair. "And no wonder! You've changed too! Two weeks ago, you practically admitted to leaving Sandra because of me, and now you're acting like you can't even be in the same space as me."

Luke's face darkened at her words. He stared at her with an intensity that made her stomach churn. The room had gone back to its dull murmur, but Kat felt exposed, vulnerable.

Without waiting for a response, she turned and fled towards the TV room, where she found Tom seated at a small table, busy with his crayons and paper. His little body was hunched over, totally focused on his drawing, Charlie asleep at his feet.

"Tom, we need to go home," Kat said, her voice shaky.

Tom barely glanced up at her, a small frown on his face. "We've only just got here, Mummy. I like it here."

Kat's spirits plummeted further.

"Why don't you like Clara, Mummy?" Tom asked, his tone edged with the curiosity only a child could possess.

"I do like her," Kat lied.

But she knew Tom remained unconvinced. He simply chuckled and returned to his drawing, as if he knew something she didn't. She desperately needed a drink to steady herself.

Leaving Tom again, Kat made her way towards the kitchen. The noise of the party continued as she moved down the hallway. The dim lights and idle chatter only added to her woes. Everybody getting on great. But then she heard something.

Footsteps. From upstairs.

She froze. The sensation that someone was watching her returned, just as the day before. Her heart pounded as she glanced up the staircase. Everyone was downstairs, right? She threw a quick glance into the dining room. The guests were still engaged in their small talk, drinks in hand, seemingly oblivious to her.

Without thinking, she moved towards the stairs, each step slow and deliberate. The house seemed unexpectedly darker, quieter, as if she'd found a place all to herself. She told herself she was being silly. And even if there was someone upstairs, maybe Clara had forgotten to mention something about a guest staying over. Or—

Suddenly, a creak above. She stopped, her hand gripping the banister. Her breath caught in her throat as she peered up into the darkness. Surely not?

With her pulse racing, Kat took another step, her foot sinking into the soft carpet…

25

Kat hesitated halfway up the stairs, her eyes locked on the shadows of the corridor above. All she could hear was the faint murmur of the party below, a muffled blur of voices and music blending into the background. But all she could see in her mind was when she thought she had seen something—a shadow in the upstairs window of Imogen's house.

She stared at her phone for a long moment before her gaze drifted across the street to Imogen's house. The curtains remained drawn, as they had for days, and the house looked empty and silent. But just as she was about to turn away, something caught her eye—a fleeting shadow in the upstairs window.

Kat froze. She blinked, trying to focus on the spot where she thought she'd seen movement, but when she looked back up, the window was empty.

. . .

She tried to shake it off. It was absurd to think anyone was upstairs. Maybe it was just a relative of Clara's—someone elderly, bedridden, unable to come downstairs. Or a guest at the party, someone staying over who had retired upstairs early. Kat had no way of knowing how many people Clara had invited. So, if there was an obvious explanation, why couldn't she bring herself to move? Her legs felt heavy, as if she had lead weights in her shoes. The logical part of her brain screamed that she should just turn around and go back to the party, where everything was normal, safe. Yet something kept her rooted to the spot.

Suddenly, the sound of footsteps echoing from below startled her. Kat whipped around to see Clara standing at the foot of the stairs, smiling up at her. "What are you doing up there?" she asked, her voice light and in no way cross.

Kat hesitated, flustered, and quickly stammered, "I-I thought I heard someone up there." Her words sounded silly as soon as she said them, and a wave of embarrassment washed over her.

Clara's smile didn't waver. Instead, she laughed softly, as though Kat had made an innocent mistake. "There's no one up there," she said reassuringly. "Come on, you're missing all the fun."

Kat was relieved, but confused. Why wasn't Clara annoyed at her for sneaking upstairs? Wouldn't anyone else have been at least a little suspicious or irritated? Shaking off her thoughts, Kat followed Clara back down the stairs, the unease lingering at the back of her mind. She allowed herself one last glance up as she trailed behind Clara into the kitchen. All remained ominously dark.

Clara poured them both a stiff drink. They sat at the

kitchen table, just the two of them, while the other guests lingered in the main room. From time to time, someone came in, refilled their drink or grabbed something to eat from the impressive buffet, smiling politely at Kat before disappearing again.

"I've been worried about you," Clara said after a few moments, breaking the silence. Her tone was gentle, understanding. "I can only imagine how hard everything has been for you lately."

Kat looked down at her drink, swirling the liquid around, the clinking of ice cubes against glass somehow soothing. "I'm fine, really," she replied, but her voice lacked conviction. Even she didn't believe it.

Clara leant in slightly, her expression serious. "Stress can take a real toll. If you ever need to talk to someone, I have some friends who work in that field who could help. There's no shame in it. You've been through a lot."

Kat forced a smile, touched by Clara's concern but also feeling a familiar tension in her chest. She recalled her mum suggesting exactly the same thing to Adam, albeit with considerably less empathy.

"You're not right in the head," Edwina said, tapping her temple with her forefinger. "You need help."

"Thanks," Kat eventually replied, recollecting the look on her husband's face before glancing at the foot of the stairwell. "I'll think about it."

The conversation shifted to lighter subjects, especially after Clara poured them both a second generous measure of vodka. They laughed, and for a brief moment, Kat let herself relax. The edge of anxiety that had gripped her since arriving at the party seemed to fade, replaced by the comforting haze of tipsiness. She realised that she was relying on alcohol far too often to help her unwind.

Just like Adam.

After a while, Luke entered the kitchen, offering a brief nod of acknowledgement before announcing that he had to leave. Something about meeting someone early the next day. He didn't even meet Kat's eyes as he said his goodbyes, leaving her embarrassed and angry. At least Clara didn't accompany him to the door.

The party continued, and Kat found herself chatting with other guests in the kitchen, Clara by her side the whole time. Clara was the perfect hostess—attentive, gracious, and unfailingly kind. Kat was beginning to feel more comfortable when she noticed the crowd was starting to thin out. People were leaving, drifting away in pairs. The noise was now reduced to soft chatter.

"Looks like it's time to wind down," Clara said, glancing around. She looked pleased, as though the evening had gone exactly as she had hoped.

Kat nodded, standing up a little too quickly. The alcohol buzzed in her head, making her slightly dizzy. "I should probably get Tom home."

Clara smiled warmly. "Of course. It was lovely having you both here."

Kat retrieved Tom from the TV room, where he had spent most of the evening absorbed in his drawings. He looked up at her with a wide grin, clearly enjoying himself. "Do we have to go?" he asked, his voice tinged with disappointment.

Kat forced a smile. "Yeah, it's getting late."

Tom reluctantly packed up his things, and together they made their way across the street to their own home. The night air was cool, and Kat felt a slight chill as they walked. But inside, the house was warm and quiet, and after settling Tom into bed, Kat finally exhaled, a sense of peace washing over her.

Yet even as she poured herself a glass of wine, lit one

of Adam's cigarettes, and sat down in the living room, the lingering unease crept back. Without thinking, she found herself glancing out of the window, her gaze drawn to Clara's house. The upstairs windows were dark, just as they had been that night when she thought she'd seen something move. But hadn't she heard footsteps earlier?

She took a long drag of her cigarette, trying to shake the feeling. But no matter how hard she tried, her mind kept drifting back to those upstairs windows. And then, more disturbing than anything else, Kat caught herself smiling.

26

K‌AT TRIED hard for the next two weeks to put her life back on track. Luke's comment about her "going the same way as Adam" had struck a nerve, and she knew he could be right. She couldn't afford to slip into that same pit of despair. She needed to stay strong for Tom. The mere thought of losing him, or anyone questioning her capacity as a mother, terrified her. But why was she seeing things, hearing things, just as Adam had?

Determined not to spiral further, she pushed herself to re-engage with the business. It had become clear that her absence was raising eyebrows, amplified by Luke hinting at her waning interest. They met a few times over coffee during that fortnight, discussing work in depth. They somehow navigated the tension that had built between them and nothing was mentioned of the party or their spontaneous argument in front of the other guests. Kat maintained a firm grip on the conversations, keeping them about business; the new analyst, Prakash, and what was next for the company.

Truth Lies Beneath

By the time the weekend arrived, now mid-March, the daffodils were in full bloom wherever she went, and Kat was pleased to greet her parents for the next few days. Despite her growing resentment towards her mum and dad—again, she recalled Adam and how he despised them—at least they made a fuss of Tom and gave her a break from the day-to-day single parent routine.

It was a sunny Friday, and Kat spent the morning tidying the house. Edwina and William arrived around midday, and Kat greeted them as warmly as she could muster, making sure to keep the mood light, hoping it would keep her nerves at bay. Her parents had been nothing but supportive through everything, but she still felt a deep-seated pressure to appear in control. Kat chastised herself for inwardly grimacing at the very sight of her own mum's face.

They brought a gift for Tom, who was ecstatic to see them when he returned home from school, and immediately ran off with William to play with his new toy in the living room. Edwina, always the sharp observer, sensed something was off with Kat. "Are you feeling alright, dear?" she asked when they were alone in the kitchen.

Kat forced a smile. "Just a bit tired, that's all. Everything's been so hectic."

"And what about Luke?" Edwina asked.

"What about him?" Kat snapped, knowing full well what her mum meant. She recalled the FaceTime call when she had made her intentions crystal clear.

"Not only is he good at business decisions, but I also always thought Luke was very dishy."

"Well, you could do a lot worse than—"

"Mum, please," Kat replied, trying to sound firm. The last thing she needed was another conversation about

Luke, especially when things between them were already tense.

"I only mention it because your dad and I think he'd be a great support to you," Edwina continued, her voice softening. "And for Tom too. You've been through so much, darling, and a man around the house would help you in so many ways."

Kat sighed, not meeting her mother's eyes. "I don't need a man to take care of me, Mum. I'm fine."

"But Luke isn't just any man," Edwina pressed. "You've said it yourself. He's been there for you. He's helping tremendously with the business. You can't shut everyone out, darling."

Kat opened the fridge, pretending to busy herself with finding something to drink, though she wasn't the least bit thirsty. "I haven't shut him out," she replied through gritted teeth, closing the door a little too firmly. "I'm just… taking my time."

Edwina's silence spoke volumes. After a moment, she added, "Just make sure you don't push him too far. You don't want to end up alone."

The words stung, and Kat felt the weight of her mum's disapproval hanging in the air. But there was something else consuming her thoughts: had she pushed Luke too far? She had only said she needed to think about the holiday, not dismissed it entirely. So why had Luke changed so quickly? It felt as though he had distanced himself from the moment she hadn't leapt at the idea.

William joined them in the kitchen, grinning as Tom ran in after him, giggling. The tension dissolved briefly as they laughed at Tom's enthusiasm, but Kat couldn't shake the unease that had settled deep inside her. William suggested taking Tom to the park and Edwina said she fancied some air too, surprising Kat as her mum was getting more unsteady on her feet every time she saw her. However, Kat was grateful for the break from the strained atmosphere and she said she would stay behind and prepare dinner. Once they disappeared, she allowed herself a moment of peace, pouring herself a generous glass of red and lighting up yet another cigarette. There were only a few left. She would need to buy a fresh packet.

As she drew hard, taking in a lungful of nicotine, Kat couldn't stop thinking about her mum's continual interference. The tension between them was becoming a genuine issue; a palpable resentment. She tried to immerse herself in preparing dinner, but something urged her to follow them. Grabbing her coat, she headed out, walking to the park, yet not having the slightest idea why she was doing so.

From a distance, Kat watched as her dad and Tom played, William's laughter carrying on the breeze. Her mum, however, sat alone on a bench, her frailty evident in the way she hunched slightly, watching the scene from afar. A slow-burning anger welled up inside Kat. Ever since she and Adam had joined Liam and Imogen's company, her mum had meddled, criticised, and judged every aspect of her life. Now, sitting isolated and unaware, Edwina seemed almost vulnerable. An intrusive thought flickered in Kat's mind — what if something happened to her? Would it change anything? She imagined her mother falling, hurting herself, and for a fleeting moment, a dark satisfaction washed over her.

Kat shook the notion away, horrified. She cursed herself under her breath and stepped back from the scene, turning on her heels to walk home. But as she did, a disquiet remained. The image had been so vivid, so real. As if some part of her had wanted it to happen.

Once home, Kat tried to forget the moment, returning to the safety of her routine.

But half an hour later, everything changed.

27

KAT WAS in the kitchen when she heard Clara's voice calling out. "Hello? Anyone home?" There was an unnerving urgency in her tone. Kat scampered into the hallway, but before she could get to the front door, it was flung open. Clara stepped inside, holding Tom's hand while gripping Charlie's lead with the other. He barked furiously at Kat. Her heart leapt into her throat, panic surging through her as she quickly looked over Tom for any sign of injury.

"What's happened?" she demanded, her voice shaking.

"It's your mum," Clara said, her voice steady but serious. "She's had a fall."

Kat's world stopped. "What? Where is she? What happened?"

"She fell in the park and hit her head. She was unconscious for a moment. The ambulance is on its way." Clara pulled hard on the dog lead, finally making Charlie drop to the floor, whimpering like a child who had been told off in front of his friends.

Tom, who had been gripping Clara's hand tightly, was in tears, his little face red streaked with panic. Clara crouched down beside him, gently pulling his head into her shoulder and murmuring something soft and reassuring into his ear. Kat noticed his sobs slow, and she felt a sudden urge to push Clara aside and comfort her son, hold him, and tell him everything would be alright, but her mind was racing towards the park, and to her mum.

She desperately tried to keep her voice steady despite the rising panic. "I need to get to her. Clara, can you stay with Tom?"

Clara nodded quickly, her face a mask of calm. "Of course, I'll look after him. We'll look after Charlie, won't we, darling?"

Darling?

"Just go!" Clara shouted.

Kat thanked her with a glance, grabbed her coat and keys, and rushed out of the door. She drove to the park, every second an eternity, despite it being a matter of minutes away. Thoughts spun chaotically in her mind. Her mum, always so fragile on her feet lately, her hips causing her nothing but pain, had still insisted on going to the park. Kat had been surprised but too exhausted to protest earlier. But she also knew why her mum had chosen to go. Because of their silly argument over Luke. It was Kat's fault she had gone at all. And then she wondered if anybody had noticed her following them.

Clambering out of her car, she spotted the ambulance straight away. Her dad stood next to it, speaking with a paramedic, his face drawn and pale. He looked older, more frail in the late afternoon sunlight, his shoulders slumped in a way Kat had never seen before. She rushed to his side, barely able to form words.

"Dad… where's Mum?"

William turned to her, his eyes filled with worry. "She's inside the ambulance. They've been checking her over. They're taking her to the hospital, Kat… It's bad. She hit her head hard."

Kat's breath caught in her throat. She glanced towards the ambulance, her legs leaden. Everything seemed to blur, the voices of the paramedics, her father's quiet worry, all blending into a disorienting haze.

Steeling herself, she climbed into the back of the ambulance. Edwina lay on the stretcher, her face pale, her eyes barely open. She looked fragile, too fragile, and seeing her like that sent a cold shock through Kat's veins.

"Mum?" Kat whispered, leaning closer. "Are you okay? You've had a nasty fall."

Edwina looked up weakly and murmured, "Kat, darling. I didn't fall. I was pushed."

Kat's heart missed a beat. "What do you mean, pushed?"

Edwina winced, trying to reach for her head. "I'm not sure, but it felt like someone caught my foot, then pushed me. It happened so quickly."

Kat swallowed hard, her throat tight. "They said you hit your head pretty hard."

"I did," Edwina murmured. "Everything's a bit fuzzy, but I'll be fine. Your dad… he's beside himself… look after him, darling."

The paramedics interrupted gently, telling Kat they needed to get Edwina to the hospital as soon as possible. Kat nodded, feeling helpless as she backed out of the ambulance. "Did you see what happened?" she asked her dad.

William shook his head. "I wasn't with her, love. I was playing football with Tom."

Kissing Kat on the cheek, he climbed in to sit beside

his wife for the journey, leaving Kat to follow behind in her car.

The drive to the hospital was a blur of anxious thoughts. Kat gripped the steering wheel tightly, the words her mother had said to her before the fall echoing in her mind: *"You can't shut everyone out, Kat. Don't end up alone."*

It was all too much to process; her strained relationship with Luke, the constant pressure of holding everything together for Tom, and now, her mother's accident. She needed to be strong, but how could she be when her whole world seemed to be falling apart?

At the hospital, Kat and her father sat with her mother as they waited for the doctors to assess Edwina. William paced nervously, his usually calm demeanour cracking under the weight of his worries. Edwina had been slipping in and out of consciousness since the ambulance ride, and every time she closed her eyes, Kat felt a stab of panic.

Eventually, the doctor came with an update. Edwina had suffered a serious head injury, and they needed to monitor her closely for the next twenty-four hours. The news hit Kat like a punch to the gut. She felt lightheaded, overwhelmed by the diagnosis. Was her mum going to pull through?

Sitting at her bedside, Kat held Edwina's hand, her mind racing with a million thoughts. She could hear William softly muttering words under his breath, though she wasn't sure he realised he was doing it. Would *he* be okay? Would she lose them both?

As she sat there, lost in her thoughts, a sudden realisation struck her with startling clarity. Clara had brought Tom home from the park. What was she doing there? Kat hadn't mentioned to anyone that her parents were taking

Tom to the park, so why had Clara been there? Kat certainly hadn't seen her, but had she seen Kat?

The question hit her like a hammer blow.

"Kat… I didn't fall. I was pushed."

But with her mother lying unconscious beside her, now was not the time to dwell on it. Kat squeezed Edwina's hand tighter, forcing herself to stay focused on the present.

28

Almost a month later, Kat sat in the back of a hearse, staring blankly at the road ahead as the car rolled through Edwina's home village. Her father, William, sat next to her, utterly silent, his frail hands resting in his lap. It had only been three weeks since Edwina's fall, but those three weeks were a blur, a period of disbelief for Kat. Her mum had never regained consciousness properly, only drifting in and out of a confused state. The head trauma she suffered, coupled with bleeding in her brain, was too severe for her body to overcome. She had passed within twenty-four hours; the doctors telling them that the impact had caused a subdural haematoma—blood clotting between her brain and the skull. It was a fatal injury, one that even the best surgeons couldn't always fix. Kat had sat at her bedside, holding her mum's hand, watching her breathe slowly until the machines finally went silent.

William had been completely devasted by the news. But the toll of losing his wife was far worse than Kat could have imagined. In just three short weeks, the man she had known her entire life had shrunk into someone almost unrecognisable. His skin had grown pale and papery, hanging loose on his face. His once-strong frame seemed to sag under the weight of grief. His eyes were bloodshot and ringed with dark shadows, a sign of the sleepless nights Kat knew he was enduring. She had made him meals, coaxing him out of Adam's old reading chair in the living room—she especially didn't want him sitting there—but he would barely touch them. She would find him muttering to himself when he thought no one was listening, pacing the floor in the middle of the night, or sitting alone in a darkened room.

Tom had noticed the changes too. Though he had taken his grandmother's passing in his stride, much like he had with Adam and Liam, he was uneasy around William. One night, he crawled into Kat's bed, his small body trembling with fear. "Grandad is scaring me," he whispered. Kat hugged him tightly, promising it would get better, but she wasn't sure if she believed it herself. William seemed to be retreating into some private world. On one occasion, Kat caught him talking to Edwina as if she were still alive, his voice carrying from the living room late at night.

And Tom... something about how he coped with bereavement worried her. His detachment, the way he accepted each death with little more than a shrug. It wasn't normal for a child of his age, as though he was holding something inside, something that helped him stay grounded despite the loss around him, but Kat couldn't determine what it was. The only person who had died where he showed a semblance of emotion was his aunty Imogen.

The funeral was a small, quiet affair, set in Edwina's picturesque village in rural Leicestershire. The church was a quaint, stone building surrounded by rolling fields, a place where Edwina had grown up and lived all her life. The service was sombre, filled with the usual condolences from friends and neighbours who had come to pay their respects. Kat stood by William's side, her heart heavy with grief, but her outward appearance composed. She'd been strong since her mum's passing, but at times, she didn't quite know where her resolve was coming from. After the funeral, she took her dad home. It was a longer journey than it should have been, William stumbling along the path as though his legs could barely support him.

Once inside, Kat helped him into his familiar armchair in the living room, the one he had always sat in to watch the horse racing on his enormous television. But that day, he didn't reach for the remote. Instead, he remained staring at the blank TV screen, his eyes hollow, his hands trembling slightly.

"Dad, are you sure you're okay on your own?" Kat asked, her voice soft. She didn't want to leave him like that, not when he seemed so lost.

William nodded, though his gaze remained fixed on the television. "I'll be fine," he said in a distant voice. "You need to get back for Tom. He's been through enough already."

Kat hesitated. Tom was staying with Lauren and Max for a couple of days, but she was reluctant to leave her dad. He was so frail, so fragile. And yet, he insisted. "Go," he said, waving her off with a feeble hand. "I'll be okay."

Kat stood in the doorway for a long moment, watching him. He was rocking gently in his chair, a motion that sent a chill down her spine. His eyes, though still fixed on the television, seemed unfocused, as though he were seeing something she couldn't. Just as she was about to leave, William turned his head slightly, looking at the empty sofa where Edwina had always sat.

"Did you see that, darling?" he asked softly, nodding towards the blank TV screen. His voice was warm, as if speaking to an old friend. "That was funny, wasn't it?"

Kat's blood ran cold. Her father chuckled lightly, his face breaking into a smile as he continued to converse with the empty chair. He seemed so at ease, so content, as though Edwina were right there beside him, sharing in the joke. Kat felt a wave of nausea rise in her throat. She wanted to say something, to tell him to stop, but the words wouldn't come. Instead, she stood frozen, her heart pounding in her chest, watching the man she had once known unravel before her eyes.

Finally, she backed out of the room, unable to bear the sight any longer. Tears stung her eyes as she closed the door quietly behind her, her chest heavy with the weight of it all. She had lost her mother, and now, it seemed, she was extremely close to losing her father too.

29

On the drive home, Kat found herself stopping at regular intervals, the loss of her mum finally sinking in. The numbness that she had held inside for the past few weeks eventually cracked, and she felt it in every inch of her body. The quiet of the car offered little comfort, her first time alone in what seemed like an age. Her thoughts cycled endlessly around her mother's death, William's slow descent into his private world of grief, and Tom, who had shouldered the weight of yet another death with eerie detachment. She wasn't sure what to make of it anymore, and the questions that had been gnawing at her since Edwina's fall were growing louder with each passing day.

Before she picked up Tom, she went to Clara's house, the nagging doubt of why Clara had been in the park that day, refusing to let go. Clara greeted her with a warm smile, as always, but Kat felt the apprehension prickling under her skin as she followed her into the kitchen.

"How was the funeral?" Clara asked sympathetically. "Did you give your mum a good send-off?"

Kat nodded, not wanting to talk about the service or her mum, and definitely not her dad. She hesitated for a moment, unsure of how to start. "I've been meaning to ask you about that day in the park," she began slowly. "Why were you there when… when Mum fell?"

Unsurprisingly, Clara took the question in her stride. "Oh, I always take Charlie there for his walks. You know that." She waved a hand as though it were the most natural thing in the world. "Tom saw me after your mum fell. He called me over, and I just acted on instinct. I'm so proud of him for how he handled it. He stayed so calm, like a little man."

Kat took in the words, unsure of how to respond. It was a perfectly reasonable explanation. And yet… "You hugged him in the hallway when you brought him home," Kat said, her voice faltering. "You whispered something in his ear, and he stopped crying instantly. What did you say to him?"

Clara smiled fondly. "He just needed reassurance. It was a traumatic thing for him to see. I told him how brave he was, and it seemed to help. Kids need that, Kat."

Something about the way Clara said it rankled Kat. The possessive, almost maternal tone in her voice made her skin crawl. Like she was his bloody mother. But before Kat could dwell on it, she asked the other question that had been burning in her mind. "Did you see anyone else in the park?"

Clara paused, her brow furrowing for a moment. "No. No one else was around, as far as I remember."

Kat felt her pulse quicken as she blurted out the words that had haunted her since her mum's last moments of clarity. "Mum said she didn't fall on her own. She thought she was tripped or pushed."

Clara raised an eyebrow, her expression unreadable

for a moment. "That's not uncommon with head injuries. People can get confused, even disoriented, after a blow like that. It's called post-traumatic confabulation. She probably imagined it. I wouldn't dwell on it too much."

Kat wasn't sure if the explanation eased her mind or made it worse. The medical jargon sounded plausible enough, but how did Clara know such information? Then Clara's voice shifted, a note of curiosity creeping into her tone. "Have you asked your dad about it?"

Kat nodded. "I did, but he's... he's not himself. He was with Tom, playing football. He doesn't seem to remember much."

Clara's face softened again, this time with what seemed like genuine sympathy. "I'm so sorry. It's been such a difficult period for all of you."

Kat thanked Clara for her time and made to leave, but when she reached the hallway, Charlie suddenly bounded towards her, his tail wagging furiously. He leapt up at Kat, his paws landing on her chest, and began clawing. Startled, Kat stumbled back, pushing at the dog weakly, but he kept jumping, his nails scraping against her arms.

"Charlie! Down!" Kat shouted, but her voice trembled, panic creeping in as she tried to shove him off. She caught a glimpse of Clara in the kitchen. Was she just watching, her arms folded, not moving to help? For what felt like a long moment, she just stood there, observing, a small smile playing at her lips. Finally, Clara called out softly, "Charlie, enough."

The dog immediately stopped, dropping back down onto the floor as though nothing had happened. Clara strolled over and patted him on the head. "He's just excited, that's all."

Kat stared at her, unable to comprehend why it had

taken her so long to intervene. She swallowed hard. "I should go. I have to pick up Tom."

Clara smiled again, her expression calm and collected. "Of course. Let me know if you need anything."

Kat left the house feeling shaken, her thoughts swirling as she made her way to Lauren's. The interaction with Clara replayed in her mind over and over, each detail scratching at her already frayed nerves. By the time she arrived to pick up Tom, she was barely holding herself together.

Lauren greeted her at the door. Once inside, she saw Tom and Max running circles around the living room. "Hey, you look like you've had an awful day," Lauren said, her tone full of concern. "Was the funeral that bad?"

Kat forced a smile, quickly gathering Tom's things as she hurried to leave. "Yeah... you could say that."

"Come through," Lauren replied, stepping aside for Kat to pass, and telling the boys to go and play upstairs for a while.

Reluctantly, Kat stepped into the kitchen and sat down at the table, her hands trembling. The numbness she had kept trapped for weeks suddenly cracked open, and the dam finally broke. Tears spilled from her eyes. She hadn't cried since the day her mum died, but now, every ounce of her grief, her fear, and her confusion came pouring out.

She sobbed into her hands, the sound of it echoing through the kitchen, her body shaking as she let it all out.

Moments later, Lauren's voice pulled her back. "Kat, you need to get out of your head for a while. Let's plan another night out, huh? I'll even promise not to wear my godawful shoes this time. They hurt just looking at them."

Kat let out a half-laugh, half-sob, grateful for the brief

moment of lightness. "I'd like that," she said, but deep down, the prospect of going out drinking as if nothing had happened was totally conflicting with the pandemonium swirling inside.

30

Twenty-four hours later, the knock at Kat's front door felt like the inevitable, and when she saw the two police officers, their solemn expressions confirmed her worst fears.

"It's Dad, isn't it?" she whispered, her voice hollow as though she had already processed the grief before they could speak. The officers exchanged a glance, confirming her assumption with a nod.

"May we come inside?" the female officer asked gently.

Kat stepped aside, gesturing them into the hallway with a slight inclination of her head. "Can I get you something? Tea? Coffee?" Without waiting for a reply, she found herself moving towards the kitchen, as if on autopilot.

"We're fine, thank you," the male officer replied, as he and his colleague followed Kat. She was aware of her voice rambling as she led them, talking about how frail William was the day before, how unsurprised she was that something had happened. He hadn't been the same since her mum died, but still, it was all happening so quickly.

"Mrs Chapman, please, stop," the female officer interrupted gently, cutting off her nervous chatter as she began to make coffee despite the declined offer. "Why don't you sit down?"

Confused, Kat turned to face them fully for the first time. Something in their behaviour had changed, and her stomach tightened with new apprehension.

"Your father... it wasn't as straightforward as you might believe." The female officer's voice was calm but direct. "It appears your father took his own life."

The words seemed to hit Kat like a physical blow. She stared blankly for a moment, struggling to comprehend them.

"That's... that's not possible," she stammered, clutching the work surface. "Dad wouldn't, he didn't... he was upset, yes, but he wasn't—"

"There was an empty bottle of whiskey by his side," the officer explained. "And three empty packs of paracetamol on the arm of his chair."

Whiskey? Kat felt like she was in some surreal dream. "No... no, that can't be right. Dad didn't drink, not really. The occasional pint at the pub, maybe a glass of wine at Christmas, but whiskey? He wouldn't even have it in the house!"

"We found no signs of forced entry," the male officer added. "The front door was locked when we arrived, and we had to break in after seeing him through the living room window. A neighbour had reported it."

Kat's thoughts were in overdrive. "But there wasn't any alcohol when I left. I'm sure of it. I would've noticed."

"Are you certain?" the officer asked. "It's possible he

could have hidden it from you. Stashed it somewhere. Had he been acting differently, more withdrawn?"

She shook her head, the questions spinning wildly in her mind. She couldn't reconcile the image of her gentle dad with the picture they were painting. "No, I mean… yes, he was extremely sad, but… he wouldn't do this."

The female officer's voice softened further. "I know this is hard to accept. Sometimes, people hide their feelings well, even from those they're closest to. It might have been a sudden decision."

Kat's hands trembled as she gripped the work surface harder, the room spinning around her. "I can't believe this. He wouldn't…"

The officers exchanged a glance again before the woman leant forward. "We can stay with you, or is there someone you'd like to call? A friend? Family member?"

Family member? Are you joking? They're all fucking dead.

Kat swallowed hard, shaking her head. "No, I'll be fine. I just need to… try to take this all in."

They left her with their contact information, urging her to reach out if she needed anything at all. Once the door clicked shut behind them, Kat moved to the living room and sat in silence.

Her father. Gone. Her mother, gone. And it was only a few short months since she had buried her husband. The grief was piling up like a mountain she could never hope to climb. And at the back of her mind came the inevitable conclusion. Retribution.

As she remained in the stillness of the room, her thoughts turned to the practical issues. Another funeral to arrange. Another trip up north. She'd need to take care of the estate, figure out what to do with the house. And Tom. What was she going to tell Tom? He'd been so resilient after the deaths of his dad and grandmother, but this… would this break him? Or worse, would he continue to accept it, like some part of him had disconnected from the reality of death altogether?

A wave of loneliness washed over her, a sharp, suffocating feeling of isolation. She had no one left. No parents, no husband, no family she could truly lean on. Her gaze drifted towards the window, out across the street, where she caught herself looking more and more often.

Clara's car wasn't there. How long had it been gone? She hadn't paid attention when she took Tom to school, but now she thought about it, Kat was sure it was missing that morning.

As if Clara's presence, or lack thereof, held some kind of answer, Kat found herself obsessively replaying moments in her mind. The day Clara had brought Tom home after her mum's fall. How she had hugged Tom in the hallway, whispered something that calmed him instantly. The way Clara had seemed to slide effortlessly into her and Tom's lives.

And now, this. Her dad… Clara had been at the park that day. Kat shook her head, telling herself she was just being crazy. And more importantly, how could Kat ever prove it?

Her thoughts snapped back to the conversation with the police. Whiskey? Her dad never kept whiskey in the house. She knew that for sure. So where had it come from?

The room felt suddenly too small, the air too thick. She stepped back from the window, pacing the floor with restless energy.

And then the sound of a car approached and Kat glanced up to see Clara pulling into the driveway.

31

Kat watched, a knot of unease twisting tighter in her stomach. She knew she'd have to tell Clara about her dad, about his sudden passing. As she stood with the front door slightly ajar, Clara finally stepped out of her car, her face brightening as soon as she spotted Kat.

"Kat?" she called out, stepping towards the street. "Are you alright? You look… Have you been crying?"

Left with little choice, Kat joined Clara in her driveway. Clara's gaze settled on the red rings around Kat's eyes.

"Come over. Come inside," Clara insisted, interlocking her arm through Kat's. The look of concern on her face again confused Kat. Was she reading her so wrong?

Once inside, the question felt impulsive, and it came out before Kat could stop herself.

"Have you been anywhere nice?" she asked, her voice a little too casual for the weight in the air.

Clara's brow furrowed, as if momentarily baffled by Kat's opening line. "What?"

"I didn't see your car this morning when I took Tom to school. Just wondered if you'd been out somewhere nice." Kat realised her attempt to keep her tone light felt forced.

Clara blinked, a flicker of something—annoyance?—crossing her face. "I was at work," she said. Then, with a hint of sarcasm, she added, "But thanks for keeping tabs on me."

Kat shifted uncomfortably. "Oh, right. But, um, what, to see a client?" She nodded towards Clara's smart-casual clothes, suddenly feeling the question was intrusive, even ridiculous, but she was beyond thinking straight.

Clara sighed, her expression softening just slightly. "Kat, I don't wear a uniform. This," she continued, looking down at her attire, "is something I throw on for meetings or consultations."

Kat's face flushed with embarrassment. Of course. She had known that. Why would she query what she was wearing? "Right," she muttered, brushing a loose strand of hair from her face. "That makes sense. Sorry, that was a dumb question."

Clara smiled, the corners of her mouth tugging upward as if she found Kat's flustered reaction slightly amusing. "It's fine. I still have to pay the bills, you know."

Feeling even more self-conscious, Kat cleared her throat and pressed on. "So, where have you been?"

There was a slight pause, so brief that if Kat hadn't been watching Clara closely, she might have missed it. But there it was, a flicker of hesitation before Clara responded smoothly, "University College Hospital. I'm the financial advisor for two doctors there."

Kat felt her heart skip. University College Hospital. She was momentarily swept back to the memory of

Adam frantically searching for Luke after his alleged attack.

"That's close to Regent's Park, right?" Kat said, her voice trailing off as her thoughts raced. Right near the office. The sheer coincidence left her reeling, but again she stopped herself from being so bloody paranoid.

Clara didn't seem fazed by the comment. She nodded. "Yes, I guess it's not far from there."

Before Kat could go further down the proverbial rabbit hole, Clara's expression shifted, her eyes scanning Kat's face with renewed concern. "But never mind all that. You still haven't told me what's going on. What's happened? You look like you've been through hell."

The question snapped Kat back to the present. The grief she'd been attempting to avoid came rushing back all at once. She took a shaky breath, trying to steady herself, but her voice cracked when she finally spoke. "It's my dad."

Clara's eyes widened. "Oh, no... what's happened?" But again, Kat noticed the slightest hesitance before Clara asked. Did she already know?

"He's..." Kat's throat felt dry, the words catching as she tried to explain. She swallowed hard, not wanting to reveal the truth about how he had died. Instead, she wanted to gauge Clara's response, to catch any telltale sign. "He's passed away."

Clara's reaction was immediate. She turned away from Kat, covering her face with her hands, her body shaking as if sobbing uncontrollably. The intensity of her display took Kat by surprise.

Kat hesitated, instinctively moving towards her to offer comfort, but Clara raised a hand, keeping her at a distance.

"No, it's okay," Clara choked out through her tears. "I'll be fine. I just… I can't believe it. Not William…"

Kat felt her heart constrict with confusion. How could it hit Clara so hard? She'd only met her parents a couple of times, scarcely long enough to form any deep friendship. "I didn't realise you were so close to him," Kat said. "I mean, you barely knew him."

Clara slowly lowered her hands, wiping away her tears, though her face remained red and puffy. Her expression was a mix of sadness and something Kat couldn't quite read. "I just, I really liked your dad. He was such a kind man. The way he adored Tom. He was the perfect grandad for him. I could see how much love he had for him."

Kat stood there, uncertain. There was something about Clara's reaction that felt both sincere and off. She couldn't quite place it. Was Clara genuinely that upset, or was she putting on a performance?

Clara's voice softened again as she added, "I really liked both your parents. I can't imagine what you're going through right now."

Kat watched her closely, noting how Clara's expression had shifted from devastated to composed so quickly. The tears had been there, but had they been real?

Clara looked up, her eyes now clear, though still red-rimmed. "I'm sorry," she said. "I know this must be such a shock."

Kat nodded slowly, though her mind was racing. Clara was always there, always offering comfort. But was it the kind of comfort Kat needed, or was it something more manipulative?

As she left her house, Kat couldn't shake the unsettling feeling that Clara was somehow gaslighting her.

32

Kat sat Tom down at the kitchen table after school, not really knowing where to start, but realising she had to break the news quickly. She took a deep breath, trying to steady herself before speaking. "Tom, I need to talk to you about something," she began, her voice wavering slightly. "Grandad has... gone to sleep. He's with Grandma now, and they're both at peace, looking down on you. And I want you to know how proud they are of you."

As the words left her mouth, Kat felt the tears she'd been holding back fill her eyes once more. She couldn't help it. But what startled her most was Tom's reaction. Or rather, his lack of one.

He sat there, calmly, without a flicker of emotion crossing his face. His manner was unsettlingly unmoved, while Kat broke down beside him. It wasn't just that he wasn't crying; he didn't even look surprised.

"Tom," she said, wiping her tears and trying to regain her composure. "Are you okay? Why... why aren't you upset?"

Tom paused, tilting his head as if the question confused him. "Everyone has to die, Mummy," he said matter-of-factly. "Grandma and Grandad had good lives. They were happy, and now they're together again."

Kat stared at him, stunned by his casual tone. He was only a child, and yet he was talking about death with such maturity, as though it was the most natural thing in the world. Where had he got such ideas from? And now that she thought about it, his reaction had been eerily similar when her mum had passed away. He'd shown no tears, no sadness. It was as if he'd already come to terms with it before it even happened. Just as he did with his dad.

"Darling, I know you're strong," she said, trying to find the right words, "but it's okay to feel sad, you know? It's okay to cry. Losing someone… it's hard."

Tom shrugged, unbothered by her concern. "I'm happy they're together again. Like you just said, they're watching over us now, Mummy. I think it's nice."

Kat sat back in her chair, reeling from the conversation. How could her son be so detached? Was he hiding his feelings, or was something else going on? The thought unsettled her even further.

On Monday, still disturbed by Tom's reaction, Kat called Luke and arranged to meet him at the café. She needed to tell him everything that had happened, to explain how much time it would take to deal with yet another funeral and her parents' estate.

When she arrived, Luke was already perched at a corner table, a cappuccino untouched in front of him. His face brightened briefly when he saw her, although she sensed something was wrong.

"Hey," Kat began, her voice low as she scanned the

customers sitting close by. "I've got some bad news. My dad passed away."

But before she could continue, Luke interrupted her. "Yeah. I already know. I'm sorry…"

Kat sat back in her chair. "What? You already know? How?"

"Clara called me on Friday," Luke said, taking a sip of his coffee as if Kat's question was the most stupid thing he'd ever heard.

Kat's heart skipped a beat. "Clara? Why would she call you?"

Luke shrugged, not picking up on her growing discomfort. "She was just trying to help, I presume. She figured I'd need to know, given the situation with the business and all that. She thought it would save you having to make yet another phone call when you're already going through so much."

"I don't understand why she'd go behind my back and tell you something so personal," Kat replied, struggling to keep her voice even. "It's my news to share, not hers."

Luke sighed, clearly exasperated. "Kat, you need to chill out. Clara was trying to help you. She's not the enemy here. She's been nothing but supportive, and yet you persist in acting like she's out to get you."

"I don't have a problem with Clara," Kat snapped, even though she could hear the untruth in her voice. "I just… I don't like feeling like I'm being kept in the dark. This is my family. My life."

Luke leant forward, his tone softening. Kat felt a flicker of the old Luke coming through at last. "I get that," he said. "But think about it. Clara's been doing nothing but looking out for you. She's been helping with Tom, making sure you're okay. It's not her fault you're going through all this, and she's trying to share the burden, so it's not all on your shoulders."

Kat bit her lip, fighting the urge to argue. Deep down, she knew Luke was right—Clara had been there for her in ways she hadn't even asked for. But that was the problem. It felt as though Clara was always there. It made Kat feel powerless, like Clara was quietly pulling the strings. Just as Imogen always had.

"Listen, I'm sorry you're going through this," Luke said, his tone softening even more. "I can't imagine how hard it must be, losing both your parents so close together."

Kat nodded, grateful for the sympathy. "Yeah… and it's not just the grief. It's everything. Arranging the funeral, dealing with the estate. I don't know how I'm going to manage it all."

Luke sighed and leant back in his chair. "I wish I could help more, but I'm struggling to keep things running as it is."

Kat frowned. "What do you mean? I thought everything was going smoothly with the business."

Luke shook his head. "Prakash is great, but he's new, and I'm spending more time training him than actually managing the day-to-day stuff. We've had communication issues with clients, and honestly, I'm stretched to the limit. I can't keep doing this on my own."

Kat felt a pang of guilt. She had been so focused on her personal crises that she'd assumed Luke was coping fine. But she'd not considered that he had to get Prakash up to speed too. "I'm sorry," she said. "I didn't realise how hard things were for you."

"I'm not blaming you," Luke said gently. "I know you've got a lot going on. But this can't continue. I'm not sure how much more I can take."

Kat's stomach twisted with anxiety. "What are you saying? You're not… you're not thinking about leaving, are you?"

Luke looked away, his face tense. "I don't want to, but something's got to give. We either need more help, or I don't know how much longer I can cope."

Kat stared out of the café window. Everything was unravelling—her family, her business. And now, even Luke, once her closest ally, was on the verge of breaking.

33

At the end of the week, Kat met Lauren at the Sunset bar once again. The familiar sound of clinking glasses and low chatter filled the space, but that night, everything seemed a little duller to Kat. The week had taken its toll on her. Arranging her father's funeral, online calls with the solicitor, and dealing with the related onslaught of paperwork had drained her more than she'd anticipated. And then there was work. Luke was on edge, and though she tried to help with the mounting enquiries from clients, it felt like she was barely treading water.

The thought of losing him terrified her, and every day he seemed more exhausted, more at his wits' end. She knew the company couldn't function without him, and she also knew she couldn't do it alone. But between that, organising the funeral, and dealing with her family's solicitor, it felt like everything was slipping through her fingers. Not for the first time in recent weeks, she wondered how much her mum and dad were actually worth and whether she and Tom could just run away from it all. Perhaps losing them so close together could still be in her favour?

However, the thought soon repulsed her, and she chastised herself for even letting it cross her mind. How had it come to this? She pictured Adam's smile. At least one person would be happy at her parents' demise.

With Lauren's mum babysitting the boys again, once Kat and Lauren had settled into a familiar table in the bar, Kat asked casually, "Where exactly does your mum live again? I just feel a little uneasy not knowing where Tom is."

Lauren dismissed the concern with a wave of her hand, laughing lightly. "Just around the corner from my place. Don't worry, he's in excellent hands. You really need to stop worrying so much. My mum is not a child snatcher, you know."

Kat offered a weak smile, but the joke didn't feel funny, as if intentional. Not knowing where her son was, only adding to her already overactive mind.

"So, how are you really doing?" Lauren asked. Her tone was soft, but serious.

Kat shrugged. She didn't have the energy to dive into the full weight of everything. "Getting by, I guess."

Lauren nodded, her eyes scanning Kat's face.

An hour or so later, after a few glasses of wine and a brief lull in the conversation, Lauren suddenly asked, "Tell me, Kat. What exactly happened that day with Imogen and Liam?"

The question hung in the air. Kat hesitated. Although she wondered where the question had come from, she also considered that maybe sharing would help. Perhaps letting it out would lift some of the burden that had been suffocating her for so long. She began slowly. "It was Imogen. She just snapped one day. Completely lost it. It was at her summerhouse, and she attacked Liam first. She—" Kat stopped for a moment, the image of Liam's lifeless body flashing in her mind. She closed her eyes, swallowed hard, and forced herself to continue. "She killed him with her dressmaker's scissors."

Surprisingly, Lauren's expression didn't change, but she leant in slightly, listening intently, her silence acting as a cue for Kat to proceed.

"She didn't stop there. She turned on Adam and me. I've never seen anything like it. The look in her eyes. It was like she wasn't even there anymore." Kat's heart raced as she recalled the terror of the moment. "I knew she was going to kill us too if I didn't do something. So, I grabbed a garden spade and…"

She stopped, the weight of her words sinking in. Her hands trembled slightly as she gazed down at the glass in front of her. She knew she was saying far too much, but she couldn't stop herself. "I hit her as hard as I could. I had no choice."

Silence fell between them. Kat half expected Lauren to offer some words of comfort, but when she looked up, Lauren was simply nodding.

Kat frowned. "You do believe me, don't you?" she asked, her voice now uncertain.

"Of course I do," Lauren replied without hesitation, her hand reaching out for Kat's. She sounded almost offended. "Why shouldn't I believe you?"

Kat didn't know why she'd asked that. Maybe it was the wine. Maybe it was the way Lauren seemed so calm about something so horrific.

Lauren shifted in her seat. "All that, and then what happened to Adam outside Vicky and Kevin's flat."

The mention of Adam made Kat wince. "Yeah," she murmured, taking a deep breath. "It all feels so surreal when I say it out loud."

Lauren squeezed her hand once more. "You've been through hell, Kat."

Kat forced a smile, but the tightness in her chest remained.

They soon turned the conversation onto lighter topics, talking about men, and laughing loudly as the wine finally worked its magic. Kat genuinely giggled, the tension in her body releasing bit by bit.

By the time they parted ways at the tube station, Kat was feeling lightheaded and giddy from the alcohol. She waved Lauren off, but as she started the short walk home, she couldn't shake a strange sensation. The street was quiet, the only sound her own footsteps echoing off the pavement. Something felt off. She couldn't put her finger on it, but then she felt a tingling at the back of her neck.

She glanced over her shoulder. No one was there.

She shook her head, laughing softly to herself. *You're drunk, Kat. It's just the wine messing with you.*

But as she continued walking, the sensation grew stronger. The street was too quiet. Too still. She quickened her pace, her heart thudding in her chest. She was only a few blocks from her house, but suddenly, it seemed like miles. Every sound seemed magnified—the rustle of leaves, the distant hum of traffic, the click of her heels against the pavement.

Just get home. Get inside. Lock the doors.

By the time she reached her front door, her hands were shaking. She fumbled with her keys, thinking any moment somebody would reach for her from behind. She finally got the door open, practically stumbling inside before slamming it shut behind her.

Leaning against the wall, she let out an elongated breath. She tried to laugh it off, but the unease still lingered.

She ran upstairs and grabbed the new packet of cigarettes from Adam's drawer, stalling as she looked at her husband's possessions. Several moments later, as she stood outside, her phone pinged for a second time in her pocket. She slowly retrieved it, reading the message many times over.

> I hope you enjoyed being back in the Sunset. Such wonderful memories.

34

K at sat at the kitchen table, a dull ache in her head as if it had settled in for the day. She had an hour before she had to pick up Tom from Lauren's house and her hangover clung on despite taking two lots of paracetamol.

The sharp ring of the doorbell made her jump. She pushed her chair back, heart thudding a little too fast in her chest, and opened the door to find Kevin and Vicky standing on the porch; the last people she expected, or indeed, wanted to see. Kevin wore a tense smile, while Vicky's expression was unreadable, her eyes darting over Kat as though assessing her.

"Kevin," Kat said, surprised. What did they want? The last time they'd spoken had been strained, to say the least.

"Can we talk?" Kevin asked. "About my job?"

Kat stiffened. She glanced at Vicky in the background, her face giving nothing away. Kat hadn't forgotten the phone call the day after letting Kevin go, the thinly veiled threat of retribution and a suggestion about her aunt being onto something. It had seemed almost absurd at the time, but now, seeing them standing there together, something about the way Vicky stared made the memory more sinister.

"Come in," Kat said, stepping aside. As she shut the door, she was convinced she saw movement from the house opposite.

They moved into the living room. Kevin took a seat after Kat gestured, but Vicky stood with her arms crossed, looking out of the window as if she suspected prying eyes too.

"I want my job back," Kevin said bluntly, staring directly at Kat. "I've had time to think, and I know I messed up, and I'd like another opportunity."

Kat sat down across from him, her mind racing. Yes, the business needed help, but taking Kevin Doyle back? Not a fucking chance.

"I'm sorry, Kevin," Kat said carefully, trying to keep her voice steady. "I can't offer you your position back. Things have changed since you left. We've taken someone else on."

Vicky turned from the window, speaking for the first time. "Who? They can't be as good as Kevin, and we know you need help."

Kat blinked, taken aback by the sudden venom in Vicky's tone. "That's not true. We are coping just fine on—"

"Oh, please," Vicky cut her off. "We know about your parents, about how little time you can give the business."

Kat stood, facing Vicky at the same height at least helping her feel less vulnerable. "How the hell do you know about my parents?"

Vicky laughed, prompting Kevin to stand and join his girlfriend. He whispered something in her ear before turning to face Kat once more. His tone was much more neutral. "Please, Kat. We need the money. I thought I'd easily find another job, but there just aren't the roles out there anymore."

"I'm sorry, Kevin," Kat replied, her eyes focused on Kevin once more while trying to ignore the stares of Vicky from behind. How on earth did she expect Kat to allow Kevin back with her threats and accusations? "We have all the staff we need. If anything changes, I'll let you know," Kat finished, her voice steady but firm. The tension in the room was palpable, and for a moment, it seemed like Kevin might protest, but Vicky cut in before he could say anything.

"You'll regret this," Vicky muttered, her eyes narrowing. "You think you're untouchable, don't you? You think no one knows what you did?"

Kat blinked, startled by the sheer hostility emanating from Vicky's words. Kat felt her heartbeat accelerate, her throat tightening with the tension of the encounter.

"You know what?" Vicky continued, stepping closer, her voice dropping to a near whisper. "Maybe you should be more careful who you cross."

Kat's breath caught in her throat. The veiled threat from before seemed to solidify, hanging in the air between them like a storm cloud ready to burst. Aunty Pauline? Kat knew very well what Adam had done to her and Bob. And then Vicky had mentioned Bob's children, Nathan and Belinda. Is that who Vicky was alluding to? Her heartbeat went up another notch, if that was possible.

Vicky's lips twisted into a smug smile. She knew she'd rattled Kat. "It'd be a shame if things got out in the open, wouldn't it? With everything you've got going on. Luke struggling, your parents… Tom."

Kat's eyes widened at the mention of her son, and a fierce wave of protectiveness washed over her. "You leave my child out of this," she snapped. "Whatever issues you think you have with me, they don't involve him at all."

Vicky's smile didn't falter. "Just saying," she purred, turning on her heel and heading towards the door. Kevin paused, throwing Kat an apologetic glance, but it was clear that Vicky had the final word in their relationship.

"Thanks for your time," Kevin mumbled before following Vicky out of the house.

Kat stood frozen for a moment, her heart pounding in her chest. The door clicked shut behind them, and she was left standing in the middle of the living room.

She sank back down onto the couch, rubbing her temples. The last thing she needed was more stress, especially with everything piling up. Luke had been distant lately, and the timing of Kevin's visit was too coincidental. Had Luke told Kevin he was struggling? Or was it something more?

Before Kat could dwell on it further, her phone buzzed on the table. She picked it up, her stomach twisting slightly when she saw Clara's name on the screen. With a sigh, she answered.

"Hey, Clara," Kat said, forcing herself to sound calm, though her nerves were still frayed from the confrontation.

"Hey. I just saw some people leaving your place," Clara's voice came through the line, a light note of curiosity lacing her tone. "Is everything okay?"

Kat frowned, glancing out of the window. Sure enough, she could see Clara standing in her living room across the street, phone in hand. Her eyes were fixed on Kat's house, her posture casual, but there was something unsettling about it. Why was Clara watching at all?

"Yeah," Kat replied, trying to keep her tone neutral. "Just a couple of old work colleagues. No big deal."

"Really?" Clara asked, her voice knowing. "They appeared extremely angry when they left. I couldn't help but notice."

Kat shifted uncomfortably, unsure why Clara was so interested. Was it genuine concern, or something more? The thought that Clara had been watching her house, paying attention to her visitors, sent a shiver down her spine.

"It's nothing," Kat insisted, though even she could hear the defensiveness in her voice. "Just work stuff."

"I see," Clara replied, her voice soft but curious. "Well, if you ever need to talk, you know where to find me. I'm just looking out for you. What, with all that's going on."

Kat muttered a quick thanks before hanging up the phone. She didn't have the energy for Clara's overbearing concern right then. She heard a car starting and watched as Kevin and Vicky pulled away. However, Kat then stared in disbelief as Clara left her house. She looked in a hurry, part jogging to her car. Kat couldn't help but stare as Clara's tyres screeched as she sped off in the same direction.

For a few brief moments, Kat remained at the window, contemplating whether she should follow too.

35

Kat sat across from Lauren, her hands wrapped around the warm mug of coffee, the conversation still fresh in her mind. The events in her living room with Vicky and Kevin refused to leave her thoughts. Lauren's eyes were on her, and she finally spoke to break the deafening silence which had descended between them.

"So, what was that all about? Vicky and Kevin showing up out of nowhere?" Lauren asked.

Kat sighed deeply before moving one hand from the mug and rubbing her forehead between her finger and thumb. "It wasn't just about Kevin's job. Vicky made these… threats. Something about her aunty Pauline being onto something, and how I might have my own guilty secrets."

Lauren raised her eyebrows. "Who is this Aunty Pauline? What did she mean by that?"

Kat hesitated, not sure how much to reveal, but feeling too overwhelmed to keep it all in. She'd kept it all bottled up for far too long, although for obvious reasons. "Pauline North and Bob Lane. They were… well, they worked for Liam, back when he was running things. When he let them go, they couldn't find work. They eventually took their own lives. Like some suicide pact between the pair of them."

Lauren's face contorted with shock. "What? How?"

Kat swallowed hard. "Adam found them. They'd taken a cocktail of pills, turned on the gas in their house. It was awful. They couldn't cope after losing their jobs."

Lauren leant back, as if processing the information. Kat realised just how much she was asking her friend to take on board, not to mention how much she was revealing. "Why was Adam there, though?" Lauren asked. "Did he just stumble upon them?"

The question lingered and Kat suddenly felt the room close in around her. She shifted uncomfortably, knowing she was saying far too much.

"He went there to talk," Kat said hastily, her voice a little too high-pitched, yet unable to stop herself. "They were forever calling him. About work, about how Liam used to run the business, all kinds of accusations. I think Adam went there to placate them, or tell them to back off. He couldn't believe it when he found them. It was all just… horrible."

Lauren studied her, eyes narrowing slightly. Kat couldn't determine how much she believed. However, it was the official storyline, so Kat didn't think she had anything to concern herself with.

"Wow," Lauren eventually said, her voice filled with genuine empathy. "I had no idea you'd been through so much. And now losing your parents and everything with the business, I can't even imagine."

Kat forced a smile, grateful that Lauren didn't press further. She needed to steer the conversation away from the past before she dug herself deeper into a hole. "Yeah, it's been a tough year. But hey, enough about me. How's everything with you and Max?"

Lauren picked up on the change of topic and let it slide, talking about her son and the chaos of motherhood with her estranged husband working abroad. Kat nodded along, pretending to listen, but her mind was elsewhere. The unexpected threats from Vicky—it all felt too connected now she had revealed the story of Pauline and Bob to Lauren.

The following morning, Kat tried to return to what once was her usual Sunday routine. She made breakfast for her and Tom, sipped her coffee, and sat on the couch, scrolling through social media on her phone. Tom asked if he could play in his room, and Kat selfishly agreed without thinking, knowing she should be devoting much more of her time to her son. She couldn't even recall the last time she enquired how he was getting on at school.

A knock at the door broke her out of her trance. It was still early, and she wasn't expecting anyone, especially on a Sunday. With her heart quickening, she stood up and walked towards the door, peeking through the side window.

Luke.

She opened the door, surprised to see him standing there, looking dishevelled and pale.

"Luke?" she said, peering up and down the street as though he might have been followed. "What's wrong?"

He shifted on his feet, peering down at the ground for a moment before meeting her eyes again. "Kat, can I come in?"

"Of course." She stepped aside, letting him into the

house, sensing something was wrong. "Sit down," she said, after guiding him to the living room.

"I think it's best if we both sit down," Luke replied, his voice unsteady.

Kat felt something catch in her throat. "What is it? Just tell me."

Luke took a deep breath, his hands shaking slightly as he ran them through his hair. "There was… there was a fire last night."

Kat hesitated, as if the words hadn't registered right away. "A fire?"

He nodded slowly. "At Vicky and Kevin's flat. They didn't make it, Kat. They died in the fire."

The air seemed to leave the room in an instant. Kat's vision blurred as the ground beneath her appeared to tilt. "What?" she whispered, barely able to form the word.

Luke reached out, grabbing her arm as her knees buckled. The room spun. Kevin and Vicky… dead?

"No," she whispered again, shaking her head. "It can't be true."

"It is," Luke said. "I'm sorry. I don't know what happened exactly, but the fire… it spread fast. They couldn't get out. It must've started while they were asleep. Smoke inhalation… it can knock you out before you even realize there's danger. And carbon monoxide…" he exhaled sharply. "It's silent. No smell, nothing. They probably never even woke up."

Kat's breath came in short, ragged bursts, her chest tightening with the shock. She felt Luke's arm around her, guiding her to the couch as she collapsed into the cushions, her mind unable to process the news.

"They're gone?" she asked, her voice barely audible.

Luke nodded, sitting beside her, his face pale and

drawn. "I don't know all the details, but yeah. The police called me early today. They're gone."

Kat stared blankly ahead, her mind reeling. Vicky's words from the day before rang in her ears, sharp and chilling. *Retribution*. Kat also recalled the time when Luke had told her that Kevin thought somebody was hanging around outside their flat.

As the thoughts swirled in her head, a darker one surfaced. How much easier her life would be if Kevin and Vicky were no longer around. The idea was both terrifying and strangely calming, like a solution she hadn't allowed herself to consider until then.

It felt like a nightmare, like she was trapped in some cruel, twisted version of her own life, where people kept dying and she couldn't stop it.

Her parents, now Kevin and Vicky. What was happening? She glanced at the reading chair in the corner. Adam's chair.

Luke's voice broke through her spiralling thoughts. "I thought you needed to know before you heard it from someone else."

She nodded, unable to speak, her heart pounding in her chest. Tears prickled her eyes, but she couldn't cry. Not for them. So why was she close to breaking down?

"They were just here," she whispered. "They were just here yesterday."

Luke's grip on her hand tightened. "I know."

Kat closed her eyes, trying to steady her breathing, but the weight of it all was crushing her from the inside. How was this even possible?

Kevin and Vicky, dead in a fire. It didn't feel real, despite her knowing it was.

But even as her mind did cartwheels, she recalled what Luke just said.

"I know."

36

Luke followed Kat into the kitchen, her hands trembling as she took two mugs from the cupboard. The familiar routine of making coffee felt alien; slow and disjointed, like her awareness was floating somewhere else entirely.

More killings. More deaths.

As the machine whirred into action, she glanced back at Luke, who sat at the table, leaning forward with his hands interlocked. His words echoed in her mind: *"I know."*

"How did you know they were here yesterday?" Kat asked, her voice quieter than she intended, almost as though she feared the answer.

Luke looked up, his face serious but calm. "Clara told me."

Kat was taken aback. "Clara?"

He nodded. "Yeah, she called me soon after they left. She was worried about you. Asked if I knew who they were."

Kat felt a strange chill crawl up her spine. "She called you?"

Luke stood up, walking over to join her as she poured the coffee. He leant against the work surface, his arms folding and unfolding like he couldn't make his mind up. "She said she was keeping an eye out. When she saw them leave, she was concerned. She thought they looked angry, as if something might have happened inside. So, she phoned me. Wanted to ensure everything was okay."

Kat stirred the coffee absentmindedly. Clara had called her too after they left. She had asked if everything was alright. And then, in an almost eerie way, she had sped off without another word. So she must have called Luke from her car.

"I didn't recognise who she was talking about at first," Luke continued, "but when I asked her to describe them… yeah, it matched Kevin and Vicky to a tee."

Kat set the spoon down with a slight clatter, gripping the edge of the counter as another wave of nausea hit her. "She said she was worried about me?"

Luke watched her carefully, sensing her unease. "Yeah. She even called me later to ask if I thought she was interfering too much."

Kat snorted softly, unable to suppress the sound. Interfering too much? That seemed like an understatement, considering it felt as though Clara knew what she'd had for breakfast.

"What did you say to her?" Kat asked, trying to keep her voice steady.

"I told her nonsense," Luke said, taking a step closer. "I told her it was good that someone was looking out for you."

Kat felt a rush of irritation, but it quickly fizzled out. Despite her overbearing tendencies, Clara had been there when Kat needed her. Maybe Luke had a point. But still, the woman's presence was suffocating.

Luke's voice softened. "I don't get it, Kat. Why aren't you more appreciative? You've got someone looking out for you when you've been through so much."

Kat wanted to tell him. The way she thought that Clara had stared out of her window soon after she moved in. The discarded cake on top of the rubbish pile for all to see. Allowing her stupid dog to jump up at her despite it being obvious Kat despised canines. The muddy paws on her dress. Not informing her that her party was formal wear. Asking when her parents were next over and being there when her mum fell. And the other thing: looking just like Imogen. She knew there were other things too, but she couldn't recall with her head in such a spin.

So, instead, she didn't mention any of those things.

"I don't know," Kat mumbled, avoiding Luke's gaze. "I just… I don't like being watched all the time."

She sensed Luke seemed to know that she wasn't telling him everything, but he didn't press her. Instead, he sighed and took a sip of his coffee, his expression thoughtful.

After a long silence, something else tugged at Kat's memory. Something Luke had said earlier—about the police. She turned towards him, her heart quickening again.

"Wait. Why did the police call you?" she asked, trying to keep her tone casual. "You know, about Vicky and Kevin."

Luke lowered his mug. "They found Kevin's phone."

Kat's pulse spiked. "And?"

"There were several calls made to me over the past week."

She narrowed her eyes. "Why was he calling you?"

Luke hesitated, glancing away for a moment before meeting her gaze again. "He was begging for his job back, Kat. Every call, every message—he was desperate."

Kat's fists clenched. "And what did you say?"

"I told him the same thing each time," Luke said quietly. "It wasn't my decision to make. It was yours."

Kat's throat felt tight. Kevin had been desperate for his job back, but she'd told him there was no room for him. But now… now he was gone. The guilt clawed at her, despite the obvious relief that he and Vicky could no longer dig up the past. No more Bob Lane and Aunty fucking Pauline.

Finally, Luke set his empty mug on the counter. He looked like he wanted to say more, but was holding back. Kat's hands trembled as she cleared the mugs, the weight of everything pressing down on her harder than ever.

"I should go," Luke said, turning towards the door. "Leave you in peace on a Sunday."

Kat nodded numbly, following him as he walked to the front door. But as he reached for the handle, he paused, his back still to her.

"Oh yeah," he said, his voice ominous. "Vicky and Kevin…" He turned to face her. "They weren't alone in the flat."

Kat's breath hitched. "What?"

"There were two other bodies found with them," Luke said, his expression grim. "The police haven't identified them yet."

Kat stared at him, her mind spinning, trying to make sense of what he'd just said. Two other bodies? Who else had been in that flat with Vicky and Kevin? And why had Luke only mentioned it as he was leaving?

The questions swirled in her head, but she couldn't find her voice. She could only watch as Luke opened the door and stepped outside before returning to the living room once more.

Without realising, she found herself sitting in Adam's reading chair in the corner, and from nowhere, her lips curved in a small smile.

37

Kat eventually stood by the door and called for Tom, her mind still deep in thought after the conversation with Luke. She needed to clear her head, to think, and figured some fresh air might help. "Get your shoes on, Tom. We're going to the park," she shouted.

Tom appeared in the hallway, beaming. "Can I bring my football?"

Kat nodded absently, grabbing her coat as Tom hurriedly searched for the ball, his excitement infectious despite her state of mind.

The park was a short walk away, and the early spring chill made the air crisp, helping to calm her thoughts. When they arrived, Tom was already bouncing the ball before kicking it towards the open field. Kat found a bench nearby, taking a seat with a huge sigh.

She focused on Tom, running after his football, and her heart ached—not just with the grief of losing Adam, but with the pain of Tom not having his father there to kick the ball back. Adam would have been out there, sharing in the joy of their son's excitement, teaching him tricks, showing him how to beat an opponent. She imagined his face, red through exertion yet beaming with pride. Tom turned to look at Kat and smiled broadly. Kat smiled in return and blew him a kiss.

Lost in thought, Kat's eyes followed the ball as it rolled across the grass, triggering another vivid memory. A few days after Adam had misplaced the very same ball in the park, her dad had found it again, triumphantly returning it to Tom with a smile as wide as the sun. Kat had laughed at the time, thinking how lucky they were to have her dad's help in the simplest of things. She also recalled Adam's envious streak that her dad had found it when he himself had searched in vain in the exact same spot.

But her dad was gone now too. And her mum. She glanced over to the other bench, the one where her mum had fallen and hit her head. But quickly, she looked away, the memories too raw. The grief that she had somehow pushed aside came rushing back, crashing against the walls of her heart in relentless waves. Her parents—how was she supposed to grieve them properly when so much was going on around her?

She had spent the days since their deaths tying up loose ends, dealing with their estate, planning funerals, and talking to solicitors. She still didn't know exactly how much money she would inherit. Maybe that would help with the pain? Yet the raw, personal grief was still a festering wound she hadn't allowed herself to touch.

Would she ever grieve properly?

Kat squeezed her eyes shut, hoping to block out the overwhelming thoughts. But it was no use. Everything was blurring together.

When Adam died, she had thought the past would finally be over, that all the painful memories and dark secrets would die with him. But now, she realised nothing would ever be over, not truly. She knew Adam had always blamed Liam's and Imogen's deaths for the downturn in his life. After they were gone, it was as though he had nothing left to give. He lost interest in the business, in everything, and that had been the beginning of the end.

And now Kevin and Vicky were gone too. It had only been a day since they'd stood in her living room, begging for Kevin's job back, and now they were dead. Burned in a fire. The same day they had visited her. The synchronicity was too stark, too real. Would the police get involved? Kat's stomach twisted as she wondered.

She hadn't asked Luke how the fire started. Would he know if the police suspected anything? Should she call them herself and ask? But what would that accomplish? What would she even say?

And then there were others in the flat.

Kat pulled out her phone, her hands still trembling. She opened the browser and typed in 'London news, flat fire'. Her fingers moved automatically, scrolling through the results until she found a report.

Her eyes skimmed the headline: Tragedy Strikes in East London – Four Bodies Discovered After Flat Fire Near Liverpool Street Station.

The article offered little more than Luke had already told her. The fire had broken out late in the evening, and police were still investigating the cause. Four bodies were discovered, but authorities hadn't released the victims' names to the public. No foul play was mentioned—yet.

Kat's breath caught in her throat. The lack of information was more unsettling than if the article had confirmed her worst fears. She was sitting on the bench once more, her thoughts whirling, when suddenly a familiar sound pulled her back to the present.

A bark echoed through the park. Tom's head shot up from his football, and a wide smile spread across his face.

"Charlie!" he screamed, abandoning his ball without a second thought as he ran in the direction of the approaching figure.

Kat squinted against the low sun, following her child's excited movements, and then saw Clara walking towards them with her dog, Charlie, trotting alongside.

Clara waved as she drew closer. "Fancy seeing you here," she said with a smile, though it faltered slightly as she looked at Kat's pale face. "Are you alright?"

Kat tried to muster a smile, but it came out strained. "Yeah, just… it's been a long weekend."

As Tom played with Charlie, Clara sat beside Kat on the bench. "You look like you've seen a ghost. What's going on?"

Kat hesitated for a moment, unsure whether to share the news. But there was no point in holding back. "It's Kevin and Vicky. The couple who came round to my house yesterday. They died last night."

Clara's face twisted in shock. "What? How?"

Kat swallowed hard. "There was a fire. In their flat. They didn't make it."

Clara blinked several times, clearly taken aback. "That's awful. Obviously I didn't even know them, but that's… that's terrible."

Kat nodded, the numbness settling in again. They walked home together in near silence, Tom running ahead holding onto Charlie's leash. Kat wanted to ask Clara where she went in such a hurry, so soon after Kevin and Vicky left. She also wanted to know why she'd called Luke so quickly. But she neither had the energy nor the desire. She couldn't risk saying too much. When they reached their street, Clara gave Kat a final hug before heading into her own house.

Kat unlocked the door and let Tom, who was still buzzing with excitement, inside. "Have you got my football?" he asked.

Kat's heart dropped. In all the excitement of Tom playing with Charlie, she'd forgotten to collect it.

"No, sweetheart. I think we left it there."

Tom's face darkened, his expression shifting from disappointment to anger in seconds. "You left it in the park on purpose! Why didn't you bring it back?"

Before she could answer, he stormed off to his room, slamming the door behind him.

Kat stood in the hallway, the guilt about her son's bloody football only piling on top of everything else.

38

THE NEXT DAY, Kat sat in her living room, staring blankly at the floor, when a sharp knock at the door pulled her from her thoughts. Slowly, she made her way to the hallway, and her stomach clenched when she saw two police officers standing on her porch. Kat didn't know how much more she could physically handle.

"Mrs Chapman?" one of them asked, though it wasn't really a question. Kat immediately recognised them: Officer Anderson and Officer Rodriguez. The same two officers who had visited after Adam reported their front door being smeared with red paint. The incident made her blood run cold. No one had ever figured out who was responsible for that.

The officers exchanged a quick glance before stepping forward slightly. "Can we come in?"

Kat nodded and opened the door wider, letting them in. She shut it behind them with a soft click, trying to calm her erratic breathing.

As the officers took seats on the couch, Anderson

spoke again. "We recognised your name and address from our previous visit." He paused, as if to gauge her reaction. "Your husband, Adam, reported an incident with the red paint on the door. Do you remember?"

Kat felt a cold sweat on the back of her neck. Of course, she remembered. "Yes," she answered quietly. "But nothing ever came of it."

The officers exchanged another brief look. "We understand. And we're sorry about what happened before Christmas. We heard about your husband. And we were wondering how you've been doing?"

The question threw Kat off balance. "How I've been…?" she faltered, trying to comprehend what they were implying. Surely they hadn't called round to enquire about her wellbeing.

Rodriguez leant forward slightly. "We mean, has anything unusual happened recently? Any incidents like that one?"

Kat shook her head, feeling increasingly uneasy. "No, nothing like that." She paused. "I've just lost my parents, though. My mum fell, and my dad… well, he couldn't cope." She found herself not wanting to go into the full details with the officers. The police looked at each other again, something passing between them that Kat couldn't read.

Finally, Anderson cleared his throat. "We're very sorry for your loss, Mrs Chapman. We're not here to pry into your family matters. We're here because of Kevin Doyle."

Kat stiffened at the mention of his name. "What about him?"

Rodriguez spoke next. "We understand Kevin and Vicky Doyle visited you recently. When did you last see them?"

Kat's pulse quickened. "Saturday," she answered cautiously. "They came around. Kevin wanted his job back."

"And how did you respond to that?" Anderson asked, his voice deceptively calm.

"I told him no," Kat said carefully, avoiding the memory of Vicky's threatening manner. "I said we didn't need him anymore. He accepted it."

Anderson raised an eyebrow. "He accepted it? Just like that?"

"Well…" Kat hesitated. "He didn't argue. He just accepted it."

The officers exchanged yet another glance, making Kat feel like they knew much more than they were letting on. Rodriguez cleared his throat. "Why was he let go in the first place?"

Kat frowned, her discomfort growing. "What does that have to do with anything?"

Rodriguez leant back. "We're just trying to get a clear picture, Mrs Chapman. Understanding his circumstances might help us."

Kat sighed heavily, the weight of their scrutiny becoming overbearing. "Kevin was slacking. He wasn't doing his job properly, and I confronted him about it."

"Was there an argument?" Anderson asked, his voice carrying a slight edge.

Kat flushed. "Not really. I mean, a small one, maybe. But nothing major." She didn't understand why they were so focused on Kevin's employment situation.

Finally, after what felt like an eternity of uncomfortable silence, Rodriguez shifted in his seat, preparing to stand. "That's all for now. Thank you for your time, Mrs Chapman."

Kat felt her tension begin to ease, thinking the interrogation was over. But just as they stood to leave, Anderson turned back to her, his expression darkening.

"One more thing," he said. "Do you know a Nathan or Belinda Lane?"

Kat felt the blood rush to her head. "No, I don't think so," she managed to say.

Rodriguez narrowed his eyes, watching her closely. "And what about Bob Lane?"

All the names became a fuzz in her head, and Kat felt the room spin around her. She grasped the back of the sofa to steady herself. "Bob Lane?" she replied quietly. "He worked with Liam and Imogen. Years ago."

Anderson nodded grimly. "That's right. Bob Lane was discovered alongside Pauline North. Your husband, Adam, found them in Pauline's house."

Kat's head swam with memories, her conversation with Adam when they revealed all to each other…

"I can just imagine how you made Pauline and Bob a nice cup of tea before slipping the capsules into each mug. How many did you actually give them?" She laughed. "Mind you, turning the gas on afterwards was a stroke of genius, darling. The police were convinced it was suicide, especially after you left the blister pack on the table."

"So what?" she shot back defensively. "They killed themselves. Everything was proven at the time. My Adam had nothing to do—"

"Because Nathan and Belinda Lane are Bob's children," Anderson said quietly. "And their bodies were recovered from Kevin and Vicky Doyle's flat two nights ago."

The officers exchanged another look as Kat stood there, feeling the walls of her world closing in around her. The air in the room felt suffocating, and the weight of everything she had kept buried for so long threatened to break free.

"Thank you for your time, Mrs Chapman," Officer Rodriguez said softly, the two officers turning to leave.

But Kat barely heard them. Her mind was racing with a thousand questions, none of which had answers.

39

The more she thought about it, the more her mind spiralled. She and Adam were the only ones who knew what really happened with Bob Lane and Pauline North. The police had been in the dark about that. They obviously still were, otherwise, their questions would've cut deeper. They would have dug further into the circumstances of their deaths and Kat's potential connection. But they hadn't. And that should have been a tremendous relief.

Except it wasn't.

The weight of everything crashed down on her, suffocating her, pushing her to a breaking point. How much more could she take before she unravelled completely?

After pulling herself together as best she could, Kat grabbed her bag and set off to meet Luke for their pre-arranged café meeting. But as she made her way towards the tube station, a strange feeling gnawed at her. She could sense someone watching her—she was certain of it. Her palms grew clammy, and she kept glancing over her shoulder, certain she'd catch sight of someone lurking just out of view. Yet each time she turned, no one was there. And this wasn't the first occasion she'd suspected she'd been followed.

It reminded her too much of Adam, of how paranoid he'd become in the final few weeks of his life, jumping at shadows, convinced that someone was always one step behind him. Was this how it started? Was she on the same path? But again, that word, coincidence? Shaking her head, Kat picked up her pace and finally made it to the café, her nerves almost shot.

Luke greeted her with what Kat considered a strained smile, but it quickly faded when he noticed her fraught expression. "What's wrong?" he asked, pulling out a chair in front of a table with two fresh drinks already in place.

Kat sat down across from him, barely able to keep her hands from trembling. "The police came to see me earlier," she started. "They told me that the other two people found in the flat were Bob Lane's children. Nathan and Belinda."

Luke's face remained unreadable. "Who's Bob Lane?" he asked.

Kat hesitated. She couldn't very well tell him everything—not without risking exposure, not without tangling herself in the truth she'd spent so long burying beneath the surface. "It's complicated," she said finally, fumbling over her words. "Bob… he used to work for us. For Liam and Imogen. Adam knew him pretty well. It's just strange that his children would end up dead in the same flat as Kevin and Vicky."

Luke raised an eyebrow, sensing her unease but not pressing her. "Strange, yeah. But maybe it's just a coincidence?"

She couldn't help but laugh bitterly. "Bob and Pauline, they killed themselves after Liam let them go.

They couldn't find work. It was a mess. Adam found them. The whole thing was awful." She spoke rapidly, her thoughts tumbling out before she could stop them.

Luke frowned, clearly disturbed. "I didn't know any of that. It sounds like hell, Kat."

Too much, she thought. More than anyone should have to handle. And still, it kept piling on.

Retribution.

Luke must have sensed that the conversation was veering into territory she didn't want to go, so he shifted it elsewhere. Not that it helped Kat's mood at all. In fact, it made it even worse. "Look," he began sheepishly, his eyes not leaving his coffee. "I don't want to add to your stress, but Clara asked me out for dinner."

Kat's eyes widened. "Clara?" She couldn't hide her shock. It was bad enough to discover that Luke was taking another woman out, but of all people, Clara was the last name she wanted to hear.

"Yeah. She called me yesterday and invited me to that Italian place down the street—Ristorante Giovanni. Do you know it?"

She knew it well. It was too close to home for comfort. Her surprise quickly morphed into something more complicated—an odd mix of unease and jealousy. She had no right to feel that way. She and Luke weren't together. She'd pushed him away, kept her distance since that one night, so why should it matter?

Kat forced a smile, doing her best to keep her voice light. "No, that's great. I hope you have an enjoyable time."

But her thoughts were anything but light. Bloody Clara. And now she was asking Luke out to dinner.

Luke talked a little about work, trying to ease the tension, but Kat's mind wasn't there anymore. She was trapped in her own thoughts, her own fears. She returned home in a daze, unsure of how much more she could cope with.

She walked into the kitchen, hoping to distract herself, but the sight that greeted her stopped her dead in her tracks. There, in the middle of the back lawn, lay Tom's missing football; the very one they had left at the park the day before.

Just like your dad finding it, Kat.

How the hell had it got there?

Simple.

Someone had been in her garden. And therefore, someone had known they'd left it in the park. The same person who Kat was sure followed her that morning too?

40

THE FOOTBALL LYING in her back garden filled Kat with horror. Her mind raced as she moved to the living room and stared out of the window at Clara's car parked across the street. She was convinced it must have been her. Who else but Clara could have snuck into her garden and put it there? She would have known they left it at the park the previous day, too. Unable to suppress her anger any longer, and without thinking, she grabbed her keys and stormed out of the front door, crossing the street before she could stop herself. She had to blame someone, just like Adam did.

Clara greeted her with a smile, but it quickly faded when she saw the intensity in Kat's expression. "Kat? Whatever's wrong?" Clara asked, her brow creased with concern.

"You know damn well what's wrong," Kat snapped, her voice trembling with anger. "You put Tom's football in my garden."

Clara's eyes widened in confusion. "What? I don't know what you're talking about."

Kat crossed her arms, her frustration bubbling over. "Don't play games with me, Clara. Who else could it have been? You knew it was missing yesterday, and now it's back. In the middle of my lawn."

Clara was clearly taken aback. "Kat, I swear I have no idea what you're talking about."

"Then explain how it got there!" Kat's voice was rising, and she was losing control. Every part of her wanted to scream. "You're always watching me, always checking in. You never leave me alone!"

Clara frowned, her eyes darting up and down the street before she motioned for Kat to step inside. "Calm down, Kat. Please. Come in. We can talk about this." She gently took Kat's arm and led her into the house.

Kat followed reluctantly, her mind still spinning. As soon as they were indoors, she turned on Clara, her hands trembling. "I need answers."

Clara closed the door and sighed, shaking her head. "I don't know what you're accusing me of, Kat, but I didn't put a football in your garden. When did you even notice it?"

"This morning. It wasn't there when I left at eleven, but when I came back… there it was."

"I've been at work since seven this morning," Clara explained patiently. "I had to meet a client at the hospital. A doctor who was due to go on duty. I didn't get home until just before you came over. I've been home for, what, ten minutes? How could I possibly have had time to sneak into your garden and put a football there?"

Kat's mind raced. If Clara was telling the truth—and it seemed plausible—then it couldn't have been her. But that left an even bigger question hanging over her: who did? She thought back to the unsettling feeling she'd had earlier, the sensation of being watched on her way to the café. Could it be related? She had suspected Clara was behind that too, but now she wasn't so sure. The more Kat tried to make sense of it, the more everything twisted.

Her voice softened, tinged with doubt. "If it wasn't you, then who could it have been?"

Clara shrugged, watching Kat closely. "I don't know, but you need to stop jumping to conclusions. You're wound up so tight. You're going to drive yourself mad."

I think I already am.

Kat bit her lip, feeling more foolish with each passing second. And she knew Clara was right. She was losing it. The paranoia that had consumed Adam before his death was creeping into her life, and she couldn't shake it. It felt as if whoever was responsible for his decline was behind hers too.

To defuse the tension, she changed the subject abruptly. "Luke told me you invited him out for dinner."

Clara's cheeks flushed, a rarity for her. "Oh. How did you know about that?"

"He mentioned it when we met at the café."

Clara's blush deepened. "I hope that's okay. I didn't think it would be a problem. I mean, you and Luke aren't… well, I didn't realise you were still… you know."

Kat hesitated. "It's not a problem," she lied, though her face betrayed her with a soft blush of her own.

Clara raised an eyebrow, clearly sensing the irritation in Kat's tone. "Are you sure? Do you still have feelings for him? I don't want to step on anyone's toes."

Kat exhaled slowly. "No. It's not like that. But we, Luke and I, we slept together. Twice."

Clara's eyes widened in surprise. "Twice?"

Kat nodded, feeling the weight of her confession. "Once was recently, and once when Adam was still alive."

Clara's shock deepened. "You slept with Luke while Adam was alive?"

Kat felt the flood of guilt rise again, overwhelming her. She had only come to confront Clara about a stupid football, and now here she was, confessing her darkest secrets. "It was a mistake," she said quietly, her voice cracking under the pressure of the memories. "I've never told anyone until now."

She remembered the first time vividly. She and Luke had stayed up late, talking in the living room long after Adam had gone to bed. They were both tipsy, and when she showed him to the spare bedroom, they kissed. It was innocent enough, and it never progressed beyond a kiss, but when Adam asked her later why it had taken so long to come to bed, she'd made some excuse, laughing it off. But the second time... the second time had been different. Luke had come over while Adam was out. They had planned it, and when it happened, there was no denying it anymore.

Clara sat back, her expression full of disbelief. "I had no idea."

Kat shook her head, her voice barely a whisper. "No one does."

Silence hung between them, thick with unspoken emotions. Kat wasn't sure if she felt lighter or more burdened by her confession. All she knew was that guilt had taken up permanent residence inside her, and she wasn't sure if she could ever dislodge it. She silently yearned for Adam.

After a long pause, Clara stood up and motioned for Kat to follow her outside. "Come on," she said quietly. "I want to show you something. Something to take your mind off this."

Confused, Kat followed her out into the rear garden.

Clara led her towards where the summerhouse used to be. But now, where it once stood, there was nothing but a vast, open space. The memories of what had happened there—the blood, the scissors, the horror—came flooding back in an instant, making Kat's heart beat so fast, she was sure it wouldn't be able to cope.

"There," Clara said softly, taking Kat's hand. "Doesn't it look better now it's gone?"

Kat felt another sudden surge. She stared at the empty space, the visions of what happened flashing vividly before her eyes.

But the thing that played on her mind the most was, did Clara know what happened inside that summerhouse that day?

41

KAT STOOD IN THE KITCHEN, staring at the football lying in the middle of the lawn, her mind circling back to Nathan and Belinda Lane. Luke had brushed off their deaths as mere coincidence, but Kat couldn't accept that anymore. Coincidence didn't exist, not in her world. Just like the football—that wasn't a coincidence either.

Her mind flashed back to the time when Clara had invited her to the dinner party, and Kat had shown up wearing jeans and a jumper, while everyone else was dressed to the nines. Why hadn't Clara told her about the dress code? It was a small thing, perhaps, but was it important? And then there was the day her mum fell in the park.

"It felt like someone caught my foot, or pushed me... It happened so quickly."

Clara had been in the park that day, taking Charlie for another bloody walk. Always coinciding with Kat or her family being there. But where else was Clara supposed to take her dog? That was the logical explanation, wasn't it?

And yet, Kat couldn't shake the doubt creeping

through her thoughts. What about her father's death? The tears Clara had shed. Were they just for show? Crocodile tears? Every single incident seemed to have Clara lingering somewhere nearby, always just close enough to be involved, yet denying any wrongdoing whenever Kat asked.

Then there was the night Vicky and Kevin died. Kat recalled seeing Clara's car screech off down the street, just after Vicky and Kevin had left Kat's house. The memory struck her like a blow. Clara claimed she had nothing to do with it, but Kat had seen her, hadn't she? Too many things were starting to align, creating a picture Kat couldn't quite see.

Her eyes drifted back to the football. Clara had insisted she'd been at work all morning. University College Hospital—just the thought of that place sent a shudder through Kat. But could she check if Clara had really been there? Maybe she could call and ask for the name of the doctor she said she'd seen?

But just as she began formulating a plan in her head, she noticed the obvious flaw. It was a ridiculous idea. Where would a receptionist even begin?

The thought rattled her. Clara had slipped into her world so seamlessly, like a shadow, always present, but never revealing too much about herself. It wasn't until then that Kat realised how little she actually knew about the woman who had become a presence in her life. The woman who looked uncannily like Imogen Daley.

All that time, she had assumed she knew Clara, but in reality, the woman was practically a stranger. Panic rose in her chest. How had she let it happen? How had she allowed Clara to become so enmeshed in her life without knowing the simplest details?

She glanced at her phone. Could she speak to Luke

about her? No, that would raise too many questions. She didn't want to tip him off to her suspicions. What about Clara herself? Could she somehow ask the name of her client without making it obvious?

Kat's thoughts spun in circles, and she felt the weight of her paranoia pressing down on her. Every direction she turned led to more uncertainty. Could Clara be behind everything? Was there some way to pin the blame on her? It was certainly possible that she somehow orchestrated the deaths of Vicky, Kevin, and even Nathan and Belinda Lane. The thought seemed absurd, but the coincidences were too many, too perfect.

Suddenly, Kat felt an overwhelming sense of isolation. She couldn't talk to anyone about it; not Luke, not the police, and certainly not Clara.

She paced around the kitchen. There had to be a way to put a stop to everything once and for all. She couldn't continue living like this, consumed by doubt and fear. But who could she turn to? Who could she trust?

Her thoughts drifted back to her mum, to the way she had fallen in the park. The memory haunted her. Clara had been there that day.

Was it possible? Could Clara have done something to her mum? The idea seemed farfetched, but after everything that had transpired, Kat couldn't rule anything out. And then her dad. Did Clara know where he lived? Could she have driven to Leicestershire, given him a cocktail of whiskey and drugs, then driven home as though nothing had ever happened?

She stared at the football again, lying so innocently on the grass. She had definitely left it in the park, and now it was back, just like that.

Kat felt trapped in her thoughts, unable to trust anyone, not even herself. She needed to get out of the house, to clear her head. But the thought of leaving, of stepping outside into a world where danger seemed to lurk around every corner, filled her with dread.

Her phone buzzed on the counter, and she jumped at the sound. She picked it up, half expecting to see Clara's name flash across the screen. But it was Luke, asking if she was okay. She stared at the message, unsure of how to respond. Was she okay? Could she even pretend to be?

Her fingers hovered over the screen, but she couldn't bring herself to type a response. Instead, she set the phone down and turned back to the window, staring at the football once more. The answers were out there, somewhere. And she had to find them—before it was too late.

42

A WHOLE WEEK PASSED, and Kat drove in silence on the way home from her father's funeral, glad of a conclusion at least. She took great solace from the thoughts of her parents' friends and neighbours, knowing they were reunited again after such a brief separation between. As she proceeded steadily along the M1 motorway, something about the sombreness of the funeral ignited a new determination in her. She couldn't keep living in the same nightmare over and over again, the web of lies and half-truths suffocating her from every angle.

By the time Kat arrived home, night had settled over London, and the oppressive quiet of the empty streets greeted her like an old foe. After collecting Tom from Lauren's house—they again arranged an evening out that coming weekend—Kat moved through the rooms of her house slowly, half expecting something, anything, to leap out from the shadows and drag her deeper into the nightmare she was living. But the house remained still, and the only sound was her own breath, quick and shallow.

. . .

The next morning, a call from Officer Rodriguez was the last thing she needed. He asked to meet her at the station, his voice as unreadable as ever. Kat agreed, dread settling in her stomach.

The police station was as cold and uninviting as they appeared on the TV shows. She was led into a private room, grey and drab, with a single metal table and two stiff chairs positioned under harsh fluorescent lights. The room had no personality—just the suffocating, sterile feel of a place where secrets were dragged out, layer by layer, until there was nothing left.

Officer Rodriguez entered with his usual partner, Officer Anderson, in tow. Kat couldn't help but wonder why they always worked together, as if one couldn't function without the other. Was it to keep each other in check, or was it part of the psychological game they played with suspects? Or was it just for her and Adam?

Rodriguez's voice broke the silence. "How much did you know about Nathan and Belinda Lane?"

Kat shuffled in her seat, confused by the opening question. "I've never met them."

Rodriguez and Anderson exchanged a glance, and Kat's mouth turned down at the corners, as if to say, *look all you want, but I didn't know them at all*.

"Are you sure about that?" Anderson leant forward, his tone as harsh as the room's fluorescent lights. "Did your husband ever meet them?"

Kat frowned. "I very much doubt it."

Rodriguez's lips curved into a small, humourless smile. "You might not know, Mrs Chapman, but Adam could have met them at some point. Maybe when he was meeting Bob Lane and Pauline North?"

Kat faltered, considering it for a moment. Could Adam have known Nathan and Belinda? Surely, he would have told her. "No," she said, shaking her head. "I don't think so. He would've said."

Rodriguez's expression shifted, and his next question hit harder than the last. "Did Adam tell you everything?"

Kat felt her cheeks flush.

What, about fucking Imogen while I was staying at my parents' house?

She had no answer for that.

"I don't understand why you're asking about them," she said finally, trying to regain her composure. "Why Nathan and Belinda? We didn't know them."

Rodriguez straightened, his manner unreadable. "Nathan and Belinda Lane rented a place together last autumn. Near to Regent's Park, actually."

Kat raised an eyebrow. "What does that have to do with anything?"

"They both took long-term absences from their jobs," Anderson interjected. "Nathan did something in Leeds and Belinda was a veterinary nurse in Cornwall. She took a sabbatical."

Kat cocked her head to one side, struggling to piece together the scattered bits of information. "So, they rented a flat in London?" She felt her frustration bubbling up. "I still don't know who they are, or were," she added with a wry smile, which she instantly regretted.

The officers exchanged another glance before Rodriguez continued. "They rented a flat not far from your office. Do you not find that interesting?"

Kat shook her head. "I don't understand what you're implying."

Rodriguez leant forward slightly. "Nathan Lane owned a white BMW."

Kat stared at him blankly. "And?"

"The same BMW had front-end damage, consistent

with the marks left by a hit-and-run," Rodriguez said, his tone carefully measured.

Kat's breath caught in her throat. "What are you saying?"

"The car is with forensics now," Anderson added. "We're checking the damage against the scene of Adam's accident."

Kat's heart pounded in her chest. "A white BMW?"

Rodriguez nodded. "A witness saw a car like that speeding away near the scene of Adam's accident. And now, the two people who owned that car, as well as the couple Adam visited that night, Vicky and Kevin, are dead."

Kat's world tilted yet again. Nathan and Belinda had been in that car. They had hit Adam, and now they were all dead in the same flat fire. Her body convulsed through every interaction, every piece of the puzzle she knew the police couldn't solve. But Kat knew, and she averted her gaze from the officers'. Bob and Pauline had told Bob's children what they had discovered, or at least what they thought they had.

She stared at the two officers, their faces unreadable. "But… I don't even know them. Why would they be involved?"

"That's what we're trying to figure out, Mrs Chapman," Rodriguez said. His eyes bored into hers, like he was daring her to lie, to crack under the weight of the questions. "And we think you might have some answers."

43

KAT SAT IN SILENCE. Nathan and Belinda Lane had been complete strangers to her. She'd never met them. She repeated this to Officers Rodriguez and Anderson, who eventually had little choice but to accept her response. However, they told her they'd be in touch if anything else came to light, a wry look on their faces suggesting that might not be far away.

The following morning, she had to go to the office to get a document signed by Luke. It required the signatures of both directors, and though she wasn't keen on facing him after their awkward conversation about Clara and dinner plans, business had to be handled. She arrived at the office, but Luke wasn't there. Curious, she stepped back out onto the street to make her way to the café, and she was just in time to see him disappearing into Regent's Park.

Kat followed at a distance, careful not to be seen. Luke walked with purpose, yet his head was tilted down, like he was lost in thought. As she pursued him through the park, she tried to quiet the growing tension within her.

She didn't want to believe Luke was hiding something, but why would he take time out from running the business, especially with how much work Kat continued to pile upon him?

Finally, he stopped at a small coffee kiosk and ordered two drinks. Why two? Kat's eyes scanned the park, looking for whoever he was meeting. She couldn't see anyone—no one who seemed like they were waiting for him, at least. Then, as if from nowhere, a figure appeared across the park, walking over the bridge of one of the lakes.

Sandra.

His ex-wife.

Kat's heart dropped. She had completely forgotten about Sandra. Ever since the day she had visited her, talking about Luke offering support and being her rock. Kat had written her off as someone inconsequential, someone she didn't need to worry about. Maybe bitter and twisted that her marriage was ending, but in light of everything, Sandra was the least of Kat's worries. But why was Luke meeting her now? And why there, in the middle of Regent's Park, when he was supposed to be at work?

She watched as Luke handed Sandra one of the drinks. They exchanged a hug, and Kat felt her chest tighten. Was this what Luke had been hiding? All this time, Kat thought his feelings were tangled up between her and Clara, but now... Sandra?

Kat felt like she'd been punched in the stomach. Luke had told her he and Sandra were done, that he'd left her because of his affection for Kat. And yet here they were, sitting on a park bench, sipping coffee together like old lovers. From where Kat stood, she couldn't hear what they were saying, but their body language was clear—intimate, close.

They stayed on the bench for what felt like hours, although it was probably just minutes. Then, just as easily as they had met, Luke and Sandra hugged again. But this time, it wasn't a casual hug. It was intimate. Too intimate. And then, to Kat's horror, Luke leant in and kissed Sandra—a soft, lingering kiss that made Kat's stomach turn.

A rush of adrenaline rushed through her, and she fought the urge to storm over and confront them. But she didn't. She stayed rooted to the spot, watching, waiting.

Luke stood up first and began walking back in the direction of the office. Kat waited, her heart pounding in her chest, as Sandra lingered by the bench for a few moments longer. She wondered what Sandra could possibly be thinking. And then, out of nowhere, Clara appeared.

With her dog, Charlie, by her side, she walked directly into Sandra's path. Charlie, clearly excited, jumped up at Sandra, his paws scratching at her legs. Kat watched in disbelief as Sandra shrieked, trying to push the dog off her. Clara didn't seem to be making much of an effort to stop him. In fact, it appeared she was enjoying the spectacle.

The two women exchanged heated words. Kat couldn't hear what they were saying, but the finger-jabbing and aggressive body language spoke volumes. Sandra looked as though she was about to kick the dog at one point, trying to shove him away, and for a brief moment, Kat felt a flicker of amusement—until she remembered the growing mess she was entangled in.

After what seemed like an eternity, Clara finally yanked Charlie away, and the two women left the park in opposite directions—Sandra stomping off angrily, and Clara looking disturbingly pleased with herself.

Kat stood frozen in place, her mind whirling. What had she just witnessed? First Luke meeting Sandra, and then Clara turning up. Were Luke and Clara in cahoots? But how could they be, given the intimate kiss between Luke and Sandra moments earlier?

Kat eventually moved to the coffee kiosk herself, needing something, anything, to steady her nerves. She ordered a drink and sat down on a nearby bench, the events of the exchanges replaying in her mind.

As she sat there, she realised she was no closer to resolving anything. Luke's strange behaviour, Clara's sudden appearances, and now Sandra being dragged back into the picture; it was all too perfectly connected.

She sipped her coffee, the warm liquid doing little to thaw the icy fear gnawing at her insides.

44

Kat entered the office to find Luke sat his desk, his face tense, his mind anywhere but on the monitor before him. He looked up when she came in, but quickly turned away. Something was clearly wrong, but when Kat asked, Luke simply waved her off. "Nothing," he said, but his tone was far too clipped to be casual. Kat didn't press him immediately. Instead, she pulled out the document she needed him to sign.

"Work stuff," she said lightly, placing it on his desk. Luke took the pen from her hand, then hesitated, realising he should read what the hell he was about to put his name to. "It's for the bank," Kat reassured him. Luke nodded and turned the paper over to find where he was required to sign.

"Did you and Clara have a good time at the restaurant?" Kat asked, trying to sound offhanded, as though she cared little about the answer.

Luke looked up, his eyes narrowing. "It was supposed to be this coming Friday, but I've knocked it on the head."

Kat's eyes widened. "Cancelled it? Why?"

"Yes. I cancelled it," Luke replied too quickly. "Something's come up."

She tilted her head, scrutinising his face. "What's come up?"

Luke's shoulders slumped, and he sighed heavily, as though the weight of the world was pressing down on him. "I... I've been back in touch with Sandra."

The words hung in the air. Kat no longer cared that much about Luke's romantic life, but the way he said it made it sound like there was more to it than just a reunion.

"Back in touch? I thought you left her?"

"I did. But she found something out." He looked away, swallowing hard, his hands fidgeting nervously. "It's... complicated."

Kat's lips parted slightly, but no words came out, just a low exhale of frustration. "What did she find out, Luke?" she finally asked.

Luke hesitated, his hand still hovering over the papers. "It's nothing," he eventually replied.

Kat felt her head spin. What was it with everyone keeping secrets?

As if she could talk.

"So, what is it? Is she blackmailing you to get back together?"

Luke let out a heavy breath. "No. Nothing like that." He laughed nervously before signing the document and passing it back to Kat. Her eyes didn't leave his. She knew he was holding something back, something he didn't want Kat to hear. The business? The past?

"Are you two getting back together?"

Luke gave a humourless laugh. "It's too early for that. But I must admit, I do still have feelings for her."

Kat raised her eyebrows, surprised by his honesty. "Feelings? After everything?"

He looked at her, his eyes dark. "We go back a long way, Kat. Longer than you think. Back to the days when Adam was in a relationship with her."

Kat froze. "What?"

Luke sighed again, clearly not wanting to delve into it. "Yeah. Didn't you know?" He held a smug look, a look that said he knew something she didn't. "Adam went out with Sandra for quite a while. Didn't he ever tell you?"

"No, he didn't," Kat said, feeling her blood turn cold. She'd never known. Why would Adam have hidden that from her? Her mind spun. So that's what Sandra had meant the day she turned up and Kat invited her in for coffee. She knew Luke had just left. She must have.

"We all need someone we can rely on during difficult times…"

Sandra had meant Adam.

"He's been a rock for you, hasn't he?"

Adam had been her rock.

Luke shrugged, trying to make it seem insignificant. "It was years ago. Before you two even met. Adam and Sandra got together when we all worked at the software company. He got in there first," he added with an unconvincing grin.

Kat's mind whirled. Why had Adam never told her? It seemed like another layer of secrecy on top of everything else. Luke was watching her, as if trying to gauge her reaction.

"Why does it matter?" Luke asked gently. "That's ancient history."

Kat swallowed hard. "Maybe it doesn't," she muttered. But it did. Everything mattered.

Luke shifted in his chair, looking restless. His fingers

tapped incessantly on the edge of the desk, a habit Kat hadn't noticed before and now it grated on her nerves.

"Look," Luke said. "Sandra's back in the picture, but it's not like she's moving straight back in. I'm just trying to figure things out. As I said, it's complicated."

Kat stood up, straightening her coat. "Does Clara know about all this?" she asked, her tone tinged with sarcasm.

Luke chuckled, but it was hollow. "Clara? No. She's got nothing to do with it."

Kat raised an eyebrow. "Well, you've already cancelled dinner with her. What if she asks me about your past? About why you called off your romantic rendezvous?"

Luke shook his head. "There's no need to be like that, Kat. Besides, I have every intention of telling Clara that Sandra is back in the picture. It's better she hears it from me than finds out another way."

As he spoke, Kat noticed something else she had paid little attention to before. Luke's voice was strained, his movements erratic. His leg bounced beneath the desk, and his eyes kept darting towards the door, as though he was expecting someone to burst in at any moment. It wasn't just nerves. It was something deeper. An instability Kat had glimpsed occasionally, but had never truly considered.

"You sure you're okay?" she asked, more seriously this time.

"Yeah, fine. Why?"

"You seem… I don't know, on edge."

He gave her a tight smile. "It's just everything. Sandra, the business. It's a lot right now."

Kat watched him closely, but decided not to press further. She gathered her things and walked towards the door. "Well, good luck with that. But be careful, Luke. Everyone seems to have their secrets these days. And you're no different."

Luke looked at her, his face tightening, but he said nothing as she left.

As Kat stepped out into the cold air, her mind buzzed with new information. So, everyone around her had skeletons in the cupboard—Luke and Clara, as well as those already departed. And now Sandra was back in the picture, holding something over Luke's head. And she was linked to Adam, and if she was linked to Adam, she was linked to Kat as well.

45

On Friday evening, Kat sat across from Lauren in the Sunset, watching her friend as she spoke freely about inane matters. Kat couldn't recall the last time she didn't have something dreadful on her mind.

"Is your mum okay looking after Tom and Max again?" Kat asked, swirling her glass of wine.

Lauren nodded, glancing at her phone. "Yeah, they went straight over after school. My mum loves having them, you know that."

Kat forced a smile, but the truth was she wanted to be the one keeping an eye on Tom. She had the sudden urge to be there with him, but she fought it down. She had to trust Lauren. She had to trust someone.

"I know," Kat replied, forcing herself to relax. "Tom always comes back and says what a great time he's had."

Lauren smiled, leaning back into her chair. "Yeah, my mum is brilliant with kids. Adores the pair of them."

The conversation drifted into more light, meaningless chatter, the kind of topics that usually helped Kat switch off. But that night, a feeling of discomfort bothered her.

She couldn't stop thinking about Luke, Sandra, and Clara. Then the revelation that Adam had once dated Sandra. Was it important? Kat could no longer piece it altogether, like when you find a particular piece of a jigsaw puzzle only to find you then need to start all over again for the next one. It was like a runaway train that she just couldn't get off.

They had nearly finished their bottle of wine when the door swung open, and Kat's stomach dropped. From the chilly spring air, in stepped Clara.

"Unbelievable," Kat muttered under her breath.

But then, to her amazement, Lauren shot up from her chair, waving her arm. "Over here!"

Kat's head whipped around to stare at her friend. "You know each other?"

Lauren smiled brightly as Clara approached the table. "Yeah! We met at the school gates. She was there tonight. She wanted to see Tom, to show him Charlie." Lauren looked at Kat like it was the most normal thing in the world. "We got talking, and I told her she should join us for a drink."

Kat's heart hammered in her chest. The room felt smaller, more suffocating. Clara gave her a friendly smile as she made eye contact, but Kat could barely manage to return it.

"So... you just invited her?" Kat asked as Clara went to the bar, trying to keep her voice steady.

Lauren grinned. "Yeah, thought it'd be fun! You don't mind, do you?"

Kat forced a tight smile. "No. Of course not. It's just a bit of a surprise, that's all."

Clara quickly joined them with a clean glass and a fresh bottle of wine to share. After formalities, the evening continued, but Kat retreated into her own mind.

Clara and Lauren were laughing, bonding over stories of their youth, and Kat only chimed in when she had to. Every time Clara said something that made Lauren laugh, Kat's chest tightened. Lauren was supposed to be *her* friend. Her *close* friend. And then there was Clara, sliding in so easily again, taking up space that didn't belong to her.

Kat sipped her wine and tried to quell the bubbling resentment. But it was impossible to ignore the mounting tension, the jealousy twisting inside her. She recalled her drunken nights with Lauren, nights when she'd shared secrets about her relationship with Adam. About their past, about Kevin and Vicky. Surely Lauren wouldn't disclose such personal information to Clara when she wasn't around? *When I'm not around?* Shit. Kat hadn't even considered that they might become close. Would Clara take Lauren away from her, just as she'd tried to seduce Luke?

It was paranoia, Kat told herself. She was spiralling. But there was something about this new connection between Lauren and Clara that made her feel boxed in, as if the entire world was against her.

The laughter at the table continued, the wine flowed, and Kat felt like an outsider. It should have been her relaxing, her finding some peace. Instead, she was simmering with anxiety.

By the time they left the bar and said their goodbyes to Lauren at the tube station, and began walking home, Kat could barely hold her emotions together.

"Hey, do you want to come in for a nightcap?" Clara asked as they reached their street. "It's still early."

Kat hesitated, her instincts screaming at her to decline. But something made her nod. Maybe she needed to confront the feeling. Or maybe she just wanted to see more of Clara's life, the woman who was quickly becoming entangled in hers.

They stepped inside Clara's house, and the warmth hit Kat like a wave. It was cosy, too cosy; pictures of Charlie hung on the wall, soft cushions lined the couch, and the smell of lavender filled the air. Kat fucking detested the woman.

Clara poured them both a small glass of whiskey, sitting down opposite Kat. "So," she began, a soft smile on her lips, "I got the sense tonight that maybe you weren't too happy to see me."

Kat nearly choked on her drink. "What? No, it's not that," she stammered, feeling her cheeks burn. "I was just surprised, that's all. I didn't realise you and Lauren even knew each other."

Clara nodded slowly, watching her with an unreadable expression. "Lauren's nice. Easy to talk to."

Kat clenched her jaw. "Yeah. She is."

Clara raised an eyebrow. "But are you sure that's all it is? You seemed off tonight."

Kat's heartbeat quickened, but she refused to let Clara see how much she was affecting her. "It was just a shock, that's all."

Clara's gaze lingered on her, too long for Kat's liking. She felt like Clara was looking straight through her, seeing things Kat didn't want anyone to see.

After an uncomfortable silence, Kat finished her drink and stood up. "I should get home. Thanks for the nightcap."

Clara didn't protest, but as she walked Kat to the door, there was something in her eyes, something knowing. It made Kat's skin crawl.

When she finally stepped back into her own house, Kat shut the door and leant against it, her chest hammering. Once again, she found herself in the living room, staring out of the window, looking across the street at Clara's house. Her heart thumped in her chest. And then her gaze made its inevitable journey to the window upstairs.

Unsure whether it was the drink, or something else entirely, Kat smiled openly when she imagined seeing the curtains part.

46

On Monday morning, following the longest Sunday Kat could ever remember, her phone buzzed, making her jump. Everything made Kat jump those days. She continually picked at her fingers too, biting calluses until they bled. But it didn't hurt, which surprised Kat. Collecting the phone, she noticed it was Kathy from the accounts department. Luke hadn't shown up for work.

Kat felt the tension ripple through her. After all that had transpired when they met early the previous week—the odd behaviour, the sudden change in his relationship with Sandra…

"I haven't heard from him," Kathy added. "We've tried calling his mobile, but there's no answer. Do you think everything's alright?"

Kat swallowed hard. She'd known something was off with Luke the last time they spoke, but she'd somehow dismissed it. Luke was going through a lot, dealing with the aftermath of Sandra's sudden reappearance, but this? Not showing up at the office? Luke was reliable, a rock. Something must be wrong.

"Thanks, Kathy," Kat replied. "I'll handle it."

Her thoughts twisted as she dashed out of the house and ran to the tube station to get to the office. What if Luke had left the business altogether? Fled the country? The pressure he had been under the past few weeks, and now with Sandra back in his life. Perhaps it was her fault, and she'd somehow persuaded him to get away, start afresh. But without him, the business was done. There was only one junior analyst left, and he was barely coping as it was.

When she arrived at the office, a sea of worried faces greeted Kat. No one had heard from Luke. She tried his mobile again, her hands trembling as she pressed redial over and over. Each time, it rang out. No voicemail. No answer.

Kat stared at her phone, feeling a rising sense of dread. She couldn't involve the police. Not yet. Maybe not at all? She couldn't keep involving the police. What were their names? Rodriguez and Anderson. The last time they'd called round, informing her they'd be in touch if anything else came to light, a wry look on their faces that might not be far away. Shit.

Her mind flickered back to watching Luke in the park. Seeing him kiss Sandra, rekindling feelings for her after everything. She hadn't asked him much about it, but perhaps she should have.

She made up her mind. She had to check Luke's flat. Kat didn't know exactly where he lived, but she remembered him mentioning a place near Russell Square. She'd never been, but now wasn't the time for hesitation. She couldn't just sit at the office and wait. Quickly, she got his address off the payroll system and found herself out on the streets once more.

Her cab wound through the busy traffic, pulling up to

a modest apartment block at the end of a quiet cul-de-sac. Kat felt a rush of unease as she rang the buzzer. No response.

After a few minutes, a tenant opened the door to leave. Kat took her chance, wedging her foot in the gap before it closed. Glancing around nervously, she slipped inside, her heart pounding as she made her way to the second floor.

When she reached flat 203, she stopped to regulate her breathing. The hallway was dark and silent, unnervingly so. She knocked gently at first. No reply. She knocked again, louder this time, panic creeping into her chest.

"Luke?" she called, her voice small in the dim corridor.

For a moment, nothing. And then—a sound. Faint, but unmistakable. A muffled shuffle, someone moving inside.

Kat knocked again, this time with more force. "Luke! It's Kat. Open up!"

She heard footsteps approaching the door. It creaked open slowly, revealing Luke—dishevelled, unshaven, and looking like he hadn't slept in days. His shirt was wrinkled, and dark circles surrounded his eyes. He was a ghost of the man she knew, barely holding himself together.

"Luke," Kat whispered, stepping closer. "What's going on? You've missed work. I've been calling—"

He didn't speak at first, only held the door open a little wider, a silent invitation for her to go inside.

Kat hesitated before stepping over the threshold, the smell of stale alcohol hitting her immediately. She glanced around the small living room, taking in the scene. An empty bottle of scotch sat on the table, cushions were strewn haphazardly across the floor, and the kitchen was a mess of dirty dishes. The whole place screamed of someone who had let things go.

"Luke," she said, softer this time. "What's going on? Talk to me."

He sat down heavily on the sofa, rubbing his face with both hands. "It's Sandra," he muttered, his voice cracked and hollow. "She's dead."

Kat froze. "What?"

Luke finally looked up, his eyes glazed and distant. "She was killed on Saturday night. They found her body yesterday, in the canal."

Kat stared at him, her mind whirling. "Killed? What the hell happened?"

"A dog walker found her," Luke continued, his voice thick. "The police think she was pushed. They're still investigating, but she's gone."

"Oh my God," Kat whispered, sinking onto the arm of the sofa. "Luke, I'm so sorry. I—"

He cut her off, looking at her with an intensity that chilled her to the core. "It wasn't anything to do with you, was it?"

The question lingered, sharp and dangerous. Kat blinked, her heart hammering in her chest. "What? No! Why would you even ask that?"

Luke leant back, staring at the ceiling. "I don't know," he admitted. "I don't know anything anymore. Everything's just… fucked up."

Kat's shoulders slumped. Sandra, dead. In the canal. But why would Luke ask if she had anything to do with it? Had something happened between Sandra and Luke after their meeting in the park? Had Sandra threatened him? Could Luke have been involved and now he was trying to cover his tracks?

"…she found something out…"

She didn't know what to say. Didn't know if she should stay or leave. Luke looked like he was on the verge of collapse, but his question had left her rattled.

"Luke," Kat said carefully, "I didn't have anything to do with Sandra. You have to believe me."

He glanced at her, his expression softening slightly. "I don't know what to believe, Kat. Not anymore. So many deaths, and every single one connected to Adam, you…"

She sat in silence for a moment, trying to process it all. Luke was falling apart, and now Sandra was dead. And he was coming to his own inevitable conclusions. Why wouldn't he? She'd come to the same conclusion herself weeks and weeks ago. She tried to recall Saturday night. Where had she been? Kat couldn't remember anything anymore. Her movements, her whereabouts. She was crumbling by the day, by the hour.

"Luke?" she asked quietly, almost afraid to ask. Luke glanced up. "What did Sandra find out?"

But Luke just shook his head slowly from side to side, like he couldn't stop it. "She never told me."

Was he telling the truth?

Eventually, Kat stood. "You need to rest," she said. "I'll cover for you at work. Just let me know if you need anything."

Luke didn't respond as she left. But as Kat stepped out into the mild early May air, a chilling thought crept into her mind.

Sandra was dead, and she didn't know if she had played a part in it.

47

Kat arrived at the office the following morning; it was the last place she wanted to be. She had never felt at ease in that kind of environment, and that day felt a hundred times worse. The quiet buzz of activity, the soft clatter of keyboards, and the distant hum of conversation were suffocating. Her mind was full of thoughts about Luke and whether he would turn up for work. But it was brimming with other things too.

She had been trying to reach Luke since leaving him the day before—calls, texts—nothing. She didn't want to panic, but each missed call, each unanswered message, made her anxiety swell. Could she allow the business to fail? Hadn't Adam lost all interest too?

Walking past the open-plan office area, Kat briefly greeted a couple of the employees, her mind already in tatters. Kathy stopped her just as she was about to proceed to her own cubicle.

"Have you heard from Luke?" she asked hesitantly.

"No," Kat snapped. "Why, have you?"

The girl shook her head, concern etched across her

face. "No one's heard from him. I've tried calling but nothing. Do you know if everything will be alright if he doesn't show?"

Kat felt the weight of the situation hit her. People were worried about their jobs. She forced a smile, not wanting to appear as rattled as she was. "I'll get hold of him. Don't worry."

Once inside her cubicle, she slammed the door behind her and pulled out her phone, dialling Luke's number again. It rang and rang. She sent a text…

> Where are you? Call me.

Then she threw her phone onto the desk in frustration.

Kat leant back in her chair, rubbing her temples. She couldn't afford for Luke to go AWOL, not now, not when the company was already on shaky ground.

A knock on the door pulled her from her thoughts. "Come in," she called out. Prakash, the junior analyst, stepped inside. He looked uneasy, and Kat, in her current state of mind, wasn't exactly in the mood for more drama.

"Mrs Chapman," he said softly, closing the door behind him. "We need to talk."

Her eyes narrowed. She wasn't sure she could take any more surprises, but she gestured for him to sit down. "Please," she said, rather too aggressively. "Call me Kat."

Prakash fidgeted, avoiding eye contact. "Okay… Kat. I… I don't know how to tell you this."

"Tell me what?" she asked, her voice sharper still. She needed to calm down.

"I'm leaving the company."

Kat's chest tightened. "You're what?"

He swallowed hard, the silence between them thick and uncomfortable. "I'm sorry. I just… I can't stay anymore."

Kat shot up from her seat, anger bubbling to the surface. "Why, Prakash? Why would you leave? What's going on?"

Prakash shifted uncomfortably. "It's not the job. I mean, I enjoy working here. It's just…" He hesitated, and Kat felt her frustration growing.

"Spit it out. What's going on?"

"I've been getting these messages," he said, lowering his voice as if someone might overhear him. "On WhatsApp. They're telling me to leave the company, warning me that I shouldn't be working here anymore."

Kat stared at him. "What? Who are they from?"

"I don't know," he admitted, shaking his head. "It's just a number. No name, nothing. I tried calling it back, but it always goes to voicemail. At first, I ignored it, but then, I started feeling like someone's watching me. You know, when I go to lunch or leave the office. It's freaking me out."

Kat crossed her arms and turned her foot at a right-angle. She stared at Prakash, attempting to digest what he was saying. Was it for real, or was he just trying to bail out? "Let me see the messages."

Prakash shifted in his seat, looking embarrassed. "They're deleted. It happened over the weekend. The entire chat disappeared. I don't know how it happened."

Of course, Kat thought, her patience wearing thin. "So, let me get this straight. You're quitting your job, a good job, because of some anonymous messages that you can't show me?"

He nodded, looking as though he wished the ground would swallow him up.

"Prakash, come on. Is this really about the messages, or is there something else going on?"

"I'm serious, Mrs Chap… I mean, Kat," he said, his voice quivering. "It's not just the messages. I've been getting this feeling, like something bad is going to happen. I can't explain it. It's just—whoever's sending these, they somehow know about me, what I do. I don't feel safe."

Kat's frustration turned to disbelief. Everyone around her was falling apart. First Luke, now Prakash. She couldn't lose him too, not with the business hanging by a thread. But his comments also unnerved her. The feeling he was being watched and something bad was going to happen.

Something bad is fucking happening.

"Fine," she said, her voice laced with bitterness. "Put it in writing. But you know what? I can do better than you. If you're going to let some mysterious messages scare you off, then maybe you shouldn't be here."

Prakash looked taken aback by her sudden shift in tone. "I didn't want it to come to this. I'm sorry."

"Just go," she snapped, her voice rising. "And don't expect me to chase after you for your resignation letter. I'll give you a month's pay, but apart from that, I don't owe you anything."

Prakash stood up, clearly shaken, and mumbled something about sending the letter in the morning. As he left, Kat slammed the door behind him, her hands trembling with a mix of anger and frustration.

She walked to the window, needing something—anything—to calm her nerves. And that's when she saw her. Clara. A tube stop from home. Entering Regent's Park opposite, with Charlie on his lead.

48

THE OFFICE SUDDENLY FELT STIFLING. Kat paced her cubicle, aware of glaring eyes from the other side of the glass, yet she had no time for any of them. Stepping back to the window, she glanced out at the park again, but there was no sign of Clara. But Kat's suspicions, already simmering beneath the surface, were flaring once more. Why was she walking her dog there, of all places?

Kat's phone buzzed on her desk, interrupting her thoughts. It was Lauren; her supposed best friend. Until she invited bloody Clara out with them.

> How are you? Fancy a coffee sometime?

Kat ignored it, Clara's figure on the periphery of the park still etched in her mind. She looked out of the window again, but there was still no sign of Clara or her stupid damn dog. Both had vanished as if they had never been there at all.

Without hesitation, Kat grabbed her jacket and headed out of the office. She needed fresh air, but more than that, she needed to find Clara. The situation had gone on long enough.

The moment she stepped outside, the warm spring air hit her skin, although she wished it were cold after the oppressive heat of the office. As she crossed the street and entered the park, she scanned everywhere, looking for any sign of her neighbour and dog. But neither were to be seen.

Kat walked deeper into the park, her eyes darting around, searching for the woman who seemed to be everywhere and nowhere at once. The park was quieter than usual, just the hum of a lawnmower in the distance and the sound of a group of small children playing at the far end of the green. But still no Clara.

Her phone buzzed in her pocket again. Another message from Lauren, probably. But she ignored it, keeping her focus on the task at hand. As she walked the path she had taken many times before, she replayed the past few weeks in her head. Every strange coincidence, every uncomfortable interaction. It felt like Clara was always there, even when she claimed she wasn't.

That night at the pub, with Lauren, still lingered in her mind. Clara's sudden appearance, how easily she had inserted herself into Kat's evening. Then there was the football incident—Tom's ball reappearing outside Kat's house. Clara had said she was at work that morning, but something didn't sit right with Kat about that.

She ran her hands down her face, her fingers lingering at her temples, trying to stop the pounding inside her skull, replaying every detail, every odd thing about Clara. Could she be involved in what was happening at the office too? Was it just a coincidence that Prakash had received threatening messages? Kat was unable to shake the feeling that all these things were connected, even if she couldn't yet see how.

Her phone buzzed a third time, but after retrieving it, this time the number was withheld. She stared at the screen, her breath catching in her throat. Kat's hand trembled as she clicked on the messages icon.

> Are you sure you know who's watching you?

Her pulse quickened as she scanned the empty park, her heart hammering in her chest. There was no one around. Her mind immediately flashed back to the cryptic messages Prakash had received, the ones he claimed had made him feel like someone was following him. Could this be the same person? Or was it something else entirely?

She quickly responded:

> Who is this?

But no response came. The message hung in the air like a silent threat, its meaning unclear but unmistakably sinister.

Kat shoved her phone into her pocket and kept walking, her pace quickening as the hairs on the back of her neck stood on end. She felt the eerie sensation of being watched, but every time she looked over her shoulder, the park remained as empty as it had been when she'd arrived.

But Clara had been there. Kat had seen her with her own eyes. Hadn't she?

Sandra's death, Luke's non-attendance at the office,

Prakash's sudden resignation, the strange events circled around her life like a tightening noose.

As she exited the park, Kat found herself at a crossroads. She could continue ignoring her instincts, chalk it all up to paranoia and coincidence, or she could finally dig deeper. She had always trusted her gut, and right now, it was screaming at her that Clara wasn't just an innocent neighbour.

Quickly, she returned to the office and collected her laptop and other items, and offered a brief nod of her head to Kathy, who looked just as pale as she had earlier. Kathy opened her mouth to speak, but Kat half-smiled and raised the bag in her hand as if to say, 'I'm in a hurry'.

After catching the tube, Kat half walked and half ran to her house. Once on her street, her eyes drifted across to Clara's house. All appeared eerily quiet. However, her pulse quickened again when she was sure she caught a glimpse of a shadow at the upstairs window.

49

Three days later, Kat sat at her desk, the soft hum of her laptop barely cutting through the oppressive silence of her home office. It was Friday, and she was meant to be working, but her mind simply wouldn't allow her to concentrate. Her focus on the business, once her number one priority, was dulling by the day—by the hour.

She stared blankly at the screen, her fingers frozen over the keyboard, no longer able to summon the energy to care about the work in front of her. Adam had gone through the same thing. She could see him sitting in his old chair, staring into space, just like she was now, slowly unravelling under the pressure of forces he couldn't control. She recalled the days when she told him to get help, just as Clara had suggested to her.

"Stress can take a real toll. If you ever need to talk to someone, I have some friends who work in that field who could help. There's no shame in it. You've been through a lot."

Kat bit her lip, the memory of Adam pulling at her. The image of him looking at her from the upstairs window from the house opposite. Was it him? He'd been driven mad by what they'd got themselves into. Recruiting Kevin was their first mistake. He had a knack for playing mind games, and his girlfriend, Vicky, had made it worse, pushing Adam to the brink. But it hadn't ended with Adam. Vicky had threatened Kat too, and now Kat was facing something eerily similar. Sandra then returned out of nowhere, pulling Luke back into her web, just as she'd once done with Adam. And that was why none of them were still around. Just like Mark Harris—Kat almost laughed, remembering his name. The first person to suffer under Liam and Imogen's scheme's. Adam had seen to him, passing the blame onto George—another name from the past who had fallen victim to Adam's unnerving skill to rid every single person who blocked his path to success. Then there was Bob and Pauline, before Liam and Imogen themselves. So much death. And what about Kat's parents? Why hadn't she grieved as she should have done? Once so close, yet driven apart by the web Kat and Adam had become entangled in. A web that just wouldn't let go.

Her thoughts shifted to Luke, and a cold suspicion crept into her mind. Luke had always been close, always ready to help, but maybe that was the plan. Maybe he was trying to take the business from her, just as he had tried to take Adam's stability. It seemed everyone was losing control, and Kat couldn't help feeling that she was next.

Too late for that.

The sudden sound of her doorbell jarred her from her thoughts, making her heart leap. She wasn't expecting anyone, and for a moment, she considered ignoring it. But something pulled her from her chair, and she walked to the door, her feet heavy with dread.

She opened the door to find Luke standing there,

looking like a ghost of the man she once knew. His hair was matted, his clothes dishevelled, and there was a faint but unmistakable odour clinging to him. He couldn't have showered in days. His eyes, once sharp and alert, were dull and vacant, and when he smiled, it wasn't the warm grin she remembered. It was unsettling, almost manic, his teeth already yellowing from days of neglect.

"Luke?" Kat said, her voice barely above a whisper.

He didn't answer, just pushed past her, letting himself into the house as if he owned the place. Kat's heart raced, her skin crawling as she closed the door behind him.

"I'm done, Kat," Luke said, his voice flat, emotionless. He walked into her living room and slumped onto the couch, his hands trembling slightly as he rubbed them together. "I'm leaving the business. It's yours. You can have my directorship. I don't care anymore."

Kat stood frozen by the door, watching him, her own hands trembling as if in sympathy with the mess that sat before her. What the hell was happening?

"What's going on?" she asked, trying to keep her voice steady despite the rising fear in her chest.

He laughed, but it wasn't a sound of amusement. It was hollow, almost desperate. "It's too much. All of it. I can't do it anymore. Kevin was right that day he called me. He knew. He was warning me."

"Of what?" Kat pressed, stepping closer but still keeping her distance. Something about his demeanour frightened her.

Luke's eyes darted around the room as if he expected something, or someone, to jump out at him at any moment. "I've been seeing him. Everywhere I go."

"Seeing who? What the hell are you talking about?"

"I don't know who. But he's definitely there, watching me."

Kat's blood ran cold. "What do you mean? What the fuck are you talking about?" She glanced across the road at *that* house once more.

Luke stood abruptly, pacing the room, his hands running through his hair. "I don't know! I know it can't be real. But someone's there. At the office, at home, even when I'm walking down the street. I see him, Kat. He's following me."

Kat's throat tightened, her heart pounding in her chest. Luke sounded deranged, his words tumbling out in a rush of panic. She didn't know what to say. Was he having a breakdown?

"Luke, you're not well," Kat said softly, trying to calm him down. "You need help."

He spun around to face her, his eyes bloodshot and wild. "I'm not crazy! I know what I'm seeing! Someone is there, watching me, just like they're watching you."

The words hit her like a punch to the gut. "What do you mean, watching me?" She recalled Prakash and his disappearing WhatsApp messages and the one she'd received in Regent's Park.

Luke's face twisted into a grimace. "You think I don't know? You think I haven't seen the way you act? You're losing it too, Kat."

Kat took a step back, her pulse racing. This was madness. Luke was unravelling right in front of her, and she had no idea how to stop it. Her mind raced through the events of the past few weeks— Sandra's death, Luke's refusal to go to work, the strange occurrences around her. Could the loss of Adam still be haunting them, even now?

"Luke, listen to me," she said, her voice firm. "You're not seeing anybody. You're just under a lot of stress, and it's messing with your mind. We both are. But we need to stay focused."

Luke shook his head, his expression frantic. "No, Kat. You don't understand. It's real."

Kat felt a wave of nausea wash over her. She didn't know what to believe anymore. But she knew Luke was right. She was convinced she was being watched. And she knew who he was talking about. Adam. She'd seen him too.

"I'm leaving," Luke said suddenly, breaking the tension. "You can have it all. I don't want it anymore."

He turned and walked towards the door, his movements sluggish, as if the weight of the world was bearing down on him. Kat watched him go, her heart pounding in her chest, her mind spinning with confusion and fear.

50

A WEEK HAD PASSED since Luke's unbelievable and yet unsettling visit to Kat's house, and in that time, she hadn't heard a word from him. Although somewhat relieved she'd had no contact—his behaviour that day had left her badly shaken—something still tormented her. Perhaps it was guilt, or maybe it was fear of what might become of him. Either way, she felt obligated to attend Sandra's funeral. Not for Sandra, but for Luke. The slag had once been Adam's girlfriend and Adam belonged to Kat, however, she still held feelings for Luke and she knew she was responsible for dragging him into the whole sorry mess. It was she who insisted Adam employed him. She'd also allowed herself to fall for him, and betray her husband as he himself fell into despair. Perhaps this was her punishment?

Retribution.

On the morning of the funeral, Kat stood in front of the mirror, fussing with her clothes. She had chosen dark trousers and a white short-sleeved shirt, an outfit that was simple and respectful, but she couldn't help feeling underdressed. It wasn't the first time lately she'd felt insecure about her appearance. Clara had a way of making her feel small, insignificant even. But today, Kat wasn't there for appearances. She just wanted to get through the service and show Luke some kind of support, whatever that might look like.

She'd called Lauren earlier, asking her to come along for backup. Kat didn't want to admit it, but she was scared of how Luke might react if he saw her there. His downward spiral had been alarming, and she wasn't sure what state she'd find him in. She needed Lauren by her side.

The day was unseasonably hot for mid-May, the sun shining with a surprising intensity, and Kat found herself grateful when she and Lauren stepped into the cool, dim church. The small building was sparsely occupied—just a few scattered mourners dressed in black, heads bowed. The smell of incense persisted, mingling with the scent of lilies arranged by the altar. The old stone walls seemed to absorb the heat, providing a welcome respite from the outside. Dust motes floated through the beams of sunlight that streamed in through the stained glass, giving the church an almost otherworldly glow.

Kat and Lauren quietly entered from the back, trying to be as inconspicuous as possible. As Kat's eyes adjusted to the dim light, she spotted Luke at the front, stood by himself, staring at the coffin that held Sandra's body within. She froze when he turned, locking eyes with her.

He looked worse than before; his hair stuck out at odd angles, greasy and unkempt, his shirt half-tucked into wrinkled trousers, the tail hanging out to one side. His eyes were bloodshot, dark circles framing them as though he hadn't slept in days. His skin was pale, almost sickly, and as he stared at her, his lips twitched, forming an almost delirious smile. There was something feral in his gaze, and for a moment, Kat felt the walls of the church closing in on her. Her breath caught in her throat. He looked deranged, like a man teetering on the edge of madness. And she should know the signs.

She clutched Lauren's arm instinctively, but Luke made no move towards them. He just stood there, his eyes never leaving Kat, until the vicar began the service and Luke turned back to face the coffin. Kat couldn't dispel the sensation of his gaze, even when it wasn't on her. There was something unsettling, something almost dangerous, about his presence.

The service passed in a blur. Kat barely heard the vicar's words, her mind too preoccupied with Luke. Every so often, she glanced at him, hoping for some sign of normalcy, some indication that he wasn't as far gone as he appeared. But each time she looked, he was the same—silent, tense, his fingers twitching as if struggling to contain some inner turmoil.

As the service came to an end, Kat felt a wave of relief. She couldn't wait to leave, to escape the oppressive atmosphere of the church and put as much distance between herself and Luke as possible. But as the mourners shuffled out, she spotted Clara at the rear of the church.

Kat's heart lurched. What was *she* doing there? Not only that, but Clara was dressed impeccably in a fitted black dress, her dark hair pinned back elegantly, a small, stylish hat perched atop her head. She looked as though she belonged in a fashion magazine rather than at a sparsely attended funeral. Once again, she outshone Kat, who felt frumpy and under-prepared in comparison.

Clara's eyes met Kat's, and for a moment, they simply stared at each other. Clara's lips curled into a small, knowing smile, one that made Kat's skin crawl. It was the same smile she'd seen before, the one that always left her with the sense Clara knew something she didn't.

Kat's gaze followed Clara as she stepped towards Luke, who had walked out of the church ahead of them. To Kat's disbelief, Luke was smiling now, a stark contrast to the haunted figure she had seen just minutes earlier. He hugged Clara, and she rested her chin on his shoulder, her eyes drifting over to Kat. It was as though Clara was silently mocking her.

As Kat and Lauren exited the church, Clara called out to Lauren, her voice warm and inviting. "Lauren! Over here."

Kat watched as Lauren broke away from her side, walking towards Clara with an eager smile. They hugged, and Kat felt an inexplicable surge of anger. Why couldn't anybody else see what she could?

Hesitating before joining them, Kat stood awkwardly to the side as they chatted. Clara turned to her, her smile softening. But there was no offer of affection. "How are you, Kat?" she asked, her voice as smooth as ever. But there was something behind the words, something that made Kat's skin prickle.

"I'm fine," Kat said, her voice clipped. She could barely look at Clara, the tension between them palpable.

As the small group of mourners gathered around the freshly dug grave, Kat's breathing quickened, and she had to press a hand to her chest to keep it steady. She watched as Luke, still grinning oddly, dropped a handful of soil onto the coffin. The vicar invited the others to do the same, but Kat found herself frozen in place. She couldn't bring herself to follow suit, couldn't bring herself to participate in the macabre ritual.

As the crowd drifted away, Kat's eyes darted to Luke

and Clara once more. They stood together, talking quietly, Luke looking almost… normal. The stark difference in his appearance from earlier left Kat shaken to the core.

And then Clara glanced over at Kat again, her eyes gleaming, that same cryptic smile on her face. Kat's breath caught as a chilling realisation crept over her. Luke had looked at peace with Clara, as if he was under her spell.

51

OVER THE COURSE of the next few days, Kat's vigil at the spare bedroom window became a routine. For hours at a time, she sat perched on a small stool, curtains scarcely parted, her gaze fixed on the house across the street. Clara's house. Imogen's old house. And watching Clara's comings and goings was becoming an obsession. She barely knew what she was looking for, but something in her gut screamed that Clara was hiding something.

Kat had even brought a kettle up with her to brew endless cups of black coffee, snacks as well, to keep herself going. It was a ridiculous setup, Kat understood. She must look completely deranged sitting there like a frantic spy, but she couldn't stop herself. Everything was falling apart. Luke was nowhere to be found. The office was in chaos, so much so, she had turned her work mobile off.

On the following Saturday morning, the bedroom door swung open, distracting her from the window. It was Tom.

"Mummy, can we go to the park? I'm really bored of watching movies."

Kat bit her lip, guilt plaguing her. She should have been paying more attention to her son, especially with the gorgeous weather outside. Tom should be out enjoying the sunshine, not stuck inside glued to the TV. But the thought of tearing herself away from the window, from Clara, made her stomach twist.

"I'm really sorry, sweetheart," she said, trying to keep her voice light. "Something's come up with work, and I need to deal with it. But I'll call Lauren, and she can take you and Max to the park. Maybe even a sleepover?"

Tom didn't answer right away. When he finally did, his voice was soft, resigned. "Okay, I guess."

Kat's heart sank. She was failing him. She was failing everyone. What would Adam think? As soon as Tom disappeared, she called Lauren. Thankfully, her friend was more than happy to help. "I'll pick him up now," Lauren said cheerfully. "Don't worry about a thing, Kat. I can take him overnight too, if that's easier."

"Thank you, Lauren. I owe you one. It's just… everything's been so crazy with Luke disappearing. It's the business, you see…"

"Don't even worry about it," Lauren cut in. "That's what friends are for. You focus on what you need to do."

As Kat hung up, her jealousy towards Lauren's friendship with Clara surfaced again, but she forced herself to push it aside. It wasn't Lauren's fault that Clara had wormed her way into her life. Still, the feeling nagged at her, leaving an unpleasant taste in her mouth.

She watched from the front window as Lauren's car pulled up to the house and Tom climbed in, looking excited at the prospect of spending time with his friend.

Kat's heart clenched as she waved him off, but not once did Tom look up. Then, she resumed her post in the spare room upstairs, watching, waiting.

For hours, the neighbourhood remained quiet, uneventful. Kat began to question her sanity. What was she even doing? Clara had done nothing overtly suspicious; she just lived across the street, occasionally walked her dog, and went to work like everyone else. But that nagging feeling of wrongness persisted. Kat was sure something was off.

Then, just as the clock hit four in the afternoon, movement caught her eye. A sleek black Mercedes pulled up outside Clara's house. The man who stepped out looked professional—tall, dressed in an expensive-looking suit, someone Kat had never seen before. Her breath caught as she watched him walk straight up to Clara's front door and ring the bell. Almost immediately, Clara appeared, wearing her all too familiar smile. She greeted the man warmly, kissing him on both cheeks before ushering him inside. Kat ducked instinctively, her heart racing as she peeked through the narrow slit in the curtains. Did Clara just see her? And was that a small, knowing smile on her lips?

A wave of unease swept over Kat. She wasn't sure why, but something about the scene felt deeply wrong. Before she could think, she grabbed her keys and dashed outside. She looked ridiculous, her slippers still on her feet, her hair unkempt, and her nerves frazzled. But that didn't stop her from creeping across the street, determined to find out who the man was and what Clara was up to.

When she reached Clara's house, she paused, unsure

of her next move. Why was she even there? What was she hoping to discover? The sound of voices drifted from the back of the house, and Kat's curiosity got the better of her. She crept around the edge of the property, remembering the nights of barbecues they'd once had with Imogen and Liam, when times were so much happier. Until the night Adam slept with Imogen.

As she neared the rear garden, she heard the guy speaking. His voice was calm, authoritative. Kat quickly crouched low against the wall, straining to hear the conversation.

"…so this is where it happened with that guy you were talking about?" the man asked. "Chapman wasn't it?"

Kat's breath caught in her throat. Chapman? What the…

"Yes," Clara responded, her voice smooth. "Adam Chapman. It was over there, where the summerhouse used to be. I've had it removed…"

Kat's heart pounded in her ears. They were talking about her husband. Why on earth was Clara discussing Adam?

The voices grew fainter as Clara and her colleague walked away, their conversation becoming muffled as they stepped across the lawn towards the space once occupied by the now infamous outbuilding. Kat remained frozen, her mind reeling. Adam. Why was Clara discussing her ex-husband at all?

Kat's legs felt weak as she slowly emerged from her hiding spot. She needed to get out of there before they saw her, but her mind was spinning.

As she made her way back to her house, her head swirled with questions. Adam had always been haunted by what happened in that garden, but why would Clara be talking about it with a stranger?

Kat leant against her cool hallway wall, staring blankly. If Clara was hiding something, was it tied to Adam? And if she were, that meant it was tied to Kat too. A shiver ran down her spine as she realised she didn't know the woman opposite at all.

52

KAT STOOD MOTIONLESS, unable to think straight. Clara had just been discussing Adam Chapman, her late husband, with a complete stranger. It wasn't just that—Clara had specifically mentioned the very event in which Kat took a fundamental part: the deaths of their neighbours. But why was she discussing that? What connection or interest could Clara possibly have in Adam's past?

However, what scared Kat the most wasn't Clara's secrecy, it was the growing realisation that she had somehow inserted herself into her life for a reason. All the strange connections, the way she moved in on Luke behind Kat's back, turning up at Sandra's funeral like a long-lost friend, befriending her parents as if they were her own, not to mention Tom and taking that bloody dog for a walk. Then she'd even attempted to ruin her friendship with Lauren.

Kat found herself staring at the house across the street once more. Everything about the exterior seemed so normal, so benign. But Kat knew better now. She knew that something sinister lay beneath the surface. The figure in the upstairs window. The noise from above when Kat was at the party.

She hurried upstairs, rushing to the spare bedroom where she had set up her makeshift surveillance station. The kettle was still warm from earlier, her half-empty mug sitting on the windowsill. But Kat ignored it, desperately trying to think on her feet.

Unable to pull herself away from the window, Kat watched as Clara's guest left the house soon followed by Clara herself. But she didn't get into her car, instead she walked purposefully in the direction of the tube station. Her steps were hurried, her face unusually tense. She didn't have Charlie with her, something that struck Kat as odd. Clara always took the dog when she went out. Where could she be going?

Just as Kat wondered if she should follow, her phone buzzed. The name "Luke" flashed on the screen, sending a jolt of anxiety through her. She hadn't heard from him since Sandra's funeral, and the cryptic message that appeared now did little to soothe her nerves:

> He's found me.

Luke had been silent for days, and now this? What did he mean? Who had found what?

Kat stared at her mobile, half expecting another message, but nothing came. She dialled Luke's number. No answer. She tried again, each ring echoing in the silence, amplifying her sense of dread. After everything Luke had been through—the trauma with Sandra, her death, the cryptic details he'd hinted at—had something finally caught up with him? Or had he spiralled so far out of control that he was no longer even coherent?

Kat rushed to get dressed, her nerves shot. The

journey to Luke's flat felt interminable, every passing minute adding to her anxiety. By the time she reached Russell Square, her heart was pounding. As before, she waited for someone to leave before clambering inside. She climbed the stairs to his flat, her stomach twisted in knots as her thoughts ricocheted in all directions. What if something had happened to him?

He's found me…

When she finally arrived at Luke's door, she stopped short. It was slightly ajar. Her breath caught in her throat as she hesitated, her hand hovering above the handle. She called his name softly, barely above a whisper. No reply. The hallway was silent, save for the distant hum of traffic. She glanced around nervously but saw no one. Should she go in?

Her fingers gripped the edge of the door, and she gently pushed it open, the hinges creaking as it swung inward. The flat was dark, the stale air carrying an odour that made her gag. Something felt very wrong. The last time she visited, Luke's place was a mess, but not this bad. Piled-up laundry overflowed from the corners, plates with dried food were scattered across the table, and there was an overwhelming sense that no one had cleaned in weeks.

Her nerves frayed, Kat moved cautiously through the flat, calling Luke's name again. Still no answer. Her stomach twisted as she made her way farther inside. The stench of neglect grew stronger as she passed between the kitchen and the living room. It wasn't just messy, it felt abandoned, like someone had left in a hurry, with no intention of returning. Taking out her phone, she dialled Luke's number once more.

Suddenly, a sharp sound broke the eerie silence. Kat jumped, her pulse skyrocketing. She quickly realised it was a phone ringing. Luke's phone, from somewhere inside. She followed the sound, her hands trembling as she traced it to the bedroom. Pushing open the door, her eyes landed on the source of the ringing: his mobile lying on the unmade bed. She picked it up, her breath catching when she saw the screen. Four missed calls. All from her.

Panic tightened its grip on her as she stared at the mobile. Luke had clearly left in a hurry, but where had he gone, and why hadn't he taken his phone? Her head reeled with implications, filled with horrible possibilities.

He's found me…

Luke's cryptic message replayed in her mind, adding to the growing fear. She turned, scanning the room for any clue that might explain his sudden disappearance. The scattered clothes, the unwashed dishes—everything pointed to a man on the run, fleeing from something, someone. But what, who?

Kat's thoughts were spinning, the pieces of the puzzle refusing to fit together. And then, as her panic reached a fever pitch, her own phone buzzed. She pulled it from her pocket, her hand shaking as she saw an unknown number flashing on the screen.

She hesitated before answering.

"Hello?" she said, her voice barely steady.

There was a pause on the other end, followed by a familiar voice. "Mrs Chapman?"

Her blood froze.

It was Officer Anderson.

"Where are you right now?" his voice held a strange tension.

"I'm… I'm out. Why? What's going on?" Kat asked, her stomach lurching with dread.

"When you're home, call me. We'll be right over." The line went dead.

Kat's heart raced as her thoughts spun out of control.

Truth Lies Beneath

The police were coming. Something was terribly wrong. She looked down at Luke's phone again, the four missed calls staring back at her like a silent accusation. What was she supposed to do? Could she really tell the police everything she knew, everything she suspected?

Her hand went to her throat, trying to steady her breathing as the weight of the situation pressed down on her.

53

Kat hurried home, Luke's mobile clutched in her trembling hand. The air felt dense around her, each breath shallow, each step heavier than the last. She had grabbed the phone without thinking, her mind a blur of panic and confusion. But now, she wasn't even sure why. What was she trying to hide? Her calls to him? But what if Luke wasn't dead? What if he came back? How would he contact her without his phone? She wrestled with the questions swirling within her, but they all led to the same conclusion: she was losing control.

As she neared her street, something caught her attention, snapping her out of her thoughts. A dark car was parked outside her house, its presence sending a wave of dread through her. The police. They were already there, waiting. Kat's stomach twisted as her head spun in frantic disbelief. She had told them she would call as soon as she got home, within the hour. But now, standing in front of the car, she knew the situation was more serious than she had previously considered.

The car doors opened, and Officers Anderson and Rodriguez stepped out, their expressions unreadable. Kat's pulse quickened further still, and her immediate thought was of Tom. She still hadn't collected him. What time had she told Lauren she would pick him up? She was neglecting her own son, lost in her labyrinth of fear and secrets, and now she was being pulled deeper.

"Good morning, Mrs Chapman," Officer Anderson greeted, his voice calm but laced with tension.

Kat tried to steady herself, her legs shaky as she ushered them inside. As she closed the door, her gaze darted across the street. There it was again, movement in the upstairs window of Clara's house. A shadow, flickering like a ghost. How many times had she seen it now? It always seemed to appear when she felt most vulnerable, most watched. Or most insecure?

"Would you like some coffee?" Kat offered, her voice brittle and thin.

Both officers shook their heads. "No, thank you," Rodriguez said.

They gestured for her to sit, and she obeyed, her hand trembling as she tried to settle into the chair. She quickly tucked it into her lap, hoping they hadn't noticed, but Officer Anderson's sharp eyes missed nothing.

"Mrs Chapman," he began, his voice now more direct. "We need to talk about a recent development."

Kat's heart hammered in her chest. She knew what they were going to say. It had to be Luke. He was dead, just like Sandra in the canal. Just like all the others.

But it wasn't what she expected.

"We've had the forensic results from the fire at Victoria's flat," Rodriguez continued. "It was started deliberately."

Deliberately? Kat's mind went blank for a moment. That wasn't possible. That fire, it had been an accident. Who was she kidding? She breathed deeply, trying to regain her composure, but her body betrayed her. She felt the corner of her mouth twitch, an involuntary urge to laugh. What was wrong with her? Why couldn't she react the way a normal person would?

"I'm not sure I understand," Kat said, her voice low, almost detached.

Rodriguez leaned forward, his gaze narrowing. "It's all too much of a coincidence, Mrs Chapman. The fire, then Sandra Law's death. Not to mention the deaths of your parents."

Kat felt her blood turn to ice. Her parents?

"My parents' deaths aren't suspicious," she said, her voice stiff. "My mum fell and had bleeding on the brain. My dad... he couldn't cope after she passed."

But even as she spoke, she heard her mother's voice echo in her mind—*I was pushed*. Kat had brushed it off, convincing herself everybody would believe it was the delusion of an ageing woman, even though she knew she was herself indulging in just that: denial. And her father. The combination of whiskey and painkillers. More than he should have. And yet, at the time, she'd pushed the obvious underneath the rug. Denial. As if not thinking about it would somehow make it untrue.

"It doesn't look good, Mrs Chapman," Anderson said, his tone neutral, but the weight of his words undeniable. "There's a pattern here, one that ties back to you and your family time and time again."

Kat's stomach churned, her mouth as dry as dust. She had been expecting this moment, in some form or another, for months. How had she ever expected to get away with it? Adam had killed Liam, Bob, Pauline, and

Mark Harris. They were all tied to him. And then Imogen. Down to her. But she had got away with it. She had to keep calm. Nobody could prove anything.

She couldn't say a word. Not without implicating herself. Not without revealing everything.

Anderson leant back in his chair, glancing at Rodriguez before he spoke again. "Where were you, Mrs Chapman, when the fire started at Victoria's flat?"

Kat's heart thudded so loudly she could hardly think. The question hung heavy, almost absurd in its simplicity, but its implications were terrifying. Where had she been?

"And Sandra Law too," Rodriguez added with a twist of the knife. "The night she *fell* into the canal."

"I—" Kat faltered. She tapped her fingers against the table in rapid succession, trying to remember where she had been, what she had been doing at the times these people had died. The timelines blurred together, and suddenly she felt trapped. Was she imagining things, or was there something she'd missed? Had she been at the wrong place at the wrong time too many times? Or had someone else orchestrated this, using her as the perfect scapegoat?

"I wasn't there when they died," Kat finally said, her voice small but firm. "You can check. I wasn't involved."

Anderson raised an eyebrow, but he didn't say anything immediately. Instead, he let the silence stretch, the tension in the room palpable. It was clear they weren't buying her answers, at least not yet.

Rodriguez spoke up again, his tone quieter but no less forceful. "You know, Mrs Chapman, people around you seem to have a habit of ending up dead. And right now, it's all pointing to you."

Kat felt the walls closing in. They were suspicious of

her—that much was certain—but they didn't have enough. Not yet. She had to keep it that way.

"I have nothing to hide," Kat said, standing abruptly. "I told you everything I know. I'll cooperate fully, but I'm not responsible for their deaths."

She could see the doubt lingering in their eyes, and they weren't quite finished.

54

Kat stood frozen as the officers' expressions darkened. Anderson's words hung in the air, thick with implication. "We'll be back soon," he said, his eyes narrowing as if assessing her every twitch. "And next time, we'll need an alibi."

Kat's stomach lurched. Alibi? She couldn't breathe. Were they accusing her? "Am I a suspect?" she asked, forcing herself to meet Anderson's gaze, though she could feel her body trembling.

"No, not yet," Anderson replied, his voice low and neutral, but the look in his eyes said otherwise. His partner, Rodriguez, shifted beside him, his face unreadable. They weren't saying it, but Kat could sense it. They suspected her. How could they not? The string of deaths, the strange coincidences—they were all weaving a noose around her neck. Why hadn't she acted before?

Retribution.

Kat swallowed hard, trying to keep herself together, but her fear was mounting. She needed to stay calm, needed to think. Then Anderson's gaze fell on the kitchen counter. "Whose phone is that? You keep yours in a blue case, don't you?"

Her heart leapt. Luke's phone. She cursed inwardly. She had been so careful, or so she thought, but in her panic, she had left it sitting there in plain view. "Oh, that… it's, uh… it's a colleague's," she stammered, her voice weak. "He left it at the office. I was going to return it."

The officers exchanged a look, a silent exchange that screamed louder than words. They didn't believe a word she was saying. They knew she was lying.

Rodriguez folded his arms. "You know, Mrs Chapman, keeping the truth from the police is a crime in itself. Is there something else you're not telling us?"

Kat felt her pulse in her throat. What could she say? She was cornered, and the walls were closing in. "No… no, it's just a phone," she managed, but her voice wavered, betraying her.

Anderson leant forward, his tone sharper. "Mrs Chapman. We need to know if there's anything, anything at all, you're hiding. Believe me, now would be the time to come clean."

Kat opened her mouth to say something, anything, but the words wouldn't come. Her mind swirled with confusion, trying to figure out how to explain herself. And then, in her desperation, she blurted out something she hadn't intended to. "There's a woman across the street. Clara Denton. She's been watching me."

The officers paused, their attention now fully on her. "Watching you?" Rodriguez asked, his brow furrowing. "What's your neighbour got to do with all this?"

Kat faltered. She hadn't thought it through. It sounded ridiculous, and she knew it, but she had already opened the door. "She… she's always around. She turned up at Sandra's funeral, when my parents were visiting, even when my mum died in the park. She had her dog… Charlie. She… she…" Kat was rambling, her words coming out faster than she could control.

Rodriguez cut in, his voice calm but sceptical. "You said earlier your mother's death was normal, given the circumstances. Now you're telling us your neighbour was there when she fell? Why would that matter?"

He said 'fell' as if in inverted comma's. Like he was ridiculing her.

Kat knew she was sinking deeper, but she couldn't stop herself. "She… I don't know, but she's been watching me. Every time something happens, Clara's there. I think she's involved in all of it. She even had Tom, my son, walk her dog. She's always turning up when I least expect it, like she's… like she's planning something."

The officers exchanged another glance, and Kat could see the amusement in their eyes. They didn't believe her. It sounded absurd, even to her own ears. She was making things worse.

"And she threw a party," Kat added, her voice breaking. "A party where everyone was dressed up, and she told me to come casual. I looked ridiculous. She humiliated me."

There was a moment of silence, and then the officers laughed. It wasn't cruel, but it wasn't kind either. Anderson shook his head. "Mrs Chapman. Are you seriously suggesting that because your neighbour made you feel out of place at a party, she's part of some grand conspiracy?"

Kat's face flushed with humiliation. "No, I… that's not what I meant. I just… she's had the summerhouse taken down."

Rodriguez raised an eyebrow. "The summerhouse?

The one where Liam and Imogen Daley died? Where you struck Imogen in self-defence?"

Again, he emphasised the words that would cut the deepest.

Kat froze. She had said too much. She had brought up the summerhouse, and now she couldn't take it back. The officers' interest was piqued, their expressions shifting from amused to serious. Anderson's eyes bored into her.

"Did you say her name was Clara Denton?" Anderson asked slowly, turning to Rodriguez.

Kat nodded, unsure of where this was going.

"Is she a financial advisor?"

"Uh-huh? Why does that—"

Anderson leant back, crossing his arms. "That's interesting. Clara Denton… my wife knows her. She's the financial advisor my wife uses."

Kat stopped in her tracks, stunned. It was as though the ground beneath her had opened up. Clara was even connected to the fucking police officer sat opposite her.

"Your wife?" Kat asked, her voice barely above a whisper.

Anderson nodded, his expression casual but deliberate. "Yes, my wife's a neurologist at University College Hospital."

That place again.

"She works privately. Clara Denton's been handling her financial affairs for a while now. Says she's very good at what she does."

Of course she fucking is.

Kat felt the walls closing in again. "So… that's it? You're just going to let her off because she handles your wife's books?" Her voice had a sharp edge to it, panic morphing into anger. They were all in this together, weren't they?

Rodriguez's face turned stony. "Being facetious isn't going to help you, Mrs Chapman. We're trying to assist you, but if you keep making these wild accusations, we're going to look at this in a different light."

Kat's breath quickened. They weren't going to believe her. They were going to let Clara off completely. Not even question her. She had to do something, but what?

Anderson stood. "We'll have a word with Ms Denton. See if there's anything there. But you'd do well to cooperate with us fully. This situation isn't looking good for you, Mrs Chapman."

Kat watched as the officers made their way to the door, her heart hammering in her chest. She followed them outside, watching as they stepped across the street towards Clara's house. She knew they wouldn't find anything. Clara was too smart, too calculating. The police would speak to her, ask a few questions, and then they'd leave. And she'd get away with it. All of it.

Kat closed the door, sickened by the grin etched across Clara's face as she welcomed the officers. If Kat was going to clear her name, she knew she couldn't rely on the police. She'd have to do it herself.

55

Kat stood at her upstairs window, her eyes fixed across the street, waiting impatiently for the officers to leave. Her mind wandered back to something the police had told her on a previous visit. A white BMW had been found with damage consistent with a hit-and-run. They hadn't mentioned it earlier, which left Kat wondering if they'd dismissed it from their investigation. Could that car still be important? Kat cursed herself for not asking more questions; she should have clarified everything to clear her name, but she had been too rattled to think straight.

She tried to recollect; had Adam, during his dark, erratic last months, ever mentioned a white BMW to the police? She sifted through the haze of her memories, trying to pull something relevant from the fragments of their conversations. Nothing came to mind. Adam had been too far gone at that point, spiralling out of control faster than she could keep track of. But had there been any mention of that car? A nagging sense of guilt crept up on her as she struggled to remember.

Her thoughts were interrupted as she glanced back at

Clara's house. The police were already leaving, and as she had feared, laughing as they walked away from Clara's door. Even from this distance, she could see Clara's smug expression as she called out to say something to the officers. Then all three of them turned to look at Kat's property. They were laughing again, their easy camaraderie clear as they waved Clara a cheerful goodbye and got into their car.

Kat's face burned with anger and humiliation. Clara had them wrapped around her little finger, just as Kat knew she would. There was no question now: Clara could get away with anything, even murder. The police clearly knew her, and any doubts Kat had raised about Clara were obviously being dismissed as nothing more than paranoid ramblings.

As Kat was about to retreat from the window, Clara looked up directly at her. Their eyes locked for a moment, and then Clara waved, a sweet, mocking gesture that made Kat's skin crawl. As if that weren't enough, Clara raised her hand to her lips and mimed a cup, beckoning Kat to come over for coffee.

Kat felt a surge of panic, but she knew she had no choice. To refuse would be to admit that she sent the officers over because she believed Clara to be guilty. So, despite the dread pooling in her stomach, Kat reluctantly left her house and crossed the street.

Clara met her at the door with a smile that didn't reach her eyes. "Come in, Kat," she said cheerfully, stepping aside to let her enter. "The police just left. But of course, you already know that, don't you?"

Kat froze in the doorway. Clara's tone had shifted ever so slightly; there was a sharp edge to it. It wasn't the friendly invitation she'd made it out to be. Clara was baiting her.

"I… I thought maybe you'd seen something," Kat stammered as she stepped inside, trying to gather her composure. "I just sent them over in case—"

"In case I'd seen something?" Clara interrupted, her voice dripping with scepticism. Her smile was gone now, replaced by a cool, calculating look. "Kat, why would you send the police to my house? If you've got something to accuse me of, why don't you just say it to my face?"

Kat's throat went dry. She had walked right into a trap, and now Clara was closing in. "I… I wasn't accusing you of anything," she said quickly, her voice trembling. "I just… I had to think on my feet. I was scared. The police think I'm involved somehow, and I—"

Clara cut her off again, this time with a laugh. It wasn't a warm laugh; it was a sharp, almost cruel sound. "You think they're going to pin all of these deaths on you?" Clara shook her head in mock sympathy. "Well, Kat, I can't say I blame them. There have been an awful lot of people getting killed surrounding you, haven't there?"

Kat's heart raced. This was it. Clara was cornering her, and there was no way out. She had spent too long avoiding the truth, too long pretending that she wasn't in over her head. Now it was all coming out.

They continued to stumble through a stilted conversation, Clara's mood switching erratically between cheerful and accusatory, like a pendulum swinging between extremes. One moment, she was making light of the situation, the next, her eyes were dark, filled with accusation. Kat could barely keep up, and she was growing more and more desperate to escape the suffocating tension.

Finally, Kat saw her opening. "I should really go," she said abruptly, rising from her chair. "I need to collect Tom."

Clara's eyes followed her as she stood, but she didn't protest. Instead, she simply nodded and said, "Of course. Tom needs his mother."

As Kat moved towards the door, something caught her eye—a vase of yellow roses sitting prominently on Clara's dining room table. The flowers were striking, their bright yellow petals catching the light in the otherwise subdued room. Without thinking, Kat said, "They're pretty. I didn't know you liked yellow roses?"

Clara glanced where Kat's eyes were set, a small smile playing on her lips. "A friend sent them," she said. "Just a little gesture. Why? Is there a problem?"

Kat's blood ran cold. Yellow roses. They were Imogen's favourite. Imogen Daley, the woman who had died in her summerhouse—the same summerhouse that Clara had torn down. Was Clara mocking her from every perceivable angle?

Kat forced a smile and mumbled something vague before making a hasty exit. As she stepped outside into the warm air, her mind whirled. Whatever game Clara was playing, she was winning. And Kat was rapidly running out of moves.

56

Kat drove to Lauren's house with an unsettled feeling, her mind buzzing with all that had happened over the past few hours. She was desperate to collect Tom and get home. She had to act fast, find answers. However, she knew she had to maintain appearances. Lauren had been a close friend, and Kat couldn't afford to alienate her—especially now.

When she arrived, Lauren greeted her warmly and invited her inside. "The kids are playing upstairs," Lauren said, gesturing towards the staircase with a smile.

Kat nodded, her mind already racing ahead. She'd have preferred not to linger, just wanted to grab Tom and go, but she forced a smile, knowing that rushing out might raise questions she didn't want to answer. "Thanks for looking after him," she said, her voice strained but polite.

As they settled into the kitchen, Lauren made them both a cup of coffee. Kat couldn't hold it in any longer. The tension was unbearable, and she needed to talk to someone, anyone, about what was happening. "The police were at my house today," Kat began, setting her mug down with a slight tremor in her hand. "They're asking a lot of questions. About all the people who've died. And they said Vicky's flat fire was started deliberately."

Lauren's face remained calm, but Kat noticed a subtle shift. Her friend's posture stiffened ever so slightly, and though she listened attentively, there was a flicker of something in her eyes; something like doubt, or was it fear of who sat opposite her?

"They asked if I had anything to do with it," Kat continued, her voice trembling. "They think I'm somehow involved in all these deaths."

At first, Lauren seemed empathetic, leaning forward as if to comfort her, but then she slowly pulled back, both physically and emotionally. "I mean, it doesn't look good, Kat," Lauren said, choosing her words carefully. "All these things happening around you. What are you going to do?"

Kat could hear the hesitancy in her voice, and panic welled up inside her. Lauren wasn't convinced. "I think it's Clara," Kat blurted out, her voice rising with urgency. "I don't know how, but she's involved. She's manipulating people, even the police! And all the blame is going to fall on me."

Lauren gave a nervous laugh, shaking her head. "Clara? Kat, she's one of the most delightful people I've ever met. I can't imagine her being involved in something like this."

Kat's frustration boiled over. "That's exactly it! She's too perfect, too sweet. Can't you see it? She's playing everyone… making sure I take the fall."

Before Lauren could respond, the doorbell rang, echoing through the house. Lauren froze, her eyes widening in surprise. There was something in her expression that unsettled Kat. She looked almost afraid of who it might be.

"I'll be right back," Lauren said, getting up from the table. Her movements were quick, nervous, and she shot Kat a glance before closing the kitchen door behind her.

Kat sat in the silence, her heart pounding. Something wasn't right. Why had Lauren looked so uneasy about someone calling round?

Curiosity got the better of her, and Kat crept to the kitchen door, pressing her ear against the frame. She could just make out the sound of Lauren's voice in the hallway, but the words were muffled. Then she heard Lauren's voice, light and cheerful. "They're beautiful. Thank you."

Kat's stomach lurched. Beautiful? What was Lauren talking about? She strained to listen, but the conversation ended quickly, and she barely had time to scurry back to her seat before Lauren re-entered the kitchen, carrying an enormous bouquet of yellow roses.

"Look at these," Lauren said, her voice tinged with delight. "Aren't they beautiful?"

Kat's breath caught in her throat as she stared at the flowers. Yellow roses. The exact same kind she had seen on Clara's table less than an hour ago. A chill ran through her. This wasn't a coincidence. It couldn't be.

"Where did they come from?" Kat asked, trying to keep her voice steady.

Lauren shrugged, setting the vase on the counter. "They were just delivered. No note, though. Isn't that odd?"

Odd wasn't the word Kat would have used. Terrifying was more like it. There was no way it was a random delivery. Clara had to be behind it. She knew Kat was going to

Lauren's house to collect Tom. She'd just told her so. And she'd sent identical flowers to mess with her.

"They're the same," Kat muttered, almost to herself.

Lauren frowned. "The same as what?"

Kat swallowed, feeling the weight of her suspicions crushing down on her. "The same as the ones Clara has on her table. She said they were from a friend."

Lauren's smile faltered, and a flicker of doubt crossed her face. She glanced back at the flowers, her brow furrowing slightly. "That's a strange coincidence," she admitted, though her tone lacked conviction.

Kat leant forward, her voice low and urgent. "It's not a coincidence, Lauren. Clara knew I was coming here. She's messing with me, making sure I know she's always one step ahead."

Lauren's scepticism returned, though now it was tinged with unease. "Kat, that's a little farfetched, don't you think? I mean, how could she possibly have flowers arranged for delivery within the hour?"

Kat shook her head, her thoughts spiralling out of control. "You don't understand. She's been doing this for weeks. She's always there, always watching. And now, she's got the police on her side, they're not going to believe anything I say."

Lauren looked down at her hands, the air between her and Kat thick with tension. She seemed to consider Kat's words, but the doubt still lingered in her eyes. "I don't know," she said quietly. "This all sounds… it sounds like you're totally overreacting."

Kat felt a stab of betrayal. She had hoped that Lauren, of all people, would understand, but now it seemed like she was losing her too. "I'm not overreacting, Lauren," she insisted, her voice desperate. "I'm telling you, Clara is dangerous. And if I don't figure out what she's up to, I'm going to take the fall for everything."

Lauren sighed, standing up from the table. "Look, I don't know what's going on. But maybe you need to take a step back. You're coming across a little unhinged, if you don't mind me saying. Do you think you might need help, you know, from a professional?"

Kat's frustration boiled over, but she bit her tongue. She couldn't push Lauren any further. Not now. Instead, she stood and forced a smile. "You're probably right," she said, though her mind was racing with plans.

57

SITTING in the driver's seat, Kat's knuckles were white against the steering wheel, her mind buzzing with chaotic thoughts. Clara. The flowers. The laughing with the police officers. She was surrounded, suffocated by these tiny, seemingly insignificant details, but they were all connected to one person. The woman was everywhere, involved in everything, and yet no one believed Kat. Not even her best friend.

Her eyes flickered to the rear-view mirror, catching Tom's reflection in the backseat. He was staring out of the window, oblivious to the storm brewing inside his mum's head. But what should have concerned her the most was that she didn't even care.

A thought flashed through her mind, one she never believed she would have entertained: the stupid dog. That fluffy little mutt that belonged to Clara. She could picture it—Charlie, darting into the street, thrown under a bus. The thought made her chuckle. It was a dark, hysterical laugh that bubbled up from her chest unexpectedly.

"Mummy?" Tom's voice cut through her reverie. "What's so funny?"

She froze, realising what just happened. She had laughed out loud. The sound was alien to her ears, unhinged and unfamiliar. She glanced back at Tom again, seeing his eyes wide with confusion in the rear-view mirror. For a moment, she barely recognised her own son.

But something else tugged at the edges of her mind, something she'd never really asked about: Lauren's mum. Why had it never occurred to her before? Why didn't she know more about the woman?

She turned sharply in her seat, trying to shake off the thought of the dog, trying to focus on something, anything, that made sense. "Tom," she said, her voice too sharp, too urgent. "What's Lauren's mum like?"

Tom shifted uncomfortably in the backseat, sensing the tension in his mother's tone. "I don't know," he muttered, turning his gaze back to the window.

"That's not an answer," Kat snapped. "Tell me. What's she like?"

"I said I don't know!" Tom's voice was rising now, defensive, as though he could sense that something was very wrong with his mum.

Kat gripped the steering wheel tighter, trying to keep her frustration in check. "It is my business. I'm your mother," she hissed. "Now tell me, what's Lauren's mum like?"

Tom hesitated, looking uncomfortable, and then, after a pause, he muttered, "It's a secret."

Kat's eyes flashed with anger. "A secret? What kind of secret? You're not going to see her again if you can't tell me." Her voice was rising, frantic now, as if somehow knowing that detail would give her some control over the madness swirling in her life.

Before she could press him further, they arrived home. Tom bolted out of the car the second it stopped, running to the front door. Kat sat in the driver's seat for a moment, her heart pounding. She shouldn't have lost her temper, but it was all slipping through her fingers—everything.

She got out and followed Tom into the house. He dumped his bag on the kitchen table and darted upstairs without a word. "Tom!" she called after him, her voice shrill, but he didn't respond. "Come back down!" she shouted, but her words were lost in the silence.

Then something outside caught her eye. In the rear garden.

The terracotta pot.

It was missing.

Kat stood frozen, staring at the empty space where the pot had once been. The very same pot Adam had accused her of moving. Back then, she'd believed it was part of his alien and confused state. But now, it really was gone. The hole by the fence where it used to sit was just an empty patch of dirt.

Her hands trembling, Kat moved to the table where Tom's bag sat. She unzipped it, her mind on autopilot, ready to pull out his dirty laundry. But as she reached inside, her fingers brushed against paper instead of clothes. She pulled out a stack of drawings, her heart skipping a beat.

At first, they seemed innocent enough—just childish scribbles. But as she looked closer, her chest tightened. They were more drawings of people. Familiar people.

Imogen. Adam. And a vase of yellow roses.

Kat's hands shook as she shuffled through the pictures, her breath coming in short gasps. She'd thought this was all over. Tom hadn't mentioned or drawn them for weeks. But there was Imogen, drawn in bright colours, standing in a garden—her garden. Another drawing showed the summerhouse. Another picture showed them at a bar, drinking. No doubt Tom's visualisation of the Sunset Bar.

No. No, no, no.

Kat's mind reeled as she frantically tossed the drawings onto the table, the floor, scattering them in her panic. Why was Tom still drawing these things?

Was this some sort of sick joke?

Her chest tightened, a mad, high-pitched laugh bubbling up again. The kind of laugh that you can't stop once it starts. She was losing it, slipping into a place she couldn't control.

"Mummy! Stop!" Tom's voice broke through the chaos.

She looked up to see her son standing in the doorway, tears streaming down his face. He was screaming at her, begging her to stop.

But she couldn't stop. She was too far gone. Her hands frantically collected the drawings, ripping them up one by one, tearing them into pieces.

"Mummy, please!" Tom cried, his voice desperate now, but Kat couldn't hear him. She was lost in the whirlwind of her own mind, her own panic.

And then, the doorbell rang.

The sound cut through the madness, freezing both Kat and Tom in place. For a moment, everything was silent.

Then Charlie, Clara's stupid dog, started barking from outside, his yapping carrying through the quiet. The doorbell rang again, more insistent this time.

Kat looked at Tom, who was standing frozen, his eyes

red and puffy. She slowly dropped the shredded drawings onto the floor, her hands trembling.

Walking along the hallway in a daze, her heart pounded in her chest. As she reached for the doorknob, her hand hesitated, hovering there for just a moment. She took a deep breath and opened the door.

There, standing on her doorstep, was the last person she wanted to see.

Clara.

58

Clara stood expressionless on the doorstep, Charlie's leash in her hand. The dog barked in quick, yipping bursts that seemed to pierce straight through Kat's skull, like tiny needles stabbing at her temples. Clara's face turned to her usual perfect politeness, but Kat saw the real expression underneath: smugness, deceit, betrayal.

"I heard shouting," Clara said, her voice calm but her eyes darting to Tom, who stood behind Kat. "I was taking Charlie for a walk and just wanted to check if everything was alright."

Kat felt the rage bubbling under her skin. Clara, with her fake smile and perfectly crafted concern, always inserting herself where she didn't belong. How fucking dare she?

She opened her mouth to tell Clara to leave, to stay out of their lives, but before she could speak, Tom rushed forward and pressed his face into Clara's side, as though seeking comfort. He clung to her the way he used to cling to Kat, and the sight sent a jolt of panic through her chest.

But instead of being offended, Kat started to laugh. The sound was harsh, jagged. It spilled out of her uncontrollably, and Clara stared, startled.

"You want to take Charlie for a walk?" Kat finally asked Tom, her voice trembling with unhinged amusement. "By all means. Take him. Go for a long walk. Take your time."

Charlie barked again, the sound scraping through Kat's nerves like chalk on a board, making her wince. Clara looked uncertain, but she smiled down at Tom, running a hand through his hair.

"Shall we, Tom?" she whispered. "Come on, let's go for a little walk."

Kat nodded rapidly, her laughter dying down but her breaths still coming out in short, shallow gasps. "Yes, yes, go. Get out of here. Go!" Her voice rose sharply, startling them both.

Clara gave her a last, wary glance before she led Tom and Charlie down the path, their figures shrinking into the distance. The barking faded, but the echoes remained, bouncing around Kat's head like ghosts of sound.

She had a plan.

The moment they were out of sight, she ran across the street, heart pounding in her chest. Clara's house loomed before her, its neat garden and pristine windows mocking her.

She's hiding something.

Kat could feel it in her bones, crawling under her skin, whispering in her ears.

She circled around to the rear of the house, breaths coming fast and shallow. The back door was locked, of course. Clara was meticulous. But Kat noticed something, a window above the kitchen sink, open just enough for a small hand to reach inside. She grinned, a wild, unhinged grin. Clara had slipped up. Finally.

Kat ran to the shed where she knew Liam and Imogen used to store their tools. Her mind was everywhere, memories flashing by in a blur. The terracotta pot, the drawings spilling out of Tom's bag, the way Clara had smiled at the police officers like they were all in on something, some grand conspiracy against her. Yellow fucking roses wherever she went.

The ladder was still there, buried under old garden tools. She dragged it out; the metal clanging loudly, but Kat didn't care. No one was watching. Clara wasn't there to stop her.

As she hauled the ladder back to the house, her breath hitched, heart hammering in her chest. What was she even looking for? She didn't know, but it didn't matter. She needed to prove that Clara was behind it all. The deaths, the police, the fire. It was all her.

Kat propped the ladder against the wall, her hands trembling as she climbed. The window was small, just large enough for her to slip her hand through. She reached inside, stretching her arm as far as it would go, her fingers brushing against the latch of the larger window below. She fumbled, fingers slipping, frustration mounting.

Come on, come on!

Her pulse pounded in her ears, louder than Charlie's barking, louder than Tom's screams. She stretched farther, her ribs pressing painfully against the windowsill, but she couldn't reach it. Her fingers scraped uselessly against the latch.

Tears pricked at her eyes, blurring her vision. Everything was slipping away.

But she couldn't let Clara win.

With a burst of desperation, Kat pushed her body farther, her foot sliding slightly on the rung of the ladder. She steadied herself just in time and made one last effort, her fingers finally catching on the latch.

Click.

The latch gave way.

Kat grinned, her breath coming in ragged gasps, and pushed the window outwards. The hinges groaned as it opened fully, and she scrambled back down the ladder, her heart pumping in triumph.

She glanced around the garden, ensuring no one was there.

With shaking hands, Kat pulled the window open wider and clambered up onto the kitchen counter, her legs awkwardly wedging themselves through the gap. The sharp edge of the sink dug into her stomach, but she ignored the pain, her mind laser-focused on getting inside.

She kicked her legs, wriggling farther, feeling the warm air of the house brush against her face as she forced her entire body through the opening. One foot found the counter below, then the other. She scrambled the rest of the way inside, her breath hitching as she finally stood on the cold tiles of Clara's kitchen floor.

Her chest heaved with the effort of it all, the adrenaline still coursing through her. She stood there, frozen for a moment, taking it all in.

The kitchen was immaculate. Gleaming surfaces, spotless floors, everything perfect in its place. The scent of lavender wafted faintly through the air, the smell so distinctly Clara that it made Kat's skin crawl.

She lingered in the centre of the room, her breath still ragged, her heart pounding in her ears.

What now?

She didn't even know what she was looking for, but

the tension in her chest told her that something was there, something important, something that could clear her name and finally reveal Clara's treachery.

Kat stood in the silence of the house, her breath coming in shallow gasps, her fingers twitching at her sides. There had to be something. There had to be.

59

Kat took a few tentative steps, glancing around the pristine space. The counters gleamed under the sunlight filtering through the window. Everything was in its place —too perfect, too controlled, just like Clara herself.

Kat yanked open a drawer. Inside were rows of utensils, neatly lined up. Nothing. She slammed it shut, her pulse racing faster. Another drawer, this one filled with neatly folded kitchen towels. Useless.

What am I even looking for? she thought wildly.

Her head twitched, and she hurried to the dining room, her fingers involuntarily fluttering at her sides. The memories hit her like a wave the second she stepped in— Adam, Imogen, Liam, all sitting at the table, laughing. The way Imogen's eyes would sparkle when she caught Adam's gaze, the way Liam would lean back in his chair with that knowing smirk. And then there was Kat, always on the outside, always watching, always second. The room felt alive with the ghosts of those moments, replaying over and over in her mind like a broken reel of film.

She could almost hear their laughter. Kat squeezed her eyes shut, trying to force the memories away, but they only got louder. She opened her eyes again and saw them—yellow roses, bright and defiant, just like Imogen had always loved. And now Clara had the very same bouquet on her dining table.

Her breath caught, and for a brief moment, her focus sharpened. Those flowers.

Kat bolted up the stairs, her legs carrying her faster than she could think. When she arrived at the landing, she hesitated. Adam had slept with Imogen here. She stared at the bedroom door, her hand trembling as she reached for the handle.

Why am I even doing this? a voice in her head asked, but she ignored it. The door creaked open, and there it was—the bed. Not the same bed, but a bed, nonetheless. The place where Adam had betrayed her. She could see it now, his body pressed against Imogen's, the sheets tangled around them.

Her head twitched violently this time, and she let out a low, guttural sound. It was as if the image of them was tattooed on her brain, a memory she couldn't scrub away no matter how hard she tried. She stumbled back, clutching her chest, her breath ragged.

"Stop it, stop it, stop it," she muttered under her breath, her voice rising to a frantic whisper. She pressed her hands to her temples, as if trying to squeeze out the recollection, but it wouldn't go away.

Suddenly, as if desperate to escape her own mind, Kat ran into Clara's bedroom—Imogen and Liam's old room. She threw open the wardrobe doors, her hands frantically rifling through Clara's clothes, her breath coming in uneven gasps. She didn't know what she was looking for, but she had to find something, anything.

But there was nothing.

She slammed the wardrobe doors shut and moved to the chest of drawers, pulling each one out with shaky hands. Clothes. Jewellery. The mundane items of everyday life. No clues, no hidden evidence, just normal, boring things. It made her sick.

"What the hell was I thinking?" she spat, her voice breaking. She was a fool. She had convinced herself that Clara's house would hold all the answers, but she was just chasing shadows, digging herself deeper into a pit of madness with every step she took.

Her heart pounded in her chest, her thoughts twisting into a chaotic jumble. The house felt suffocating, the walls pressing in on her. She had to get out.

Kat turned and practically ran down the stairs, each step feeling heavier than the last. Her brain buzzed with static, and her vision blurred at the edges. When she reached the kitchen again, she saw the key hanging in the back door. She took a deep breath, trying to steady her shaking hands, and walked over to it.

She slammed the window shut—the same one she had crawled through minutes before—and unlocked the door, stepping outside. The cool air hit her, but it did nothing to soothe the chaos in her mind. Her thoughts were a tangled mess, a storm she could no longer control.

As she crossed the street back to her own house, her legs felt weak, her steps uneven. How could she ever prove herself innocent if she couldn't find anything incriminating? Clara was too smart, too careful. She had hidden all the evidence, orchestrated everything perfectly. Kat could feel herself being pushed further and further into the role of the guilty party, and there was nothing she could do to stop it.

Once inside her house, she felt a sudden wave of

exhaustion crash over her. She stared blankly ahead, the scattered pieces of Tom's drawings still littering the kitchen table and floor. Kat moved to pick them up, her hands trembling as she shuffled the scraps of paper into a pile.

Her eyes flicked to the back garden, to the place where the terracotta pot had once sat. It was gone. Just like everything else. Nothing made sense anymore.

She stood there, dazed, staring at the empty spot where the pot had been. Her mind raced, jumping from one thought to the next. The pot, the drawings, the laughter, Clara's face, the yellow roses. It was all too much, all swirling together, blending into one big, incomprehensible mess.

And then, the doorbell rang.

Kat froze, her breath catching in her throat. Too early for Tom, she thought. He'd let himself in any way. And of course the stupid fucking dog would be barking insanely.

She ambled to the door, her heart pounding in her chest. When she opened it, her breath hitched.

It was Luke.

His beard was overgrown, his hair still a wild mess, just like the last time she'd seen him. His eyes were dark and shadowed, as if he hadn't slept in days. Neither of them spoke for a long moment. Kat just stared at him, her mind numb, unable to process what was happening.

Finally, she stepped aside to let him in.

In the kitchen, Luke turned to face her, his voice quiet but heavy. "He's back, Kat."

Kat's eyes narrowed. "Who?"

Luke's gaze was steady, his voice flat. "Adam."

60

She just stared at Luke, her mind reeling. "What the fuck are you talking about?" she asked, her voice angry.

Luke's words hung heavy in the air. The last time he had come over, he had muttered about someone watching him. *"I don't know who. But they're definitely there, watching me…"* he had said back then, his voice edged with paranoia. But now, Luke was putting a name to his stalker—Adam.

"He's not alive," Kat insisted, the panic rising in her chest. "He's not."

Luke's expression remained hollow. "I saw him, Kat. At the park, across the lake. He was there. Just… watching me." Luke's voice cracked. He ran a trembling hand through his tangled hair, his eyes wide, haunted. "Across the lake. He was staring, smiling, like he was mocking me." He paused, his breath shallow. "It was Adam."

Kat's heart pounded in her chest. It couldn't be true. It wasn't true. She had been there—they had all been there—at the cemetery, watching the coffin being lowered into the frozen January ground. She squeezed her eyes shut for a moment, willing herself to shake the creeping sense of unease. "Adam's dead, Luke. You were there. We all were. You saw him buried."

Luke shook his head slowly, his eyes bloodshot and unfocused. "I don't know what was in that coffin, but it wasn't Adam Chapman."

Kat froze, her breath catching in her throat. "What the fuck does that even mean?"

"It had to be weighted or something," Luke continued, his voice strained, like he was trying to convince himself. "He's out there, Kat. He's alive."

Kat felt like she was standing on the edge of a cliff, the earth beneath her crumbling. "That's impossible. We watched him go into the ground. I was there!"

But Luke wasn't listening. He stood suddenly, knocking his chair over as he paced the kitchen. "You need to get away, Kat. You and Tom. Leave everything behind. Just… go." His voice was frantic now, his eyes darting around the room as if someone might burst through the door at any second.

Kat felt the room spinning. "What about the business?" she asked, desperate to cling to something real, something concrete.

Luke let out a hollow laugh, turning to face her. "The business?" he scoffed. "When was the last time you even went to the office? It's over, Kat. Kathy called me. The business is in shambles. Customers are leaving. No one's written any code in weeks. It's finished."

Kat blinked, her mind struggling to process his words. The business? How had she let things get so bad? "No… that can't be true," she muttered, though even as she said it, she knew it was. She had been so caught up in the chaos of everything, she had barely noticed the crumbling of her professional life.

Luke took a step closer, his voice low, urgent. "You need to run before it's too late."

"I can't!" Kat snapped, her voice trembling. "The police are already watching me. They'd track me down in a heartbeat. They're looking for any excuse to arrest me!"

"They haven't got anything on you yet," Luke said, his expression hard. "But they will. If you stay here, they'll pin it all on you."

Kat shook her head. "No… no, I can't leave. I'm not running. I need to clear my name."

Luke gave her a long, pitying look. "There's no clearing your name, Kat. You're already guilty in their eyes." He paused, his face darkening. "Vicky's flat fire… you know that was no accident, don't you? Whoever started it knew Belinda and Nathan were inside too. It was deliberate. And you had the motive."

Kat's eyes widened, and she raked her fingers through her hair. "I know," she whispered. "I know it was deliberate. And I think…"

Luke's gaze was intense, his words clipped. "He's playing with you, Kat. If he really is behind all this, he's toying with you. You need to get out before it's too late."

But Kat couldn't move. She felt paralysed, rooted to the spot as the weight of everything pressed down on her. The fire. The deaths. The police. Clara. And now Luke, talking like Adam was still alive, lurking somewhere out there, waiting to strike. It was too much. Her head was spinning, her vision blurring as panic gripped her chest.

"I'm leaving," Luke continued, his voice hollow. "I'm packing up and getting as far away from here as I can. You should do the same."

"You've got it all wrong," Kat found herself saying,

although the words didn't appear to belong to her. She'd had that sensation before, but this time it felt more real.

"Then ask Prakash."

Kat stood perfectly still, her heart pounding in her ears. She couldn't run. She wouldn't. But what now? Her mind was racing, frantically searching for something—anything—that made sense. She needed to do something. She couldn't just sit and wait for everything to crash down around her.

With her hands trembling, Kat fumbled for her phone. She scrolled through her contacts until she found Prakash's number and pressed 'Call'. Her eyes didn't leave Luke.

The phone rang once, twice, then clicked as Prakash picked up. "Mrs Chapman?"

"Prakash," Kat said, trying to steady her voice. "I need to talk to you about those messages you were getting. The ones on WhatsApp."

There was a pause on the other end of the line. "Mrs Chapman, I told you, I don't want to get involved. I—"

"Please, Prakash," Kat interrupted, her voice pleading. "I need to know. What did they say?"

Prakash hesitated for a moment before sighing. "They were... weird. Stuff like, 'Get away from my business.' And, 'You don't belong here. Leave now.'"

Kat's heart raced. It sounded like something Adam would do, especially towards the end. But how could it be him? Adam was dead. She had seen him buried. Hadn't she?

"It's just," Prakash continued. "Whoever's sending these, they know about me. They're watching me. I still don't feel safe."

Kat's blood ran cold. The same feeling Luke had

described—the sense of being watched, stalked. Prakash too.

"Thanks, Prakash," Kat muttered, barely able to focus as her mind spun out of control. "I'll talk to you soon."

She hung up, her hands shaking. She stared at Luke once more and detected a familiar smirk on his face.

That's when she knew he'd made a huge mistake. He was next.

61

Kat stood still for a moment, staring at Luke, his smirk slowly fading into something darker. His head bobbed slightly, almost as if mocking her, like his confidence was returning bit by bit. She wanted him gone. No more smirking. No more Luke.

"You should leave," Kat said, her voice quivering but hardening with every word. "You're no longer welcome here. I don't need you at the business anymore either. I'll revoke your directorship. It's over."

Luke's laugh was low and bitter, his hair standing at odd angles, his lips cracking as spittle formed in the corner of his mouth. He looked unhinged, deluded even, and for a brief moment, Kat realised with icy clarity it wasn't Luke who was losing it. It was her. But with Luke gone, who was left? Maybe Adam could finally rest.

Luke wiped his mouth with the back of his hand, still laughing, though now it was more of a broken, desperate sound. "Bollocks to the job, Kat. Stuff the partnership." He took a step towards her, his eyes gleaming with something wild. "You know what? The worst mistake I ever made was reacquainting myself with Adam in that bookstore all those months ago. I should have ignored him, walked away."

Kat's stomach clenched at the mention of Adam. Her Adam. She didn't like how Luke said his name—as if it had a bitter aftertaste.

"And we feel the same, don't we, darling?" she said, turning her head slightly to the table behind her. "Adam never wanted you in the business. It was me. I pushed for it." She winced, suddenly feeling exposed. Her voice softened as she turned to the table once more. "I'm sorry, my darling."

Luke stared at her, bewildered. "Who the fuck are you talking to?"

Kat paused, realising what she was doing. But in her head she whispered, "it's okay," in reply to the voice only she could hear, smiling weakly as her body seemed to hum with a strange sense of comfort.

Luke took a sharp step back. His eyes widened as he appeared to register the depth of Kat's insanity. "You're fucking demented," he said, his voice low and trembling. "Just like Adam. You're just as crazy as him."

That broke something inside Kat. She snapped to attention, her body stiffening as she pointed towards the door, her voice rising into a shriek. "Get out! Now!"

Luke recoiled, genuinely frightened for the first time. His eyes darted to the door as if calculating the distance, unsure whether she might come at him. He muttered something under his breath, retreating step by step, and with each step, Kat's rage grew hotter, seething beneath her skin like boiling lava.

Luke finally stumbled out, almost tripping over his feet as Kat slammed the door behind him, the sound reverberating through the house. She stood there for a moment, breathing heavily, her pulse racing. She was shaking.

Without thinking, she ran upstairs. Into the bedroom. Into Adam's old wardrobe. She yanked the door open, rifling through his clothes with fevered intensity until she found it—the dark blue jumper with the crew neck, the one that had always been his favourite. Her hands shook as she pulled it from the hanger and slid it over her head.

It was too big, hanging off her in odd places, but she stood in front of the mirror, watching herself transform. The weight of the fabric, the familiar smell of his aftershave still clinging to it, calmed her, cocooned her.

"You look beautiful," she whispered to herself, smiling as she brushed her hair back.

"Why, thank you, Adam," she replied softly, her voice taking on a strange cadence, a touch of playfulness, as if she was flirting with him. As if Adam were right there, watching her dress.

For a moment, she felt completely at peace.

Then reality came crashing back in. She darted downstairs, glancing at the clock. Clara and Tom would be home soon.

Grabbing her car keys from the counter, she ran outside, her mind buzzing with a single thought: Luke. He had to be dealt with. She couldn't let him leave. He knew too much. He was a loose end.

Kat slid into the driver's seat, gripping the wheel tightly, her knuckles white. She spotted Luke along the street, stumbling as though he were drunk, his steps slow and uneven. Without a second thought, Kat slammed the car into reverse, the tyres screeching against the pavement as she pulled out of the driveway.

She lurched the car into drive, her foot pressing hard on the gas. The engine roared, and the car shot forward, barrelling down the street. Unbelievably, Luke didn't even turn around until the last possible second, just before the hood of the car slammed into his midsection with a sickening thud.

The world seemed to slow down as Kat watched Luke crumple onto the bonnet, his face twisted in shock and pain. She slammed on the brakes, her heart pounding in her chest, her breath coming in short, ragged gasps. She looked all around.

No one had seen. No one was watching.

Kat backed up, feeling the crunch of his body beneath the wheels as she reversed over him. Then she shifted gears, drove forward again, and left Luke's broken form behind.

She proceeded slowly back to her house, her mind blissfully quiet, free of the buzzing and the paranoia that had plagued her for so long. She parked the car carefully, as though nothing had happened, and stepped out onto the street. She smiled as she walked back inside, a calmness settling over her like a warm blanket.

In the kitchen, she calmly collected the remainder of Tom's torn-up drawings, and threw them into the bin. It was all so neat and tidy now. Everything was falling into place.

With Luke gone, was that the end? Had Adam carried out his final deed?

She made two cups of coffee, stirring the milk in slowly, savouring the way the spoon clinked softly against the cup. She sat at the table, placing one drink in Adam's place while cradling the warm mug in her hands, her mind still and quiet, as she waited patiently for Tom and Clara to come home.

62

The sound of Charlie barking broke Kat from her reverie, snapping her back to the moment. She hadn't stopped smiling since preparing the hot drinks: one for herself and one for Adam. His mug, of course, remained untouched, but it was nice to see it there, as though he would drink it when he was ready. The scene was set perfectly in Kat's mind: her and Adam, together, forever, as it should be. They'd both made mistakes, but this was their destiny. He'd come back for her, and Kat couldn't help but smile.

Charlie came bounding into the room, his excited bark filling the air as he ran to Kat's feet. She bent down to make a fuss of him, but something about her touch made the dog flinch. Bewildered, Charlie cowered back towards Clara and Tom, who stood hesitantly at the doorway. Clara's eyes, wide and unsure, watched Kat closely, as though trying to assess what exactly was happening. Tom, staring at his mum in disbelief at the attention she tried to bestow upon Charlie, clutched at Clara's leg, his little face buried into her side.

"Don't be like that, Charlie," Kat chuckled, her voice light, as though nothing in the world was wrong. "You know how much we love you."

Clara cleared her throat, trying to keep her voice calm. "Kat, is everything okay?" Her arm tightened around Tom, protectively holding him back.

Kat looked up, her smile warm and genuine, or so it seemed. "Everything is fine, thank you." She said it with such conviction that, for a brief moment, Clara almost believed her. But then her gaze fell on the full mug of coffee sitting untouched on the table, directly opposite Kat.

Clara's eyes darted back to Kat's face. She didn't have to ask. The confusion was evident in her expression. "Oh, that's for Adam," Kat said softly, noticing Clara's unease. "He likes to let it cool down first."

Clara's heart skipped a beat, her stomach twisting with anxiety. Tom, as if sensing the mounting tension, tugged on Clara's sleeve. "I'm scared. Why is she wearing Daddy's jumper?"

Clara felt her breath catch in her throat, her jaw clenching tight. She hadn't even noticed before now, but Kat was wearing a man's clothes—an oversized jumper that nearly swallowed her whole. She couldn't process it. "Tom, go to your room," she said, her voice barely above a whisper, trying to mask the panic she felt rising.

"But—"

"Go to your room, now."

Reluctantly, Tom obeyed, casting one last confused look at Kat before retreating upstairs. Clara waited until he was out of earshot before turning back to Kat. "Kat, I… I don't understand. What's going on?" Her voice was calm but strained, each word carefully measured.

Kat smiled, unfazed by the tension. "I have a confession to make, Clara. I need to tell you something important." She motioned for Clara to sit, but Clara remained frozen in place.

"Kat…" Clara's voice faltered. Her eyes darted towards the front door, thinking maybe, just maybe, she could still get Tom and ensure they both got out of there before anything went further. But Kat wasn't having it.

"I just broke into your house," Kat said simply, as though it were the most natural thing in the world. Her smile remained, calm and eerily serene.

Clara felt her knees weaken. "You… what?"

Kat waved her hand dismissively. "Oh, don't worry, I didn't mean anything by it. I merely thought you were Imogen."

"Imogen?"

Kat nodded, her voice soft, as though she were sharing a deep secret. "I thought you were her, Clara. I thought you were coming to take my Adam away from me again. I couldn't have that, you see? We could never have that, could we?"

Clara's heart pounded in her chest. "Kat, you need to listen to me—"

"No," Kat interrupted, her tone gentle but firm, like she was soothing a child. "You don't understand. I've got it all wrong, I know. I saw her, Clara. I saw Imogen in your window. At the party. I heard her calling Adam upstairs. And I thought, well, I thought Adam must have been invited too."

Clara's mind reeled. Imogen? What was she talking about? She was struggling to keep her composure. "Kat, please… You need help. I can talk to someone at the hospital—"

"No!" Kat's voice hardened for the first time, though the smile never faltered. "Everything is done now. We're all at peace. Right, Adam?" She turned her head slightly, as if expecting a response, as if Adam was sitting across from her, just out of sight.

A chill ran down Clara's spine. "Kat… there's no one there."

Sirens suddenly blared outside, their high-pitched wail cutting through the silence that had settled between the two women. Kat looked up, her expression brightening as though they were heralding something wonderful. She tilted her head slightly, listening with interest.

Clara glanced nervously out of the window. "Where are they going? Is that police, ambulances, what are they?" she asked, her voice trembling.

Kat's smile widened, a glint of madness shining in her eyes. "There's been an accident. Luke's been hit by a car." She let out a small, delighted laugh, leaning in as if sharing a private joke. "The final one."

Clara's blood ran cold. "Did you… did you do this?"

Kat shook her head, a childlike glee lighting her features. "Not me, Clara, silly. Adam. He's taken care of everything now."

Clara took a step back, her hand shaking as she reached for her phone. "I need to make a call."

Kat's expression didn't change. She stood up slowly, watching Clara with a bemused smile. "Go ahead."

Clara's fingers fumbled as she dialled, her mind flashing back to the officer's words from earlier that week. *"We think something is very wrong with Kat, but we don't have proof. Please, keep an eye on her, and call us if anything suspicious happens."* Suspicious? Clara thought grimly. This was beyond suspicion. This was insanity.

As the phone rang, Kat wandered towards the back door. Clara watched through the kitchen window as Kat stepped outside into the garden. Her movements were slow, purposeful, almost serene. She bent down, picking up Tom's football from the middle of the lawn, cradling it in her arms for a moment, like she would a baby, before walking to the garage.

Clara's heart hammered in her chest as she watched Kat momentarily disappear from view. She held her breath, terrified of what she might retrieve, but Kat emerged moments later with a terracotta pot in her hands. Clara's eyes widened even further, totally confused.

Kat returned to the lawn and carefully placed the pot on the ground where it had once sat. She stood and smiled at her handiwork, as though she had just completed some monumental task.

Clara's voice cracked as she whispered into the phone. "Please… Office Anderson. Come quickly."

Kat stepped back into the house, her smile still in place as she closed the door behind her. She glanced at Clara, her eyes gleaming. "It's done now. Adam always wondered where that pot had got to, didn't you, darling?"

Clara's hand shook violently as she ended the call. She had never been more terrified in her life.

But Kat? Kat looked like she had never been happier.

63

TEN DAYS LATER

Kat sat in a small, stark room at the police station, her hands resting calmly on the table. Her demeanour was unnervingly serene, almost as if this was just another day. Opposite her sat Detective Inspector Helen Radford and Doctor Simon Reeves, a psychiatric specialist brought in to assess Kat's mental state.

Before the interview began, Kat glanced around the room and asked, "Where's Tom?" Her tone was casual, almost as if she'd just returned from a weekend away. The DI leant forward, her voice calm yet firm. "Tom is safe," she replied. "He's staying with Lauren and Max for now."

In reality, Tom had been placed temporarily with a foster family under the supervision of Social Services. Given the gravity of Kat's actions and her mental instability, Social Services determined that a neutral and stable environment would be best for Tom's welfare until the case was resolved. However, Kat was adamant he stay with Lauren, the only person she trusted, and Social

Services would work towards that end goal. But for now, to avoid distressing Kat further and risking a volatile reaction, DI Radford decided to keep the explanation simple, hoping that mentioning familiar names would help maintain her cooperation.

Satisfied with the response, Kat nodded absently and leant back, a slight smile tugging at her lips. The DI exchanged a brief glance with the doctor before continuing the interview, her voice steady yet cautious.

"Thank you for speaking with us today, Kat," Radford said. "We'd like to go over what you remember about the past few months. Let's start at the beginning."

Kat tilted her head, a small, eerie smile spreading across her lips. "The beginning?" she echoed softly. "Well… I suppose it really began at Adam's so-called funeral."

Radford and Doctor Reeves shared another look, taking in her calm, almost dreamy expression.

"What happened at the funeral, Kat?" asked the doctor gently, his pen poised over his notepad.

"I saw him there," Kat replied, her eyes brightening with an unsettling intensity. "He was standing in the background, watching everything. Then, just like that, he disappeared. No one else saw him, but I did." She gave a small, triumphant smile, as if revealing a secret victory.

"Kat," Radford said, choosing her words carefully. "Are you certain it was Adam you saw?"

"Oh yes," Kat replied, her voice unwavering while looking at the detective as if it were she who needed a shrink alongside her. "It was Adam. I knew he'd never really leave me. He was always there, watching, waiting."

Doctor Reeves leant forward, his tone calm and soothing. "And did you see Adam again after the funeral?"

Kat's eyes flickered, as if she was recalling a fond

memory. "Yes. I saw him in Imogen's upstairs window. Several times, actually." She paused, a strange glint in her eyes. "He was trying to tell me something… that it wasn't over yet. That there were still people around who knew too much." She glanced at the doctor, her eyes glazed over. "We're a team, you know."

"Who, Kat?" asked Radford, leaning in slightly. "Who did Adam think knew too much?"

She tilted her head, thoughtful. "I went to Vicky's flat a few times. Kevin even told Luke that he knew someone was hanging around outside." Kat chuckled, her tone light and conversational, as though she were discussing an ordinary topic. "One night, I waited and saw Nathan and Belinda. They were in a white BMW. They parked around the corner, thinking no one would notice. But I did."

Radford's eyes narrowed slightly. "A white BMW was seized recently, with damage consistent with a hit-and-run. Do you think Nathan and Belinda were responsible?"

Kat shrugged, her smile unfaltering. "I knew it was them. And Adam knew too. I told him, so he… took care of it."

Doctor Reeves took a careful breath, pressing on. "Kat, what about the fire at Vicky's flat?"

"That's what I'm talking about," Kat replied with a light chuckle, as though she found the idea amusing. "Adam started the fire. He knew what needed to be done. I just told him who was responsible."

Radford looked down at her notes before glancing back at Kat. "And your mother? Did you visit her the day she fell?"

Kat's expression wavered briefly, but she steadied herself, a faraway look returning to her eyes. "Adam pushed her," she whispered. "He was always there, watching over me, protecting me from the people who wanted to take him away."

"Kat," Doctor Reeves asked. "You were seen visiting the park that day. Did you go there to push her?"

She blinked, a flicker of confusion crossing her face before she dismissed it. "It was Adam. I just... I only told him what needed to be done."

Radford continued, her tone careful. "And your father? Did you leave him with the whiskey and the pills?"

Kat leant back, a strange smile on her lips. "Adam took care of him too. He bought the whiskey, he knew what to do. It was for his own good, really. Adam knew I couldn't do it alone."

"And Sandra Law?" Radford pressed, her gaze unwavering. "Did you follow her along the canal that night?"

"I saw her, yes," Kat admitted, the smile returning, this time colder. "I knew she walked that way now and then, so I told Adam. I didn't have to worry about Sandra after that."

Doctor Reeves watched her closely, gauging her reactions. "And Luke?" he asked gently. "What happened to him?"

At the mention of Luke, Kat's face lit up, and she laughed—a chilling, almost gleeful sound. "Adam said it was my turn. He wanted me to finish one off. Just like Imogen." She closed her eyes, as if reliving a pleasant memory. "I hit him with the car, then reversed over him. I could hear his bones crunch." She laughed again, the sound echoing in the sterile room, sending a shiver down the detective's spine.

Radford's face remained composed, though her knuckles whitened as she gripped her pen. "Kat," she asked carefully. "Why do you believe Adam was still alive, even after his funeral?"

Kat's smile softened, taking on a wistful quality. "Because Adam would never leave me. We've been through so much together. I knew he was still there, guiding me, telling me what needed to be done."

Radford glanced at the doctor before continuing. "We found Adam's mobile phone at your house. There were text messages sent to you—messages saying things like 'I didn't know you liked dogs' and 'I hope you enjoyed revisiting the Sunset.' There were several others, all with replies from your phone." She paused, her eyes probing. "You sent those texts to yourself, didn't you?"

Kat's laughter filled the room once more, a mocking, hollow sound. "You don't know my Adam like I do," she replied, her voice dripping with disdain. "He was always with me."

Doctor Reeves nodded to Radford, signalling the end of the interview. Radford stood, her face a mask of professionalism, though a flicker of discomfort lingered in her eyes. "Thank you, Kat," she said quietly. "That's all for now."

As Kat was led out of the room by a waiting officer, her smile remained in place, her eyes bright with a strange satisfaction. Once the door closed, Radford turned to Doctor Reeves, her voice low.

"We know she didn't kill those people. If she had a sense of mind, she would have an alibi for each. She only killed Luke, but by then, I guess her mind had gone too far."

Doctor Reeves sighed, his face solemn. "And we know Adam Chapman is dead. However, one thing's for certain, Katrina Chapman is completely detached from reality. Whether she knows anything is anybody's guess. It wouldn't stand up in court whatever she said."

Radford nodded, a shadow passing over her expression. "So, what's next?"

"She'll remain in custody under the Mental Health Act," Doctor Reeves replied. "Likely for a very long time. I doubt we'll ever fully know the truth of what happened. But she's clearly unfit to stand trial."

Radford exhaled, glancing back at the door. "Well, whatever she believes, at least *she* can't hurt anyone else."

With that, they gathered their notes, knowing that whatever answers lay within Kat's mind were likely lost forever, buried under layers of twisted delusion and the relentless grip of her own madness.

64

THE NIGHT OF ADAM'S ACCIDENT

Lauren shivered on the bench, her coat doing little to block the December chill. Across the street, Adam's office loomed, its windows darkened against the rain-slicked street. She didn't owe him anything. She had told herself that over and over. Their brief affair had been a mistake, a lapse in judgement she was determined not to repeat.

But something about Adam's visit the previous day stuck with her. He'd been dishevelled, reeking of stale alcohol, his eyes red and hollow. Vulnerable wasn't a word she'd ever associated with him, but that's exactly how he'd seemed. Vulnerable, and somehow desperate.

It wasn't Adam she was worried about, though, not really. It was Tom. Tom adored Max, and Max adored Tom. That bond was worth something, even if Adam wasn't. She needed to know what he was up to, what kind of trouble he was in.

The office door creaked open, and Lauren straightened, her pulse quickening. A man she didn't recognise stepped out, glancing around before heading down the street. Lauren didn't think much of it until Adam followed shortly afterwards.

Her brow furrowed. Adam moved with slow, deliberate steps, his gaze locked on the man ahead. She leant forward, trying to make sense of what she was seeing. Why was Adam following the stranger?

Lauren hesitated, then stood. She didn't want to get involved, but something about the scene felt off. She kept her distance, trailing Adam as he shadowed the man through the rain-soaked streets.

They reached Baker Street Station, and Lauren watched as Adam boarded the tube, trailing his target. She paused on the platform before stepping onto the train two carriages behind. Her heart thudded with each stop, her thoughts racing.

When they emerged at Liverpool Street, the storm had worsened, the wind howling and rain driving in relentless sheets. The man seemed unfazed, striding purposefully through the crowd. Adam kept his distance, head down, but his focus never wavered. Lauren ducked into doorways and behind bus shelters, keeping herself out of sight.

The streets were crowded, yet eerily desolate at the same time. The storm seemed to drive everyone towards safety, except the three of them: the man, Adam, and Lauren. She saw Adam take shelter next to a kiosk, his eyes never leaving his prey, who was now waiting near a doorway—Wheelwright Solutions, the sign above read.

Lauren's breath caught in her throat when she saw a girl leave the building and approach the man. She didn't know who she was either, but they kissed, as if it was the most natural thing in the world.

And then—something unexpected. The pair of them

spotted Adam. But instead of fleeing, they crossed the street to meet him, speaking, the smile never once leaving the man's lips. Lauren's heart pounded. Whatever was happening, she could smell trouble. What was Adam getting himself into? She barely dared to blink as Adam began following them both down the road.

Eventually, a street sign read 'Dead End', and below it, 'No Turning'. Lauren stopped, hiding herself behind a row of cars. If she followed them any farther, she'd be spotted. Her eyes darted, her body trembling not from the cold, but from the fear of what was unfolding in front of her.

And around twenty minutes later, everything changed.

Lauren had waited patiently, the wind swirling harder, and she was about to give up and leave when Adam stepped out of the block of flats, shielding his eyes against the weather. Moments later, the growl of an engine shattered the quiet. A sleek white BMW sped past her and turned into the alley.

Within seconds, the sickening thud of metal hitting flesh followed.

Lauren froze, her breath catching in her throat. Then she ran. Her shoes slipped on the slick pavement as she skidded to the entrance of the alley. Adam lay crumpled on the ground, the BMW's taillights disappearing into the storm.

"Stop!" she screamed.

Unbelievably, the BMW's tyres screeched, the car reversing to a halt only inches away, before shifting gear once more. It sped off along the narrow street, its sound soon lost as the howling wind returned, echoing around the tall buildings. A flat door closed with a bang, but Lauren didn't see anybody.

"Adam!" she cried, dropping to her knees beside him.

His face was pale, his breaths shallow and ragged. Blood pooled beneath him, the rain mixing with it as it spread across the ground.

"Adam, stay with me," she pleaded, gripping his hand. Quickly, she retrieved her phone and dialled *999*.

His eyes flickered open, dull and glassy. "They… they set me up," he rasped, his voice barely audible.

"Who?" Lauren demanded, leaning closer. "Who did this?"

His lips moved again, but the rain swallowed his words. She pressed her ear close to his mouth.

"Kevin…" he whispered hoarsely. "And Vicky… they coaxed me…" His breath hitched, his body convulsing weakly. "It was a trap." He gurgled something else before the names Nathan and Belinda escaped his lips. "Bob's children…"

Lauren's blood ran cold. She glanced down the alley, her gaze scanning the shadows for any sign of movement. Nothing. Whoever they were, they were long gone.

"Adam…" she said, her grip on his hand tightening.

But he didn't answer. His breath grew fainter, his body limp beneath her touch.

Lauren knew it was too late. His eyes fluttered shut, and his chest stilled.

She sat back, her hands trembling. Adam was gone. What now?

She looked down at his lifeless body, her mind a whirlwind of shock, but something much darker too—opportunity. The man and the woman had set Adam up. For what, she didn't know. But Adam had money. A business. Power. And now, he was gone.

Tom adored Max. Max adored Tom. And Lauren knew what she needed to do.

She rose to her feet, her clothes soaked and clinging to

her. The storm raged on, but she was oblivious to it. Her jaw tightened, and her gaze hardened.

Whoever had done this had made a mistake. But more importantly, Kat had made a mistake. She'd let her husband down, but she must have answers too. She would know who was behind all of this, what Adam was alluding to. And Lauren intended to make her pay for it.

Quickly, she made herself scarce, the sound of sirens fast approaching. And once she was safely out of sight, she called her husband, Sean.

65

NOW

SEAN HAD ALWAYS BEEN the mastermind. Lauren might have had her moments of cunning, but Sean possessed the nerve, the vision to see the endgame clearly. That night, the night Adam was hit, it had been Sean's idea for Lauren to follow. She only shadowed Adam to Vicky's flat because he had seen a flicker of opportunity—a chance to finally secure a future that revolved around that family.

Lauren hadn't wanted Adam at her door that day, his vulnerability hanging off him like a worn coat. She'd kept the door barely open, shielding Sean, who stood silently in the kitchen. She and her husband had reconciled after a brief separation, and Sean's sudden influx of money had reignited a spark. Sceptical though Lauren was about the source of his finances, Max adored his father, and she couldn't deny the stability it promised.

So, when Sean suggested they tail Adam, she hesitated only briefly. Adam had hired Sean to kill Luke—something Lauren had found absurd at the time. But Sean, ever the opportunist, had turned the situation to his advantage, striking a better deal with Kevin and Vicky. Adam had no idea Sean had betrayed him long before that rainy night.

And that day, everything fell into place so easily. Lauren donned her coat, pretending it was her idea to follow Adam, though she had no clue what Sean truly had planned.

Three weeks after the accident, Sean attended Adam's funeral, lurking in the shadows like a ghost. He confessed later to Lauren that he had stepped out just long enough for Kat to spot him—a fleeting moment designed to haunt her.

Meanwhile, Lauren was already busy infiltrating herself into Kat's life in her own way. She'd volunteered to watch Tom during the funeral, seizing an initial chance to gaslight Kat about her parenting. Tom's odd behaviour —his quiet repetitions of "she's coming home"—played perfectly in her plans. By the time Kat returned, Lauren had planted the seeds of doubt.

"I know you're having the worst time," Lauren had said, her tone laced with faux sympathy. "But Tom… he really scared me today."

From that very early moment, Lauren noticed a real vulnerability about Kat, just as Sean had intended.

Over the following weeks and months, Lauren and Sean meticulously tightened their grip. Lauren invited Tom for a sleepover, under Sean's insistence, further cementing the bond between their families. She casually mentioned Kat's continual erratic behaviour at the school gates, a carefully crafted narrative that Sean encouraged her to spread.

Lauren's next move was to feign a tighter friendship with Kat, inviting her out for a drink. She'd even suggested the Sunset, knowing its connection to Adam would stir emotions in Kat. It worked; Kat had smiled to herself, strangely, as though the pieces in her own mind were beginning to align too.

And Kat divulged too much, far too much. She admitted her disdain for her new neighbour Clara Denton, providing Lauren with another potential pawn in their scheme. Lauren tucked the information away, already planning how to exploit it.

By now, Sean was fully involved, taking risks Lauren didn't always approve of. He'd begun shadowing Kat, as well as Kevin and Luke, incessantly escalating the paranoia.

When Edwina, Kat's mother, died, Lauren knew it wasn't a tragic accident. Sean had confessed, with a smirk, that he'd given her a hard shove at the park. The head injury that led to her death had been intentional. It was another move on the chessboard, one that had another unsuspected upturn: Kat barely appeared to grieve her own mother's demise.

A week after the funeral, Sean lingered long enough to catch Kat's father alone. He knocked on the door, a bottle of whiskey and three packets of paracetamol in hand, planting suggestions that might drive the old man to his own end. Sean's ruthlessness frightened Lauren at times, but she couldn't deny its effectiveness.

Between William's death and his funeral, tragedy struck again, and again Sean ensured Kat could easily be behind it. Vicky and Kevin, who had been growing increasingly unpredictable, met their end in a fire that consumed their flat. Sean orchestrated every detail with cold precision. He had waited patiently until he knew Nathan and Belinda were visiting, a calculated decision to ensure maximum destruction, both physical and psychological.

On the night of the fire, Sean broke into the flat below theirs, armed with a jerry can of petrol. The smell was suffocating as he poured the fuel across the floors and up the stairwell. He worked swiftly but methodically, knowing exactly how quickly the flames would spread. A single match was all it took. The inferno raged instantly, climbing through the building with a speed that would give no one above a chance.

Standing in the shadows outside, Sean watched as the orange glow lit up the night sky and sirens wailed in the distance. He felt no remorse, only satisfaction. Kevin and Vicky were no longer loose ends, and with them gone, the path forward became clearer. The tragedy hit the news the following morning—four lives lost in a horrific blaze. Lauren read the reports aloud, her tone dispassionate, while Sean merely nodded, already moving on to the next phase of their plan.

But his work wasn't finished yet. Sean turned his focus to Sandra. She had been a loose thread from the beginning, and now she was a critical piece in the game. She'd reappeared in Luke's life and Sean just couldn't allow that to happen. He followed her carefully, waiting for the perfect moment. On a cold, misty evening, she made her usual walk along the canal towpath.

Sandra paused by the water, her reflection rippling in the dim light. Sean stepped closer, ensuring she heard the faint scuff of his boots on the gravel path. She turned, startled, but Sean stayed in the shadows, just visible enough for her to make out his silhouette. Panic flickered across her face. He didn't need to say a word. His mere presence was enough to send her reeling.

The seeds were now sown for Luke's inevitable collapse. He began receiving unsettling messages, seemingly from Adam, accusing him of betrayal and warning him to stay away from the business.

By the time Sean began targeting Kat's company, everything was in motion. Sean's burner phone buzzed with messages sent to Prakash, unnerving him until he stepped away from the company. Meanwhile, Sean's surveillance of Luke had intensified. He sent texts that seemed to come from Adam, driving Luke to the brink of paranoia. Lauren had barely kept up with the details, but it hardly mattered. Sean had it all under control.

The real triumph came when Sean and Lauren turned Tom into their unwitting accomplice. Lauren had coached him to draw pictures of Imogen and the summerhouse, leaving them on top of his schoolbag where Kat would inevitably find them. She even ensured that yellow roses were delivered to both Clara and herself, further stoking Kat's suspicions.

Kat, already fragile, began seeing enemies everywhere. Lauren and Sean watched from the sidelines as she spiralled, her grip on reality slipping. It was only a matter of time.

The planting of the football and removal of the terracotta pot only added fuel to the already raging paranoia. Kat's hatred of Clara reached boiling point too. Everything and everybody around her were now working against her. She only had one person left to cling to: Adam. She'd never let him go.

. . .

By the end, Sean and Lauren's plan had borne fruit. The chaos surrounding Kat's life was more than enough to justify a custody petition.

"We're just concerned about Tom," she'd said, her voice heavy with false sincerity. "Kat's been through so much, and we want to help."

With Kat's apparent blessing, and with Sean's aid, they applied for a Special Guardianship Order. They framed their case around Kat's instability, supported by testimonies from both the police and psychiatric specialists. Lauren knew how to spin the narrative, painting herself and Sean as the stable, loving figures in Tom's life. Oh, and how he loved to spend time with Lauren's mum.

The court agreed. Tom would live with Lauren and Sean, his future secured in their home. The administrators had taken over the failing business, but the money was still there, locked away in a trust for Tom until he turned eighteen. Sean, however, was already scheming, exploring ways to access the funds much earlier.

As Sean poured himself a drink that evening, Lauren sat on the sofa, knowing Max would soon have the 'brother' she'd always wanted.

"We've done it," Sean said, his tone triumphant.

Lauren nodded, a faint smile playing on her lips. They'd won. Kat was out of the picture, and Tom was theirs, along with the future they'd been building from the shadows.

But Lauren couldn't shake a lingering unease. Sean's mind never stopped plotting, and she knew he was already onto the next step, the next move.

Maybe one day he wouldn't be around either, she thought to herself with a wry smile.

'The Family' Psychological Thriller Trilogy

Have you read the series everybody is talking about?

Available in eBook, Print & Audio

EACH BOOK AVAILABLE SEPARATELY OR AS A BUNDLE - Just search for 'Jack Stainton Books'

'I was amazed at the twists and turns in these books… brilliant... impossible to put down'

'Had to finish it quickly so I could get my heart rate back to normal...'

'I love a good psychological thriller and I have just found my new favourite author!!'

'I like to think I read enough thrillers to be able to suss them out before finishing, but this one kept me guessing until the very last sentence!'

ACKNOWLEDGEMENTS

Thank you for reading *Truth Lies Beneath*! If you've made it this far, I'll assume you've read the entire trilogy—so let's be honest, Adam and Kat had it coming, didn't they? From the very start (*The Boss's Wife*), I knew their reckoning had to be absolute, and I hope you found their journey as gripping as I did while writing it.

A massive thank you to my Advanced Reading Club. Once again, your sharp eyes and honest feedback have been invaluable. This book wouldn't be the same without you.

To my editor and cover designer—your talent and dedication continue to elevate my work, and I'm endlessly grateful.

And most importantly, to *you*, the reader—your support means everything. Writing can be a solitary pursuit, but knowing my stories reach you makes every moment worthwhile. Without your enthusiasm, reviews, and recommendations, I wouldn't have the drive to keep doing what I love.

Thank you again, and keep an eye out for my next novel, set for release in mid-2025. In the meantime, if you haven't explored all my books yet, now's the perfect time to dive in.

Happy reading
Jack

If you want to learn more about me and my books, please sign up to my FREE newsletter below…

www.jackstainton.com/newsletter

facebook.com/jackstaintonbooks
x.com/jack_stainton
instagram.com/jackstaintonbooks

REVIEWS

Enjoy this book? You can make a big difference

Honest reviews of my books help bring them to the attention of other readers.

If you've enjoyed this novel I would be very grateful if you could spend just a few minutes leaving a review (it can be as short as you like).

Thank you very much.

HE IS HERE

Grab a copy of this stand-alone Psychological Thriller set on a remote island in France…

Available online in both eBook and Print Versions

…kept me up reading chapter after chapter into the early hours!

Jack Stainton you did not disappoint. I was hooked from the beginning. What an ending.

If you want a true psychological thriller, this is your novel.

It kept my interest throughout, and the ending was totally unexpected! I highly recommend this book!

A GUEST TO DIE FOR

Jack Stainton's debut Psychological Thriller

Available online in both eBook and Print Versions

…I bought the book and read it in two sittings. Very good, lots of twists and red herrings.

This does exactly what a thriller should; it keeps you guessing until the end…

Excellent book full of twists and turns. The characters are brilliant… The ending was totally unexpected…

Sucking you in with a dreamy hope of a better start, the fear of what might happen next will keep you turning the pages!

A fantastic, gripping debut!

Printed in Dunstable, United Kingdom